PRAISE FOR JO

"Flynn is an excell

"Flynn propels his plot with potent but flexible force."
— *Publishers Weekly*

Digger
"A mystery cloaked as cleverly as (and perhaps better than)
any John Grisham work." — *Denver Post*

"Surefooted, suspenseful and in its breathless final moments
unexpectedly heartbreaking." — *Booklist*

The Next President
"*The Next President* bears favorable comparison to such
classics as *The Best Man, Advise and Consent* and
The Manchurian Candidate."
— *Booklist*

"A thriller fast enough to read in one sitting."
— *Rocky Mountain News*

The President's Henchman (A Jim McGill Novel)
"Marvelously entertaining." — *ForeWord Magazine*

Big Medicine

A John Tall Wolf Novel

Joseph Flynn

Stray Dog Press, Inc.
Springfield, IL
2023

JOSEPH FLYNN

SERIES

The Jim McGill Series
The President's Henchman, A Jim McGill Novel [#1]
The Hangman's Companion, A JimMcGill Novel [#2]
The K Street Killer A JimMcGill Novel [#3]
Part 1: The Last Ballot Cast, A JimMcGill Novel [#4 Part 1]
Part 2: The Last Ballot Cast, A JimMcGill Novel [#5 Part 2]
The Devil on the Doorstep, A Jim McGill Novel [#6]
The Good Guy with a Gun, A Jim McGill Novel [#7]
The Echo of the Whip, A Jim McGill Novel [#8]
The Daddy's Girl Decoy, A Jim McGill Novel [#9]
The Last Chopper Out, A Jim McGill Novel [#10]
The King of Mirth, A Jim McGill Novel [#11]
The Big Fix, A Jim McGill Novel [#12]
The Boy From Illinois, A Jim McGill Novel [#13]
The Man with a Plan, A Jim McGill Novel [#14]

McGill's Short Cases 1-3

The Ron Ketchum Mystery Series
Nailed, A Ron Ketchum Mystery [#1]
Defiled, A Ron Ketchum Mystery Featuring John Tall Wolf [#2]
Impaled, A Ron Ketchum Mystery [#3]

The John Tall Wolf Series
Tall Man in Ray-Bans, A John Tall Wolf Novel [#1]
War Party, A John Tall Wolf Novel [#2]
Super Chief, A John Tall Wolf Novel [#3]
Smoke Signals, A John Tall Wolf Novel [#4]
Big Medicine, A John Tall Wolf Novel [#5]
Powwow in Paris, A John Tall Wolf Novel [#6]
Top of the Mountain, A John Tall Wolf Novel [#7]

The Zeke Edison Series
Kill Me Twice, A Zeke Edison Novel [#1]

[continued]

STAND ALONE NOVELS

The Concrete Inquisition
Digger
The Next President
Hot Type
Farewell Performance
Gasoline, Texas
Round Robin, A Love Story of Epic Proportions
One False Step
Blood Street Punx
Still Coming
Still Coming Expanded Edition
Hangman — A Western Novella
Pointy Teeth, Twelve Bite-Size Stories

Dedication

In gratitude to the Choctaw Nation who helped to feed the Irish during the time of the Great Hunger. Without their generosity, I might not be here.

Acknowledgements

Catherine, Cat, Anne, Susan and Meghan do their level best to catch all my typos and other mistakes, but I usually outwit them. For this book, I've added the efforts of my Advance Reading Team. Please be kind, if one or two tiny errors remain. The fault for any flaws is mine alone.

My thanks also to Dr. Carl Arentzen and Dr. Bart Troy for the loan of their medical bags.

The beaded medicine bag on the cover and above is a design by Navajo artisans.

This novel was inspired in part by a reading of *A Warrior of the People* by Joe Starita.

Author's Notes

This is a work of fiction. Neither the characters nor the Native American reservations named in the story are real. The Bureau of Indian Affairs, of course, exists within the United States Department of the Interior, and within the BIA its Office of Justice Services is "responsible for the overall management of the Bureau's law enforcement program," but my research turned up no one who has the job description I gave to John Tall Wolf. This mixture of fact and fiction falls under the heading of literary license. If you're a purist who demands complete realism, I recommend you stick to nonfiction, and good luck finding an author in that field who doesn't make mistakes or omissions.

As to a white male writing about Native American characters, that involves a bit of license, too. From my point of view, that license is rooted in our common humanity. If writers were to focus only on characters who shared their own backgrounds, we would establish a regime of literary apartheid.

AL
Reader Discretion Advised
Contains Adult Language

Stray Dog Press, Inc.

Big Medicine
A John Tall Wolf Novel
Published by Stray Dog Press, Inc., 2023
Springfield, IL 62704, U.S.A.

Author website: *www.josephflynn.com*

Flynn, Joseph
    Big Medicine / Joseph Flynn
    246 pg.
    ISBN 978-0-9974500-9-5
    eBook 978-0-9974500-3-3

Printed in the United States of America

PUBLISHER'S NOTE
This is a work of fiction. Names, characters, places, and incidents are either the product of the author's imagination or are used fictitiously; any resemblance to actual persons, living or dead, events, or locales is entirely coincidental.

Book design by Aha! Designs
Cover photo by Gregg Daniels

Big Medicine

A John Tall Wolf Novel

Character List

Terry Adair, Captain, LAPD
Awinita, Alan White River's wife *(deceased)*
Brice Benard, real estate developer, Omaha, NE
Abra Benjamin, Director of the FBI
Thomas Bilbray, *aka Bodaway,* White River's great grandson
Rockelle Bullard, Captain, MPD, Washington, D.C.
Byron Dewitt, former deputy director, FBI; now
    President Jean Morrissey's husband
Thomas Emmett, Chief of Tribal Administration, Omaha Tribe
Nelda Freeland, Marlene Flower Moon's niece
Johanna Green Eyes, John Tall Wolf's secretary
Dr. Yvette Lisle, research physician
Arcelia Martin, office manager, McGill Investigations, LA
Jim McGill, CEO, McGill Investigations
Marlene Flower Moon, *aka Coyote,* formerly Secretary
    of the Interior
Jean Morrissey, President of the U.S.
Emily Proctor, former LAPD,
    employee of McGill Investigations, LA
Angelo Renzi, owner of LifeShare
Alan White River, John Tall Wolf's great-grandfather
Wilbur Rosewell, ex-cop, P.I., works for Brice Benard
Freddy Strait Arrow, high-tech genius and billionaire
Cale Tucker, NSA wiz kid
Hayden Wolf, John Tall Wolf's father
John Tall Wolf, federal agent of the Bureau of Indian Affairs
Rebecca Bramley Wolf, John Tall Wolf's wife, head of
    McGill Investigations, LA
Serafina Wolf y Padilla, John Tall Wolf's mother

— CHAPTER 1 —

Monday, January 23, 2017
Washington, DC

Immediately after receiving the first official phone call from newly inaugurated President Jean Morrissey and fumbling for an answer to the question she'd posed to him, John Tall Wolf wondered if James J. McGill was still hiring.

The President had asked John, "How would you feel about being nominated to be my new Secretary of the Interior? I think having a Native American continuing to hold that position is a good idea, don't you?"

Marlene Flower Moon had been the first such person to have that honor.

She'd tendered her resignation at the end of the Grant Administration.

Then she'd promptly disappeared. John had been unable to find her anywhere.

Not wanting an awkward silence to drag on too long, John had replied, "Yes, ma'am ... generically speaking, I agree."

"Generically, huh? Are you also thinking of leaving government service, Director Tall Wolf?"

"I'm not exactly certain what my plans are, ma'am. Like you, I'm a newlywed. My wife, Rebecca, has taken a job in Los Angeles, as you might have heard, and we're trying to work out a … *modus vivendi*, I'd guess you'd call it."

The President laughed. "Byron keeps asking me if I can run the government from Santa Barbara. So I can empathize with you."

"Thank you, ma'am. There's also the fact that I'm trained as an investigator, not an administrator."

The President laughed again, this time with a skeptical note.

"Byron also tells me you have a great gift for collaboration with others that produces excellent results. Something I've also noticed personally."

Byron DeWitt was the former deputy director of the FBI — besides being the President's husband — and someone with whom John had brought two cases to successful conclusions.

"That was more a matter of having the right people to help me, ma'am."

"So you're good at recruiting, too," the President said. "Or at least spotting talent."

Those were two gifts John had, but he wasn't going to admit it.

"More luck than anything else, ma'am."

"That's also good. I like lucky people."

John was stuck for a response on that point, but the President let him off the hook.

She said, "I can tell a White House cabinet position is not a long cherished dream of yours, Mr. Director, but I'd like you, please, to at least consider the possibility while I go about filling other slots in my administration. Will you do that for me?"

"Yes, ma'am, I will, and please say hello to Byron for me. I hope his recovery continues to go well."

"Thank you, John, for keeping an open mind and for your good wishes. Perhaps I'll have Byron give you a call before too long."

Then she said goodbye, leaving John to stare at the phone in his hand for a moment before putting it down.

The idea passed fleetingly through his mind that he might see if he could have his office phone number changed … but with the nation's full range of intelligence agencies at the President's command she could undoubtedly track down the new one. Or simply show up at his office one morning, wave an admonitory finger and conscript him.

He doubted that even the 13th Amendment to the Constitution, barring involuntary servitude, would stand in her way if he made it a contest of wills.

If he signed on with McGill Investigations International, though, that might give him the cover he needed. Let him continue to do the work he preferred as well. Not that his original plan in life was to become a federal officer, someone tasked with nabbing bad guys.

Marlene Flower Moon had lured him into that line of work.

John had taken the bait because he'd sensed from the beginning that Marlene was really Coyote, the Trickster of Native American lore, and quite possibly the particular beast that had tried to consume him as an infant — and would have succeeded if his adoptive parents Hayden Wolf and Serafina Wolf y Padilla hadn't arrived at the last minute to save his life.

As a vital young man, however, John had relished the chance of confronting his nemesis directly. Through the years of testing himself against Marlene, he'd more than held his own. More than that, by maintaining a more or less direct relationship with Marlene he was able to keep an eye on her. Not let her slip from the top of his consciousness. Be ready for any scheme the Trickster might conjure for him.

Only, now, things had changed.

Marlene's resignation as Secretary of the Interior had left the Cabinet seat open for John to fill. It wouldn't have been hard for Marlene to guess that Jean Morrissey would nominate him. Having John take the post might well be just one step in whatever game the Trickster was playing.

Of course, if John declined the nomination and felt compelled to leave government work, that might lead him to put a foot in another snare Marlene had set out for him. When a chess player found himself in a position where he was going to lose an important piece no matter what move he made, he was said to be in a fork. Given the appetites John suspected Marlene of having, the metaphor was particularly unwelcome.

He was going to have to work harder and smarter, whatever choice he made, and figure out where Marlene had gone and what her plans were. At least insofar as they concerned him.

His rumination was interrupted when his secretary, Johanna Green Eyes, buzzed him.

She said, "There's a big old Indian out here to see you, boss."

Johanna was seven-eighths Comanche and one-eighth Scot. The Scottish ancestor had survived his introduction to the Wild West of 19th century America and, given the absence of any bonnie lasses from back home, had married into the native population, who had given up trying to kill him after several years of making their best efforts.

At least that was the family legend Johanna had shared with John.

Considering how smart, tough and determined she was, and the color of her eyes, he was inclined to believe it.

He asked, "Did the big old Indian introduce himself by name?"

After a pause, she replied, "He says he's your great-grandpa. Does look quite a bit like you. Or what I imagine you'll look like if you make it that far."

John had gotten to his feet by the time Johanna added, "He says his name's Alan White River, and they let him out of jail early. Says you're supposed to make sure he doesn't steal any more trains."

John opened the door to his office and smiled at Alan White River. The two men embraced.

Stepping back, White River said, "They let me go from Club Fed early because my tennis game got too good for all the other over-60 inmates."

White River, himself, was well into in his 90's, and possibly older.

"Yeah, that and a presidential nudge from Patricia Grant," John replied. "They processed your release faster than I expected."

John turned to look at the striking woman — several decades younger than his great-grandfather — who stood next to White River. It was no accident that Johanna Green Eyes hadn't mentioned her. Comanches could have a sly sense of humor.

Before she could introduce herself, White River said, "My prison pen-pal, Dr. Yvette Lisle."

The French name notwithstanding, John could see the doctor was Native American. Mostly. She did have a Gallic nose. He shook her hand. "Nice to meet you, Doctor."

She nodded and said, "You, also."

"Evie needs your help, grandson," White River told John.

He looked at the old man. "With?"

White River shrugged and said, "You know how it is. If white people aren't stealing from Indians, we're stealing from each other."

"That's a real old story," Johanna said. "Usually involves land."

John gave her a brief look before turning to Dr. Lisle. "You've been robbed, Doctor?"

"I have."

"And this isn't a matter for your local police?"

She shook her head. "I don't think so. The theft involves my work. I'm a medical researcher. My project was funded in part by the federal government."

And just like that, John saw deliverance. He had a new investigation to pursue, the kind of task he loved to do. It was also a legitimate reason, i.e. excuse, for putting off a decision on President Morrissey's request. If that resulted in his being told the federal government no longer required his services in any capacity, he felt sure he'd be allowed to complete one last case for the Bureau of Indian Affairs.

At least, he hoped so.

He told Dr. Lisle, "You've come to the right place."

He ushered the doctor and Alan White River into his office.

***

The first question John asked Dr. Lisle was, "Who else besides the government funds your work?"

"Freddy Strait Arrow."

Hearing that name, John sat back in his chair and looked intently at his female visitor. Freddy Strait Arrow was a young high-tech genius and billionaire. He was also a major contributor to what had been Marlene Flower Moon's political ambitions. Implicit in that relationship, at least in John's mind, was that Freddy was or had been one of Marlene's lovers.

"Do you know Marlene Flower Moon, Dr. Lisle?" John asked.

In addition to looking at her, John kept watch on White River with his peripheral vision.

The old man maintained an impassive demeanor.

"I've heard the name, but we've never met," Dr. Lisle said.

For an uneasy moment, John thought the good doctor just might *be* Marlene. After all, the Trickster was a shape-shifter. But, no, Coyote wouldn't do that, at least not with him. She had too much invested in the Marlene Flower Moon persona to do that. It would be conceding a measure of defeat to come to John as any other woman.

Turning his head to look directly at his great-grandfather, he didn't see any skulduggery in his eyes. That was a relief. Looking back at Dr. Lisle, he asked, "What kind of research do you do, Doctor?"

She replied with a question of her own. "What do you know about MRSA?"

John had to turn the page to another part of his mind. He found the reference he sought. "That's the acronym for one of those super-bugs, isn't it? One of those illnesses with no effective means of treatment."

The smile Dr. Lisle offered John said, *Not bad for a layman.*

Verbalizing, she elucidated, "MRSA stands for methicillin-resistant Staphylococcus aureus. It's a bacterium that can cause infections in different parts of the body. MRSA is also resistant to other antibiotics besides methicillin. What's worse, MRSA is adaptive. Medicines that could once knock it out have become ineffective. Right now the bug's evolutionary speed is outpacing our efforts to fight it. Without quick and substantial advances in pharmaceuticals, the world could be right back to where it was before the advent of antibiotics, and that was not a pretty place."

John said, "Much higher mortality rates from infections?"

Doctor Lisle nodded. "For young and old and most people in between."

"Your work, the material that was stolen from you, addresses that problem in some way?" John asked.

"It does. There need to be many more steps taken in terms of peer reviews and clinical trials to determine the efficacy of what I've done, but I think the data that my approach has generated show real promise."

John was glad to hear the doctor hadn't said a cure was at hand. Overselling a proposition was something that always made him suspicious. He said, "If someone went to the trouble of stealing your work, they must also see that same potential."

John quickly followed that with two other ideas.

"Or, if there are researchers with competitive approaches, maybe someone wants to knock you to the back of the pack. That, or the theft was a random event done by an everyday criminal looking for money or drugs to steal."

The first notion, John saw, registered as a possibility with Dr. Lisle. The second one just made her laugh briefly. That was enough for him to see she was quite attractive. Up until then, he'd noticed her features only as pleasantly symmetrical. Now, he saw the lavender color of her eyes. Possibly a French trait that went with her name. Quite fetching against her copper skin tones.

Not that her appearance was alluring to him, despite its virtues.

He still got excited when he talked with Rebecca every night.

He intended to keep that chemistry strong as long as they both lived. What Dr. Lisle's comely appearance made him realize, though, was there might be a personal angle to the theft of Dr. Lisle's work. Maybe a spurned lover had sought to strike out at her.

He'd table that idea until he eliminated the most obvious one.

"Doctor," John said, "if your work passes scientific muster, and clinical trials prove its efficacy —"

"Will it make me very rich?" she asked. "Yes, it will. Well, it will make me rich, make Freddie Strait Arrow even richer. The federal government's investment will be repaid and then some."

John laughed. "Washington is going to *make* money if you succeed?"

"At my insistence. I think that might have been what put my grant application over the top. I also insisted that my drug be provided to low-income citizens at cost, and Native Americans will get theirs first and without charge."

John turned to White River. He wondered if his great-grandfather had a hand in that part of the deal. White River understood what he was thinking, but he said only, "The doctor has a good heart."

"How did the two of you meet?" John asked Dr. Lisle. "I mean, what prompted you to write to him in the first place?"

"I took a ride on the Super Chief. I felt the presence of all the spirits there."

Alan White River had had Native Americans from around the country come to see the locomotive he'd stolen and fill it with the tragic stories and laments of the people for whom the advent of a transcontinental railroad had been a calamity, not a triumph. White River had thought only to have the haunted Super Chief delivered to a railroad museum in Chicago.

It had been John's idea to have it make excursions around the U.S.

So, in a way, he was responsible for Dr. Lisle seeing him that day.

He also found it interesting that a medical scientist acknowledged spiritual beliefs.

For the moment, though, John turned the conversation back to a practical law-enforcement point of view. "I don't suppose anyone got a look at whoever stole your data and write-ups? Or was it done online by hackers?"

"I work on my computer, but not online," Dr. Lisle said. "It's a stand-alone system to make sure it can't be hacked by anyone outside my lab."

John nodded. He liked the simplicity of the doctor's solution to cyber-attacks.

Apparently, though, she'd still needed better locks on her doors.

"No witnesses?" he repeated.

"Not the flesh-and-blood kind, but we have security camera footage."

She took an iPad, one of the big ones, out of her purse, brought up a video file and handed the tablet to John.

He hit the play icon, took a look and stopped the video immediately.

"These three are the thieves?"

Dr. Lisle nodded. "No one else entered the lab between the time I left the night before the theft and when I returned the morning after."

John said, "But these guys—"

"The one on the right's a girl," White River interjected.

John took a second look and saw his great-grandfather was right.

"Still, they're all just kids."

"I think they're no more than 12," Dr. Lisle said. "Mr. White River says maybe 13 or 14 at the high end."

Great-grandfather nodded.

John asked the doctor, "Do you know of any scientific prodigies with criminal tendencies?"

She shook her head.

John thought for a moment. "Still, someone with an understanding of your work's medical significance, and its potential monetary value, knows three adolescents capable and trustworthy of pulling off this crime, even if they don't understand the value of what they grabbed."

White River said, "Maybe they do."

Los Angeles, CA

As a secret token of the homesickness Rebecca Bramley felt for Canada, she kept the current weather conditions for her hometown of Calgary, Alberta on her iPhone. That morning in late January the Calgary temperature was -8°. Of course, her phone, knowing it was in the U.S., had converted the temperature reading to the Fahrenheit scale. Using the Celsius measurement that Canada had adopted in the 1970s, the number would be -22°.

The weather in L.A. at the moment was a relatively cool 55° with a partial cloud cover, but sunny and 70° was the prediction for the coming weekend. That was the kind of weather that made Canadians, with the financial means and the free time, flock south to the U.S. in winter. Going somewhere warm when there were icicles hanging from your roof, and possibly your nose, was a treat.

However, *living* in a mild climate had made warm, sunny days routine for Rebecca. Humdrum. Unwelcome, even, for Christmas and New Year's Day. Cold and bracing were what she wanted then.

What she desired even more than that was the company of her new husband, John Tall Wolf. He, however, was on the far side of the U.S. in Washington, DC. The distance between her and John seemed immense. Canada was more than 150,000 square kilometers — there was the metric system again — larger than the U.S., but three-quarters of the Canadian population lived within 100 miles of the border with the U.S.

In a lot of people's minds, or Rebecca's anyway, that made home seem like a broad but narrow land. The U.S., by contrast, had crowds of people everywhere, coast to coast and border to border. With an astounding, sometimes appalling, number of them on their roads and highways.

Especially in Los Angeles.

She avoided the freeways at every opportunity. Surface streets were the way to go for her. Even so, she was always on the lookout for byways the locals and the tourists either eschewed or hadn't found yet. If her drive to work took longer, so be it. Arriving with her blood pressure in a safe range was more important than saving a few minutes or even an hour.

Despite any drawbacks she had to deal with, she often reminded herself that after losing her niche in the Royal Canadian Mounted Police she'd landed on her feet in a rather fine fashion. She'd married a man she loved and quickly found a new job in a country that long had been the world's magnet for people with ambitions for a better life.

Hordes of immigrants would gladly have traded places with her. Her new job with McGill Investigations International started with a six-figure salary, a housing subsidy for the rent on her new apartment, and a paid three-year lease on the new Audi A7 she was driving. The offices she was renting in Westwood — having declined a site in Beverly Hills — were first class, too.

All of her perks combined to put more than a little pressure on Rebecca to get her office up and running, providing a positive return on the money Mr. McGill had invested in her. So far, though, she'd been unable to find the four satisfactory associate investigators the business plan allotted to her office. That was just the initial personnel grouping that had been anticipated.

Los Angeles, with its huge population of wealthy, eccentric and otherwise unpredictable characters, was anticipated to be a major profit center for the company.

So far, however, Rebecca had managed only to find an office manager she liked, Arcelia Martin. Arcelia had reached the United States by way of Venezuela. Her dad had played four years of major league baseball for the Oakland A's. That and a successful career transition to the front office of the San Francisco Giants had given his family a path to citizenship and a comfortable standard of living.

Arcelia's father had paid her way through four years at the University of California at Berkeley out of his own pocket. He'd told his daughter, "Baseball makes me happy. Study something that makes you happy."

Given that measure of license, she'd accumulated a bachelor's degree and a master's degree in English. Her father hadn't asked what line of work she might find with that educational back-ground and was reassured when his daughter had paid her own way through grad school, working in human relations for a Silicon Valley startup.

"How'd you get that job?" her father had asked.

"Talked my way into it. You can't beat an English major for knowing how to use the language." True enough, but it helped to impress the start-up's CEO that she was also fluent in Spanish and French.

When Arcelia told her father she wanted to move to L.A., he gave her one of his old baseball bats and said, "See if you can learn to swing this thing better than I did."

He meant, of course, to keep anyone who wanted to steal either her heart or her TV at bay.

Arcelia was still working on her bat speed when she talked her way into a job with Rebecca Bramley. The first thing, during her employment interview, she'd nodded at the photo of John Tall Wolf on Rebecca's desk and asked, "Any more like him at home?"

That set the tone and the two women became fast friends.

After that, when they spoke of John or potential boyfriends for Arcelia, the two women used French, not English.

When Rebecca arrived at the office that morning, she asked the always earlier arriving Arcelia, "Anybody need a private eye, today?"

"Not so far."

"Damn."

"Yeah."

Even with Patti Grant out of the White House and James J. McGill having exited with her, the other offices of the new McGill enterprise still enjoyed an afterglow effect; clients found their way to them with a variety of investigative needs, corporate and personal. In L.A., however, once you stepped out of the limelight, people gravitated to those who still basked in it.

Rebecca moved on to her customary second question for Arcelia. "Any of the job recruiters turn up an investigator candidate for us?"

"Sorry, no."

"Double damn. I think maybe I better start checking with my old colleagues in the RCMP."

Arcelia feigned a look of horror. "What, bring more immigrants into our country?"

"Yeah, I know. After you and I got in, it was time to slam the door."

"Right," Arcelia said. "I mean, first we brought in farm labor, then techies for Silicon Valley and now we can't even grow our own private eyes?"

Rebecca sighed. "Apparently not any that meet my exacting standards. You think Lieutenant Proctor might chew my ear off if I ask her for any more referrals?"

Emily Proctor was with the LAPD. Jim McGill had met her working a case in town and been impressed. He'd arranged with Emily to bird-dog any prospective coppers looking to move into the private sector. Rebecca eagerly had taken advantage of the connection ... only she hadn't liked any of the six police detectives that Lieutenant Proctor had sent her way.

Three of them hadn't wanted to let her review their job records; the other three, she felt, wouldn't be comfortable working for a woman. So she hadn't even bothered asking for their records. On their way out, two of them had called her a bitch and one had given her the finger.

It had taken serious exercises in self-restraint for Rebecca not to start fights with those three. Calling on Lieutenant Proctor again probably wouldn't be either wise or helpful.

But Arcelia told Rebecca, "You don't have to call; she's waiting in your office."

"Emily Proctor is?"

"Uh-huh."

Rebecca winced. "Did she come to chew me out?"

Arcelia grinned. "No, she said something about looking for a job."

Jackson, Wyoming

Marlene Flower Moon stood on the balcony of a ski chalet adjacent to the Jackson Hole Ski Resort. The temperature was -3°, but she wore only a deerskin dress that left her arms uncovered and had a hemline that stopped just above her knees. Her feet were bare. She'd taken down the deer herself.

As the animal lay dying in the snow, she'd thanked it for giving her its hide.

She'd skinned it herself, too.

She left the meat for whatever scavengers that happened by first.

The skin was tanned by an immigrant from Italy, a couturier who'd had to leave home abruptly to escape charges of massive income tax evasion. His business had collapsed behind him, but he still had a fine eye, a deft hand and a sublime sense of design. He'd lit out for the American West as a place to disappear.

After all, who would imagine *him* taking shelter in a land of cowboys?

Marlene had spotted him the moment he'd hit town. When she'd brought him the deerskin and asked for a dress made from the animal's skin, he'd almost swooned. To use material that had so recently been alive and fashion it to flatter so beautiful a woman … he wanted to ravish her at that very moment. Take her every measurement and not just with a tailor's tape, but with his mouth, his hands, his …

Better judgment asserted itself. To make the garment and see the woman wear it, that would be his reward. Well, that and to start a new fashion line using only leather from the freshest hides of wild beasts. If the animal-rights people wailed and shrieked at him, he would spit on them in return.

The designer's new business plan was but one of a multitude he'd had that never came to fruition. After Marlene had the deerskin dress in her possession, she'd turned the couturier in to the FBI. He was shipped home and promptly jailed.

Marlene hadn't wanted anyone wearing a copy of her dress.

She wore it, though, only when she walked in the forests of the nearby national parks, Yellowstone and Grand Teton. She might just as well have gone nude. Cold air couldn't bother her. Neither would any acorn she stepped on or bramble she brushed against. She wore the dress to see if she might understand vulnerability.

The way the deer must have felt when she'd claimed its life for herself.

As she stood on the chalet's balcony, she was unable to empathize with the idea of being a victim. She'd strode fearlessly through the high woodlands that conservation efforts had plentifully restocked with predators: grizzlies, mountain lions, wolves and, of course, coyotes.

But none like her, of course.

All the carnivores of the wild gave her a wide berth.

She was something more dangerous than they were, and they knew it.

So why had she been frightened — how was it that she *could* be unnerved — by a woman's soft voice that had come to her as she slept? Even she needed her rest, and that was when the voice told her, "It is time to stop."

That was all, but said three times.

The voice's tone was gentle but its insistence brooked no refusal.

Time to stop what, Marlene had wondered.

And *who* on earth might insist that she do anything?

Didn't this foolish woman understand who she was dealing with?

Then after months of plaguing her sleep, the injunction became a warning. "It is time to stop ... or I will stop you." And that was when Marlene understood who her tormentor was. Serafina Wolf y Padilla, John Tall Wolf's adoptive mother.

Marlene knew that Serafina had sent night terrors to Bly Black Knife, John Tall Wolf's biological mother, when Bly had tried to reclaim custody of her son after he'd lived for six years with his adoptive parents. The targeted nightmares had worked. Bly had dropped her custody suit.

But did the foolish woman think she could actually scare Marlene? Impose her will upon Marlene?

Serafina was reputed to be a witch, and her husband was said to be a conjurer, but did they truly think they were of a stature to confront her? Someone whose very nature was far beyond their power to comprehend. And yet …

They had taken the risk. That had to be considered.

Coyote was nothing if not calculating. Was it possible they had some resource at their disposal that she didn't? Could they contrive some sort of a trap that might actually ensnare her? If they did manage that, what might they do next?

That was when Marlene remembered something Tall Wolf had once told her.

What if the time came when she did get to eat him and didn't like the way he tasted?

That would be a bitter irony indeed. Marlene needed time to think. She'd handed in her resignation as Secretary of the Interior and left Washington, the idea of eventually becoming president having lost its appeal. She'd seen how that job worked at close range, and the crushing burden of obligations that went with it had destroyed her taste for the job.

Taste. There was that word again. If there was no satisfaction, no pleasure, no memorable *flavor* to be had in taking revenge against Tall Wolf or anyone else, why bother?

Marlene was tempted to pay a visit to Tall Wolf's parents, get a feeling if they could do more than talk a good game. Of course, if it turned out that they could, and they were setting a trap for her, then going to them would be exactly the wrong move.

They might also be ready for her to approach Tall Wolf himself in defiance of Serafina's warning.

But what about Tall Wolf's new wife, the Canadian woman?

What about Rebecca Bramley?

Prometheus Labs, Washington, DC

The outer door to Dr. Yvette Lisle's laboratory, in a building adjacent to the American University campus in Northwest Washington, had better locks than John Tall Wolf had expected. The doctor had to swipe a key-card and submit both a thumb-print and a retinal scan to gain entry. There were no metal key or number-pad alternatives.

The door itself, John found once Dr. Lisle had opened it, was a hefty, closely fitted slab of steel. It wasn't a bank vault but it would withstand any attack short of an acetylene torch. The adjacent masonry wall was also formidable.

All of which made John wonder how a trio of middle school brats had effected an illegal entry. Of course, if guile had been used instead of brawn ... but how did you outsmart biometric protection measures? He didn't recall that being covered in the coursework at Glynco, Georgia, where prospective federal agents were sent to learn their trade. Then again, that part of his education had taken place several years ago.

Before the advent of the iPhone, even.

Could be he needed a refresher course.

Once John entered the lab with Dr. Lisle and Alan White River, he saw that the space's electrical lighting was supplemented with daylight, courtesy of a series of skylights.

So, maybe the adolescent thieves had the climbing skills of young monkeys. Make your way up to the two-story roof and you could drop right in. Climb back out again, too.

Before John could say a word, Dr. Lisle noticed he was looking up and disabused him of that line of thought.

She told her guests, "The roof has weight sensors. You put anything heavier than a chihuahua up there, you'd think there was an air-raid siren going off. And the skylights are made of polycarbonate resin not glass. You could beat on them with a hammer and the panes wouldn't break."

Then she added, "They would get scratched, though, and I

don't see any signs of damage."

Neither did John.

Dr. Lisle led him and White River into her office and invited them to sit in the two guest chairs. She stepped behind her desk and used her key-card and a thumb to open a drawer. No retinal scan was required to do that.

She took out a MacBook Pro computer and put it on the desk in front of her. She raised the lid and said, "This is one of my backup machines."

"The others are the same make and model?" John asked.

"Yes."

"How do you tell them apart?"

"Other than the fact that I brought this one from home this morning?"

She tapped the keyboard and showed John the monitor. She'd written something in a language he didn't recognize. White River did, it was plain to see.

"Grandfather?" John asked.

White River had told him not to include "great" when addressing him.

"It is a transliteration of the *Umo-ho* — Omaha — language. If I have it right, Dr. Lisle has written, 'What is your name?'"

She smiled, nodded and hit the return key.

The machine responded by producing an audio message in English, "I am number two."

John thought for a moment and asked, "Did you try to use your phone to find your missing computer? You know you can do that, right?"

Yvette Lisle smiled indulgently. "Yes, I know that."

"And?"

"That feature apparently has been disabled on number one."

"Do you know how?"

She shook her head. "Not my area of expertise."

"Mine either, but I can probably find someone who would know. Maybe the feature can be restored, possibly without even tipping off the thieves."

Dr. Lisle said, "That would be helpful, but only if they haven't already copied the data to a thumb-drive."

John sighed and nodded. "Well, if they haven't done that, and by some small chance the kids who took number one aren't tech-savvy, maybe we'll be able to turn the find-me feature back on and erase all the information on the computer remotely, too."

That caught White River by surprise. "Is that possible?"

Both John and Dr. Lisle said, "Yes."

But she added, "I've backed up all my data on this machine, but I added my commentary on the process and future exploration only on number one."

John said, "And in the name of security you didn't put your ideas on the cloud, so you can't recover them that way."

Yvette Lisle nodded.

The best-laid plans, John thought.

Then he turned to his great-grandfather and said, "Before I forget, why do you think the kids who took Dr. Lisle's computer know what they stole?"

"My speculation is the adults behind the plan told them."

"Told them what?" John asked.

White River said, "That this is how the scales will be balanced. When the white men came to our lands, they brought illnesses with them that we could not fight, and those diseases killed more of us than all of their guns combined."

John understood the corollary. "And now, if Native Americans are behind this theft, they might be the only ones who will have protection against MRSA and maybe any other super-bugs that crop up. This time it will be everyone else who suffers and dies."

John's scenario made Dr. Lisle's face go pale.

"Oh, my God," she said, "I never wanted to have anything like that happen."

John believed her. There was nothing to say someone with a medical degree couldn't also be an accomplished actor, but likely not to the point of having blood drain from her face. Then John had a thought that made him feel more than a little uneasy.

He looked at White River and asked, "Grandfather, did you ever learn what happened to your other great-grandson, Bodaway? The last I saw of him, he seemed to be plunging to a certain death, but his body was never found."

The mention of Bodaway's name made White River slump in his chair.

He shrugged in an attitude of defeat. "I have not heard of or from him. My heart breaks whenever I hear his name. I blame myself for ..."

The old man could not bring himself to complete his thought.

John felt a pang of regret for causing him pain.

He'd have to tread more carefully, should he need to bring up Bodaway's name again. He'd also have to intensify his search for Marlene Flower Moon. Bodaway had shot her, and she was not one to either forgive or forget. She was one to stalk and get even, as John well knew. If anyone had a fix on what had happened to Bodaway, it would be her.

Trying to raise everyone's spirits, Dr. Lisle said, "There is one thing in our favor."

"What's that?" John asked.

"Well, anyone who's mathematically literate can read the scientific notation in my work, but the narrative voice recounting observations, hypotheses and future direction, they're not written in English or any other Western language. Not even any Asian language."

That left an easy conclusion for John to draw. "You wrote in *Umo-ho,* the language of your tribe."

"One of them, anyway. Another part of my heritage, as you probably guessed, is French by way of Quebec."

"Your name and your eye color are clues," John said with a nod.

"Yes. Anyway, finding someone who can read *Umo-ho* might slow the thieves down a bit."

John glanced at White River, saw the old man was not as sanguine.

The reason not to be optimistic was obvious.

If Bodaway were involved, it would be a lot easier for him to find an Indian who could read *Umo-ho* than it would be for a white thief.

John stood up and helped White River to his feet. He gestured to Dr. Lisle to join them.

"Where are we going?" the old man asked.

"To the U.S. Patent Office. If someone is able to decipher Dr. Lisle's work, it's reasonable to think they'd want to establish legal ownership of their stolen goods."

"What?" Dr. Lisle said, outraged by John's notion.

"Makes sense, doesn't it?" he asked.

"Yes, damn it, it does."

John said, "I don't know where the Patent Office is, but it has to be in town here somewhere. I'll look up the address on my phone."

Dr. Lisle said, "I know where it is. It's not in DC; it's in Alexandria, Virginia."

A suburb. John said, "Close enough. Let's go."

Los Angeles, California

"I'm finished with the LAPD," Emily Proctor told Rebecca Bramley as the two women sat in Rebecca's office. "It's not official yet, but it will be soon."

Taking the most obvious of guesses, Rebecca asked, "You hit the glass ceiling already?"

Emily shook her head. "It's not that. It's ... well, my dad told me I should look for a nice young lawyer or aspiring politician, both of which he'd once been. To find the man of my dreams, he meant."

"Uh-huh," Rebecca said. "I bet that went over big."

"He told me never to date another cop. Said it'd be courting disaster."

Rebecca said, "So that was just what you did. How'd your father take that?"

"He told me he'd be there whenever I needed him. For someone with one foot in the law and the other in politics, he's a prince."

"Which is something you can't say about your cop boyfriend?"

"No."

"Does he outrank you?"

"He didn't at first; he does now," Emily said.

"Direct line of command?" Rebecca asked.

"No."

"Well, that's good. How'd he get promoted: merit, connections or both?"

"Both."

"The connections just made things faster and inevitable, right?"

"They did."

Rebecca said, "So what happened, he got bossy?"

Emily shook her head. "Just the opposite. He said he'd fix it so I got promoted within a year. He'd pave the way for me. I'd deserve the increased rank, of course, because I would earn it. He'd just see to it that my good work was never *overlooked*."

"And the kicker is?" Rebecca asked.

"After he got done outlining our glorious police futures, he asked when and where I'd like to get married."

"Romantic," Rebecca said, "but, let me guess, you don't want to be anyone's lifelong protégé, always one step down the ladder, on the job and, inevitably, at home, too."

Emily laughed without humor. "Yeah, until he retires and moves on to his next wife."

If he waited that long, Rebecca thought.

She said, "Does he know you're going to leave LAPD?"

"Not yet."

"But you haven't made wedding plans, right, so he knows things aren't quite going according to his plan."

"We've stopped seeing each other. I've told him to stop calling me. But he thinks, and even says, it's just a temporary thing. He says I'll see he's right before long."

Rebecca shook her head, and Emily misinterpreted.

"You think you're going to have too many hassles with the LAPD if you hire me?"

"Hell, no. You've got the job if you want it."

"Great ... but why'd you shake your head?"

"I was thinking about men, how some can be louses while others are so great."

Emily had noticed Rebecca's wedding ring the first time they'd met.

"Yours is great?"

"He is. But let me tell you about this other guy in the RCMP. He's why I'm living in the States right now." Rebecca told Emily about her set-to with Sergeant Serge Marchand up in Canada, and how she'd cost him one of his testicles with a well-placed kick. "I don't know how something like that would play in this country, but I'll back you up, come what may."

Emily raised a fist in solidarity. "Thank you. My dad will represent us *pro bono,* if we need any legal help."

"Good," Rebecca said. "So now that I've hired my first staff investigator, all we need to do is find our first client."

Emily smiled. "I've got one for you. I didn't think it'd be polite to show up empty-handed."

Cree Indian Reserve — Beaver Lake, Alberta, Canada

Two years earlier, Coyote had marooned Bodaway, also known as Thomas Bilbray, on the Cree Nation's reserve at Beaver Lake. The reserve was only 105 kilometers (65 miles) northeast of the provincial capital of Edmonton, which hosted a metro area population of over a million people. Bodaway, however, was confined to the reserve which, in his opinion, was in the middle of fucking nowhere, and had a population of 400 full-time resident Indians.

He might have attempted to break out after his wounds had healed and his broken bones had knitted, albeit at eccentric angles.

The locals had any number of four-wheel drive vehicles he easily might have stolen, as they left their keys in the ignitions. There were open roads leading both south to Edmonton and north to the province's largest city, Calgary. Should he be pursued by any ordinary hunter, Bodaway was sure he could have eluded capture and found a way to get back to the United States. Once there, he could have hidden out somewhere in the vast reaches of land and the hundreds of millions of people.

The problem was, Bodaway was a prisoner of neither manacles nor iron bars but of the chains of memory. He still had horrifying recollections of Coyote's teeth seizing his throat. He still felt the heat of being scalded by Coyote's piss. His ego yielded to being branded a speck of mouse shit. All these torments danced before his eyes daily and, worse, filled his sleep every night.

Coyote had told him not to set foot off the reserve or she would introduce him to further, even more gruesome, terrors. The mere idea that such things were possible made him shudder. So Bodaway wasn't going anywhere.

Not physically, anyway.

Like many other isolated rural communities, the reserve was replete with short-wave radio rigs. The Cree, in the fashion of other rustics, knew better than to count on uncertain modern communications infrastructure. When all else failed, a tried-and-true battery-powered ham radio might be the last thing to save your ass when the going got rough.

Bodaway bought an old radio that a local had replaced with a new model. He'd only had to offer a gullible Cree the promise of an eventual payment. Well, that and the thrill of meeting someone famous among his kind. Bodaway had mentioned the fact that his great-grandfather was Alan White River, the man who'd stolen the Super Chief locomotive.

News of that feat had reached even the native population of Canada.

It was a coup that was growing to mythic proportions, gladdening the hearts of native bands everywhere. When Bodaway, in all honesty, spoke of the critical role he'd played in the train's theft, his status among the Cree became one of grudging acceptance.

His welcome wasn't warmer because the locals also knew that Bodaway was being punished by a great power. Still, the reserve's chief thought he at least deserved the company a ham radio could provide — with the understanding that it would have to be paid for eventually or it would be reclaimed.

So, in the wee hours of the present night, trying to put off his inevitable nightmares as long as he could, Bodaway listened to assorted discussions of the news of the outside world. He heard what was happening in the U.S. and locally. That was how he found out that the Cree were at odds with the provincial and federal governments in Canada.

The Indians claimed that Alberta and Canada collectively had failed to "manage the overall *cumulative environmental effects* of development on core Traditional Territory."

Meaning nearby oil sands exploitation and other intrusions on nature were screwing with the Cree's treaty rights to "hunt, fish and trap in perpetuity." Indians were the original North American environmentalists.

Bodaway loved hearing news of the conflict. He saw the situation as a golden opportunity to stir up some trouble and ennoble himself within his new community. That idea also gave rise to another.

If he could cause trouble in Canada, he might also do the same elsewhere. He might not have an internet connection, but his ham radio had the U.S. within easy reach. Why not use that range to become a folk-hero south of the border, too? The quaintness of his means of communication would only make him seem more authentic.

He looked for opportunities, playing off themes and memes he heard on the airwaves. He soon had ideas aplenty. He especially liked a discussion he happened upon regarding antibiotic-resistant bacteria. The topic was almost enough to make Bodaway believe in a Great Spirit. Talk about the white man finally getting his come-uppance.

He couldn't have thought of a more fitting end to the white man's occupation of all the lands he had stolen. Well, the white man along with everyone else who'd followed him to North America. The only people who should survive were the ones who got there first.

And that was where Bodaway's glee dissolved.

Hell, if some kind of super-bug could kill everyone else, it wasn't going to give Native Americans a pass. They'd be cut down like everyone else. For their people, it would just be one final defeat by biological warfare.

In fact, Native Americans, along with other poor people, would likely be the first to go.

As part of his daily physical rehabilitation discipline, Bodaway forced himself to limp around his tiny cabin for hours on end. Logs blazed in the fireplace but still he was cold. His gene pool had been formed in the heat of the American Southwest not the cold of the Canadian Northwest.

People were supposed to adapt to their conditions, but Bodaway hadn't. Cold was yet another misery he had to bear. He was sure Coyote had considered that when she'd chosen his place of confinement.

Despite his abiding physical discomforts, Bodaway found that pacing helped him to think more clearly and, better yet, more imaginatively. His first insight had been that his engineering education and skills might be traded with the inhabitants of the reserve for tangible returns, durable goods, if not money.

The first thing he'd done was pay off his ham radio with a stove repair.

He used the same means of exchange by doing car repairs, electrical wiring jobs, plumbing projects and, most grandly, he designed a new sewage system for the whole community.

In return, Bodaway had gained triple glazed windows for his cabin, which made the winter cold somewhat less unbearable. The Cree brought him fresh fruit and vegetables in season and fine cuts of meat to see him through the winter. His body would never be truly whole again, but he was becoming stronger.

His new prized possession, to supplement his radio, was a MacBook Pro the chief had purchased for him in Calgary. The Cree had their own cell tower. The tribe held its ham radios in high regard, but they weren't Luddites. When it worked, modern technology was fine.

With his new computer, Bodaway could do more extensive research into the matter of deadly bacteria and how they might be thwarted. Preferably, selectively. That might seem to be a horrible idea to some people. Hell, most people. But Bodaway thought it was a fine plan.

After all, where were the bleeding hearts when his people all but got wiped out?

Nowhere at all.

So Bodaway searched the internet, looking for advances in how to kill superbugs.

It wasn't long before he found the name Yvette Lisle. He thought at first she must be French. But a little digging showed she was at least half Native American. A story in the *Washington Post* said she was working on a new approach to defeating MRSA.

Wanting to know more about the woman herself, his search showed she was a member of the Omaha Tribe — the Upstream People. Her immediate family, on its Native American side, had been literate for only two generations. That suggested an impressively fast-rising learning curve for Dr. Lisle.

On an impulse, Bodaway looked up the meaning of Dr. Lisle's first name.

Yvette: A French name meaning archer.

Perfect, he thought. All she needed now was the right target.

Santa Fe, New Mexico

Hayden Wolf and his wife Serafina Wolf y Padilla sat at their kitchen table having a late lunch. Each of them, as aging parents were wont to do, was thinking of the inheritance they would leave to their son, John Tall Wolf. They were well pleased with the character traits they'd helped to instill in him. He was honest, kind, generous, and a supple thinker.

He was also big and strong. The potential for those qualities had been part of his genetic legacy from his biological parents. The Wolfs had nothing to do with that, but they had nourished him through a good diet, regular exercise and unstinting love and guidance.

Financially, he would be more than well provided for. Not that he would be rich. But with his monetary inheritance, his salary and his eventual pension, he should be more than comfortable.

Both Wolfs had been delighted when John had brought Rebecca Bramley to meet them in New Orleans. They couldn't have hoped for a better daughter-in-law. Lovely, smart, strong, professionally accomplished. Now, if only she and John could find a way to live together.

The fact that John and Rebecca were separated by the width of the country bothered both Hayden and Serafina. The elder Wolfs had never been distant from each other for more than a week during their marriage. How could John and Rebecca have a life together when they lived so far apart? How could they start a family, if that was what they wanted?

Well, they could, of course, conceive a child during one of their visits with each other, but once the baby was born surely they'd have to change their circumstances. Wouldn't they? The thought that they might not was another disturbing idea.

Their final abiding concern was what they should do about Coyote?

John had come into their lives when they'd saved him from being eaten by the largest coyote either of them had ever seen. Apart from its size, the animal had seemed to be an ordinary member of its species, except for the extraordinary sense of malice it had seemed to bear the Wolfs when they'd taken its meal away.

The creature had acted as if it would neither forgive nor forget.

Not even after it had gorged on its next prey.

Hayden and Serafina still rued their decision not to kill the beast. Unlike most professionals trained in empirical modes and methods, the Wolfs made room for the mystical in their thinking. They'd seen too much and knew too much to limit themselves to reproducible laboratory results.

They knew gods, ghosts and goblins had been part of the human experience since the species began to walk upright. Many such beliefs were nothing more than the attempts of small, fragile creatures — i.e. people — to understand far greater forces of nature. That was inarguable, except for those people who did argue with it.

When it came to modern medical science, masses of research produced new advances seemingly on a daily basis. For all that, there were still many things no doctor could explain: the sudden, non-traumatic death of someone judged to be perfectly healthy or the spontaneous remission of a normally fatal disease.

There was also the phenomenon known as the placebo effect: a positive health result achieved not by a supplied "sugar" pill but by the *expectation* the pill would effect a beneficial outcome. A common explanation was the body's own chemistry could mimic that of a prescribed pharmaceutical.

Such was the best guess of the scientific community.

That same group of empirical thinkers, however, largely refused to accept that negative expectations could be planted inside someone else's head with harmful or even fatal results. But that was often exactly the intended outcome that practitioners of what was called sympathetic magic, or sometimes voodoo, envisaged.

Usually such dark psychic manipulation required a physical link, say a lock of hair, a tooth, a fleck of skin. In the case of Coyote, the Wolfs had just the connection they needed. When they'd saved John from the beast that had intended to devour him, Serafina had pelted the animal's snout with a rock. Both blood and fur from that coyote had adhered to the missile.

Serafina, of course, had bagged the stone in plastic and kept it all the intervening years.

You never could tell when you might need a tool to mess with someone's head.

If there were a paranormal link between the animal who had sought to eat John and Marlene Flower Moon, well, then they had a dedicated line into her every dream. Both Hayden and Serafina felt that was indeed the case.

That direct connection was also a feedback loop. They could feel both fear and anger building in Marlene's mind as they tormented her. She might seek them out, looking for vengeance or at least relief.

They were ready for that. Whatever the outcome of their battle, they were sure they could cause Marlene enough pain to make her rethink any hostile plans she might have for their son. They'd rescued him once, and now they intended to make sure there was no second attempt to take their son's life.

At least by Coyote.

Any good parents would do as much.

United States Patent and Trademark Office
— Alexandria, Virginia

The Director of the USPTO was an African-American woman named Hezzie Jones-Greer. After getting a Bachelor of Science degree in molecular and cellular biology at the University of Illinois, she'd gone on to the University of Chicago for her law degree. So said the diplomas hanging on her office wall. The woman herself was tall and lean with caramel colored skin and pale blue eyes.

On the drive down to Alexandria from DC, John had sent her a text from his government phone, so the note came up with his name and title, John Tall Wolf, Director, Office of Justice Services, BIA. His message said. "Three Indians, none of us little, two full blood, one half-blood, would appreciate the professional courtesy of seeing you at your earliest convenience. We'll be brief."

John thought the one-government-agency-director-to-another card might be a good one to play. The three not-so-little

Indians joke would help if Ms. Jones-Greer had a sense of humor. Turned out, she did.

Her reply said, "I'm coffee and cream myself. Come on by."

Having been forewarned, Hezzie Jones-Greer had three guest chairs set out in her office for her visitors. She gave everyone a smile and shook hands with each of them. She saved Alan White River for last, held his hand the longest.

She told him, "Stealing that locomotive and filling it with your people's sorrows was a brilliant act of civil disobedience, Mr. White River. I'm going to see the Super Chief at the train museum the next time I get home to Chicago. I'm so glad you've been released from prison."

White River nodded humbly and said, "I have not yet been freed, just paroled to the custody of my great-grandson here. I have to stay in his close keeping for two years or until I die, whichever comes first."

John gave the old man a look of surprise.

"What," White River asked, "did I forget to tell you?"

"Either that or I'm rapidly losing *my* memory," John said.

Not wanting to get involved in a family spat, Hezzie said, "How may I help you, Director Tall Wolf?"

She gestured for everyone to take a seat.

Giving White River one more glance, John turned to his hostess. "Dr. Yvette Lisle has had some very significant research data stolen. Potentially, it might be highly valuable both in terms of saving lives and making money. I'm investigating the theft. It occurred to me that the person behind the crime might try to apply for a patent on Dr. Lisle's work. My thought was if we alert you to the nature of the work, your agency might flag any incoming patent application and help us catch the thief."

Hezzie had been nodding along to John's narrative, but stopped when he finished. She'd put on her thinking cap. The one she'd earned in law school. No doubt the USPTO had its own rules and regs to consider, as well as any intellectual property laws.

She looked at Yvette Lisle and asked, "Will you please outline for me just what was taken from you? You don't have to give away any trade secrets but please be specific enough that I'll know what to be looking for."

Dr. Lisle verbally sketched the nature of her work and more generally her approach to it.

Hezzie paused to let the information sink in, and then asked, "Do you know the criteria for a grant of patent?"

Dr. Lisle nodded. "I do. An invention must be statutory. That is, it must fall within the guidelines of the patent law. It also must be new, useful and non-obvious."

Hezzie smiled. "Very good. Do you think your work meets those standards?"

"I do. My work, I think, is more than innovative; it's ground-breaking. That makes it both new and non-obvious. It also is likely to save an untold number of human lives. That would inarguably make it useful."

"And do you think you're close to completion of your work?"

"I think I'm close to starting clinical trials."

"Okay, that works for me, too. It's also the good news. What's more problematic is that just about every country in the world grants its own patents. You know that, right?"

John fielded that question. "I hadn't thought of that. The thieves could go elsewhere."

"That's right," Hezzie said, "but if that's the case, they'd probably choose an advanced country that wouldn't mind bumping heads with the United States. China comes to mind; so does Russia. What I'd suggest you do there is hire a first-rate intellectual property rights lawyer with global connections. I can recommend three firms, if you like, and you could choose one."

"Yes, please," Dr. Lisle said.

"Okay, I'll text the names and phone numbers to Director Tall Wolf. One thing I'll need to flag an application in our system is a copy of the police report describing the theft you suffered," Hezzie said.

"I can provide one," John told her.

"Okay, involving the local cops would help buttress things."

"How about I get the FBI involved since part of Dr. Lisle's funding comes from the federal government?" John asked.

"That'd be even better," Hezzie told him. "It's been a pleasure to meet all of you. Sorry about your difficulties, Dr. Lisle."

"So am I," she said.

Los Angeles, California

"What's the case?" Rebecca Bramley eagerly asked Emily Proctor

"Employment fraud. Happened to a nephew of a friend of my dad."

Rebecca understood the link to the prospective client, but not the cause of action.

"I'll need more information," she said. "You know, what we're actually looking at here. That and how we can help this guy."

"Sure, I felt the same way when my dad came to me. Here's what happened. You know about Silicon Beach, don't you?"

Rebecca shook her head. "I'm still pretty new here."

"Okay, Well, everybody knows about Silicon Valley."

"Sure."

"Well, Silicon Beach is L.A.'s equivalent to that. It's a corridor of high-tech companies along the coast stretching from LAX, the city's airport, north to the Santa Monica Mountains. Some people would generalize Silicon Beach to include all of L.A., but mostly it's snugged right up against the ocean. At least, I think of it that way."

"Okay, I'm with you so far. So where does the fraud come in?"

"Well ... do companies up in Canada use non-compete clauses when they hire people?"

Rebecca tried to think if she'd ever heard of that. "Damned if I know. I was in the public sector, and nobody in Canada competes with the RCMP. I'd think, though, that if it's prevalent in the U.S., we probably have it at home, too, at least to some degree."

"Okay, so here's the thing. Just about anybody who goes on a payroll in white-collar America these days has to sign a non-compete agreement to get hired. That means if you quit your job you can't go to work for another company that does anything like what your old company does. Courts will usually demand such agreements be reasonable in duration and scope, but going to court for any reason is an expensive proposition, and then you might lose."

Rebecca made a disapproving face. "Sounds awful to me."

"Me, too. If enough people put up a stink, there'll be a law getting rid of the restrictions or at least loosening them considerably. But, here and now, non-compete agreements are broadly used and often legally upheld, according to what my dad tells me. If you're a creative person in the arts or high-tech, it can really put you in a box in terms of job mobility."

"Sounds like indentured servitude."

"Close," Emily said.

"So that's the fix this guy is in. He signed one of these non-compete agreements?"

Emily shook her head. "He says he didn't. He says he refused to sign both the non-compete and its off-premises ideas clause."

"What the heck is that?" Rebecca asked.

Emily said, "It's a paragraph that basically says if you get a bright idea at home or out riding your bike, the company owns the commercial exploitation rights to that idea, too."

"That's horrible. Who'd ever agree to something like that?"

"People who can't be picky about finding a job, but not our guy. He says he made the company, a start-up at the time he was hired, redraft his employment contract without the offending clauses. The company wanted him badly enough to agree."

"So where's the problem?" Rebecca asked.

"The problem is there are now *two* signed and dated employment contracts: Our guy has one in his possession; the other is in the company's hands."

Now Rebecca understood. "Each contract favors the party who holds it."

"Right."

"Both contracts are *countersigned* by the other party?"

"Uh-huh."

"And our prospective client has come up with an idea of great value? Something he dreamed up at home, no doubt."

Emily grinned. "You must've done good police work up there in Canada."

"I had my moments. So what's the advantage the company has? What's tilting things in their favor? It has to be that way or the guy wouldn't need us."

"The company has a video," Emily said. "It shows our guy signing their version of the contract — with three witnesses watching him do it."

"To which our potential client replies?"

"He says it never happened. He's never met or even laid eyes on any of the three witnesses in the video. There's a problem with that, though."

"What?" Rebecca asked.

"In the video, after he signs the agreement, he shakes everyone's hands."

"And the rebuttal to *that* is?"

Emily said, "A classic: 'Who you gonna believe, me or your lying eyes?'"

Rebecca sighed. "This doesn't look promising."

Emily shrugged. "You like a good challenge, don't you?"

That was exactly the right button to push, Rebecca thought. She wondered how Emily knew that. Maybe just an on-the-mark guess by one female soon-to-be-former copper about another. A woman didn't get ahead in any police department without more than a little spunk.

It was good to know from the start that she and Emily were simpatico.

"Yes, I do," Rebecca said. "Please tell me, though, that this guy can pay our fee."

"He's stone broke. All his cash and credit are tied up in his new company, I was told."

Rebecca sighed, thinking: *Take this office's first case on spec? No way, José.*

She wondered if that was still a current American idiom.

If so, was it now considered politically incorrect? So much to learn.

Then Emily refocused the discussion. "It's okay, his father is willing to pick up the tab, and that guy's so loaded you'd think he's got his own printing press at the U.S. Mint."

That put things back into the realm of possibility, but Rebecca had one more condition to add. If it turned out to be a deal-breaker, so be it.

"Junior has to put some skin in the game," she said. "Besides our regular fee, if we save his financial backside, he hands over 100 shares of his new company to McGill Investigations International. Agreed?"

Emily smiled and nodded. "Yeah, I like that."

The White House — Washington, DC

The governing administration of the United States had changed the previous Friday, as had the occupants of the White House, but the uniformed officers of the Secret Service were holdovers from the Grant Administration. When John rolled up to the Southeast Gate — after dropping off Alan White River and Dr. Lisle at her lab — the officers on duty recognized him. Even so, one of them took a look at his BIA credentials. You never knew when a Russian agent might try to pass himself off as a six-foot-four Native American.

"How goes it, Officer?" John asked. "The new boss treating you all right?"

"Yes, sir, Mr. Director. You ask me, we should have female presidents from now on. At least if they're like these first two."

That opinion might have been influenced by the officer's own gender.

She added, "You're here to see ..."

She paused to think of how to describe John's host. He wasn't the president's henchman as James J. McGill had been, but the word hadn't been given whether he should be addressed as the First Gentleman or something else.

John resolved her quandary by suggesting, "The president's surfing instructor?"

The officer fought it but couldn't keep a smile off her face.

"Yes, sir: Mr. DeWitt."

"That's who I'm here to see."

"Very good, sir." She gave him his visitor's pass and told him how to find DeWitt's office.

Before heading off to seek a parking space, John asked the officer, "Do you think I'd make a good Secretary of the Interior?"

She thought for a second before saying, "I think that'd be a bit of type-casting, sir, if you don't mind my saying so. I'd hold out for Secretary of State if I were you. You've got the height to look down on all those foreign guys. Make them think they'd better not mess with us."

John nodded and laughed before driving off.

He found a spot to park his car and made his way to the East Wing. That was where, back in the old days, the First Lady had her office. DeWitt had chosen not to occupy that fairly generous space. He'd set up shop in what had been the First Lady's *secretary's* office. A cunning move, John thought.

He'd pre-empt any would-be critic who might accuse him of being either unduly ambitious or half the man he used to be. There was, after all, still floral print wallpaper in the former First Lady's digs, chosen by its last female occupant.

John knocked on the door to Byron DeWitt's new professional lodgings.

"Is that my art-therapy instructor come-a-calling?" DeWitt sang out.

Opening the door, John said, "No, it's just me, but my mother once showed me how to string colored beads in a Meso-American style. I could share that with you."

DeWitt grinned and said, "Maybe next time."

John closed the door behind him and took a look around. The room had a view of the South Lawn, the better to see the President depart and arrive on Marine One, John thought. The furnishings looked both tasteful and comfortable but in no way ostentatious. Photos and paintings of California landscapes and city scenes hung on the walls.

There was one conspicuous absence, however.

"Where's Chairman Mao?" John asked.

The Andy Warhol serigraph of the Great Helmsman had hung prominently in DeWitt's former FBI office, serving as both a declaration of DeWitt's independence and a rebuke to the ghost of J. Edgar Hoover, the legendary and reactionary first director of the Bureau.

"In storage," DeWitt said. "He wouldn't be comfortable in here. It's too bourgeois for his kind. I've given myself a year to find the right spot for him. If I can't locate one by then, I'm going to put him up for auction and donate the proceeds to a Taiwanese little league team."

John laughed and took a visitor's chair.

He was pleased to hear how fluent his friend's speech had become.

DeWitt sat behind his desk, cutting off John's view of the lower half of his body.

John asked, "You going to be ready to play on my lacrosse team this spring?"

"Absolutely, and if I'm not, I'll bring my girlfriend to a game and we'll cheer you on."

John could just imagine that, the President and her mate showing up to take in an amateur athletic competition. There would be more Secret Service agents in the stands than fans. Still, it might be a high old time for everyone.

"Okay, good deal," John said, "but enough with the subtlety. How are you doing, really?"

"Well, if you want reality, I'm doing better than okay. That doesn't mean I don't have a lot of damn hard work ahead of me. The docs tell me how tough it will be without blinking an eye. What they dance around is whether I'll ever get to be seven-eighths or even three-quarters of my old self."

John had heard from Jim McGill other things the medical team had withheld from Byron DeWitt: To wit, they were amazed that the stroke he'd suffered hadn't killed him. And each new step he took in his mental, physical and verbal recovery surprised them daily.

It was DeWitt's progress that deterred his physicians from criticizing the acupuncture treatments and Chinese medicines he insisted on receiving. *Cumque operatur,* John thought. Whatever works.

"You know," John said, "I bet you make it back to fifteen-sixteenths."

DeWitt laughed. "I'd try to figure out the decimal equivalent of that fraction, but no way I'm up to that yet."

"See, simple math is what you might never have again. It's about 94%, by the way."

"Show-off," DeWitt said with a smile. "Okay, friend, you've brightened my day long enough. Why are you really here?"

John got right to it. "Two reasons. The first is the President called me earlier today to ask me to become the Secretary of the Interior. She thinks it would be good to have a second consecutive Native American in the job."

"And what do you think?"

"I think every child born in this country is a Native American. Besides that, one of the Secret Service people I spoke with on my way in said I should hold out for the Secretary of State job."

DeWitt beamed. "Now, *that* is a brilliant idea, having a son of our earliest inhabitants speak to the world for our country. I *love* it. Do you want me to talk to Jean about the idea?"

That was the last thing John wanted, but he saw DeWitt was so taken by the idea he didn't want to spoil his mood. Hell, who knew if a harsh rebuttal might set back his recovery? God help him, might an outright rejection even kill his friend?

John said in a gentle tone, "Let's just give the idea a little time for reflection. See how it looks in a week or two."

"Sure, sure," DeWitt said. "Can't be too hasty. Did you say you came for another reason, too? Sometimes things slip right by me."

John silently prayed the idea of him as Secretary of State would be quickly forgotten.

"Yeah, I want to ask if you might be up to doing a little desk work for me."

"Help you with a case?" DeWitt smiled brightly again. "What is it?"

John told him about Dr. Yvette Lisle's stolen research work.

"Damn, that's awful, especially if she's really near a break-through."

"Yeah." John told DeWitt about going to see Hezzie Jones-Greer at the USPTO to alert her to the chance the thief might try to patent the stolen research. "What I need help with is someone trying to file for a patent abroad and then using that as a backdoor to a U.S. patent."

It took a moment for DeWitt to process that idea, but then he nodded. He saw what John was getting at. "Yeah, could be if the thief is slick." He paused again, either exploring possibilities or trying to gather a thought.

John thought he'd gone to his friend too soon. Maybe he wasn't ready to go back to work yet. DeWitt began to nod as if being privy to John's thought and agreeing with it.

Which was halfway right.

DeWitt said, "I think I'll need help with this. I'll call Abra Benjamin."

Benjamin was the new deputy director of the FBI, John knew.

"You think she'll help?" John asked.

DeWitt had no doubt. "Sure she will."

Just to be careful, John asked, "Will you ask her to call me, after the two of you talk?"

"No problem." To John's eye, DeWitt now seemed more energized.

Maybe one-sixteenth closer to his old self.

He only hoped there would be no backsliding.

"One more thing," John said. "You know anyone at the NSA?"

The National Security Agency — Fort Meade, Maryland

John had called ahead to the NSA before arriving, but the security protocol there was still a lot stiffer for him than it had been at the White House. An unsmiling male escort took him to what was described as a "clean" room. It appeared to be a decently furnished waiting room of the type you might find in a dental office suite. But John was told his phone wouldn't be able to place calls from the room. He'd also be unable to connect to the internet.

If he had electronic games resident on his phone, he was welcome to play them.

Then the escort left John alone in the room. He didn't hear a lock click when the door closed, so presumably he was free to leave the building. With another escort, to be sure. John didn't play video games, and there were no copies of *Modern Eavesdropping* magazine on the end tables. So he sat quietly and tried to think productively.

About his problems, not Dr. Lisle's difficulty.

His first problem, of course, remained the vanishing act of Marlene Flower Moon. Being a woman of means, she could have jetted off to any country in the world. Being Coyote, she probably had the same range without the need of an airplane. The idea that she was up to some sort of devilry went without saying. Who the target of her scheming was remained to be seen.

If it was him, he wanted a distant early warning.

Of course, he didn't have to be the target. Any number of people might have raised Marlene's ire. Still, he wouldn't be unduly flattering himself to think he was at or near the top of Coyote's list of unfinished business. Quite likely, he was number one.

As a precautionary exercise, he felt it would be wise to compose a mental list of others whom Marlene might single out. After he finished helping Dr. Lisle, such a roster might well help him find Marlene. Having been stalked by Coyote for years, though, the idea of having to hunt for her rang loud with irony.

His other worry was deciding what to do with Alan White River. He found it odd that White River had been released to his custody without him receiving a notification of that condition. Was that really the way the parole boards worked? He didn't have any experience with the situation, so he couldn't say.

He thought that as aged as White River was, the person responsible for his release had considered the old Indian to be incapable of further mischief. Physically, that might be true, but White River hadn't had to strain any muscles stealing the Super Chief. What's more, John felt Great-grandfather still was capable of having a few tricks up his sleeve.

Question was, what did he do now? He couldn't see sending the old man back to prison for the remainder of his life. That would be more than cruel; it would be wrong. Still, John had a full-time job — with another one on offer — and a new wife he didn't get to see nearly as much as he wanted. Caring for an elderly man would only complicate things further.

The idea of whether he might ask his parents to take in White River had just occurred to him when the door to the room opened and a thin, young country-looking guy with strawberry hair, freckles and a prominent Adam's apple stepped in and extended a hand.

"Cale Tucker," he said with a soft Southern accent.

John got to his feet and shook the young man's hand.

"John Tall Wolf, Director of the Office of Justice Service, BIA."

"Yeah, they told me that. That's cool. Never met anyone from the BIA before. You want to sit back down, and we can talk about how I might help you?"

"Talk right here?" John asked.

"Yeah. No offense, but they just ran a quick check on you, established your bona fides. Normally, they like to go back into a few generations of family history before you can go any further into the building."

John said, "The President offered me the Secretary of the Interior job this morning, but I'm thinking I'll hold out for running the State Department."

Tucker grinned. "That's cool, too, and you can bet any of this new administration's Cabinet post nominees will get checked out all the way back to Eden. Unfortunately, they haven't shared your biography with us. There's a nice diner a straight shot down the road a mile, if you'd rather talk there. We could get a corner booth and nobody'd hear whatever we have to say."

"They have good milkshakes?" John asked.

"Great shakes."

"Let's go," he said.

John drove, following instructions without a hitch, even though there were three turns and not the straight shot Cale Tucker had described. John also noticed, without being obvious, that the young man was subtly checking the side view mirror to see if they were being followed. John didn't say anything, but he wondered if some big but secret international confrontation was underway.

Wasn't his place to inquire, though, and as Cale had said, they got a corner booth that gave them all the privacy they needed. Assuming the diner wasn't an NSA front and their every word and facial tic wasn't being recorded. They both ordered and promptly received chocolate milkshakes.

Every bit as good as promised.

"What can the NSA do for you, Mr. Director?" Cale asked.

"You checked out whether I have any pull beyond the BIA?" John asked.

It would be helpful to know whether he was going to get more than a free milkshake here.

Or if he'd even have to pick up the tab.

Cale said, "Per instructions from on high, I did just that. You might well become Secretary of the Interior. You are wired in mightily, right through to the Oval Office. That's why I'd be happy to buy you a burger and fries, too, if you'd like."

"The milkshake is enough, thanks. What I'd like to know is whether the NSA can help me find a missing laptop computer."

"Yours?" Cale asked.

John shook his head. "A medical researcher is looking into something that could be of critical national interest."

"Are foreign power involvement or military implications involved here?"

"Good questions," John said. "I hadn't taken my thinking that far but, yes, I can see how this might relate to both of those things."

"How?" Cale asked.

"My investigation concerns a possible medical breakthrough that might produce a multi-billion dollar revenue stream for a lot of years. What country wouldn't like to have the pot of gold at the end of that rainbow?"

Cale chuckled. "Nice turn of phrase, Mr. Director. I write lyrics for a band I'm in; you mind if I use that, changed around just a little?"

"Go right ahead," John said. "As for the military implication, imagine one side has a biological weapon and the only antidote for it."

The kid was quick on the uptake. "You wouldn't need nuclear weapons anymore. You just inoculate your own forces, let the bug do all the dirty-work, plant your flag and yell, 'Victory!'"

John hadn't thought of things that graphically, but he couldn't argue with the summation.

He told Cale that the medical researcher was partially funded by the federal government, and gave him her name. The kid grinned and nodded.

"That's a big help. She'd have to reveal everything up to whether she kisses on first dates to get a grant from Uncle Sam. We'll look into her financials. Get the purchase date of her laptop, its serial number and find out where it's been stashed ..." Cale's optimism did a fast fade. He added, "That's assuming the laptop's password hasn't been cracked, the hard drive hasn't been downloaded to another machine, wiped clean and sent to a junkyard. You've improved your odds by coming to us, Mr. Director, but it's no sure thing we're gonna grab the brass ring."

Neither of them liked that possibility.

Nonetheless, a gleam in the kid's eyes said he'd come up with another line of a lyric: *There's no sure thing we're gonna grab the brass ring.* Problem was, John was sure he'd heard it somewhere before. Could be they were both out of luck.

Cale said, "If you don't mind my asking, this Dr. Lisle, how'd she wind up turning to you for help?"

"My great-grandfather brought her to me."

"He's with the government, too, or another research doc?"

John said, "Neither. He's an ex-con."

Florida Avenue — Washington, DC

In the fashion of many densely populated American cities, Washington had become too expensive a place for the people who provided its basic services to find decent domiciles. Providing affordable urban housing had become a prominent political issue in California, which, as usual, was ahead of the rest of the country in social trends. Still, the same discussion was getting underway elsewhere, including the nation's capital.

Rebecca had told John she'd found a cozy one-bedroom apartment on a nice street in Santa Monica just a few blocks east of Ocean Avenue. The rent was less outrageous than normal because the building was owned by a Canadian friend of her father. Given her new digs' location, she could get up early, jog over to Palisades Park, turn on the jets and run for a couple of miles with a great ocean view. John knew the park from his own visits to Los Angeles. Signs said the bluffs there were subject to collapse if an earthquake jolted them hard enough.

John told Rebecca to run inland as fast as she could if things ever got shaky.

She promised she would. Any other threats to life and limb

would be handled the old-fashioned American way. In other words, she was applying for a concealed carry permit. She was counting on her RCMP experience, being married to a federal copper and working for James J. McGill to help her gain permission to pack heat legally and discreetly.

John had repressed a sigh upon hearing that.

As far as he knew, Rebecca never had fired a shot in the line of duty in Canada. The fact that he was comforted that she would be armed in L.A. made him sad. He and Rebecca had discussed the notion of having a child or two, but there were times when he doubted the wisdom of that idea.

At the moment, he and Alan White River got out of the government sedan John had parked in front of the dwelling where he was subletting a flat from a neighbor of Margaret Sweeney and Putnam Shady. The townhouse's owner was an archaeologist working on a dig in Rome. Excavation for a new line on the Rome Metro subway had revealed remnants of the city as it had existed 1,800 years earlier.

The scholar had been recruited by Italian authorities to consult on the job. He was expected to be away for at least two years and possibly five. He'd passed the word to people on the block that he was looking for respectable tenants to rent the place while he was gone. Rather than charge prevailing rents, he'd peg the cost to covering his property taxes and the building's routine maintenance needs.

In other words, it was a steal.

A retired cellist, Barbara Lipman, late of the National Symphony Orchestra, took the second- floor apartment. She still kept up with her instrument, something John, the new first-floor tenant, found relaxing. The basement space, as of now, remained vacant.

Margaret Sweeney had seen the basement flat and said it was easily as nice as the one she'd first rented in Putnam Shady's townhouse.

As John and White River got out of his car, the old man took in the building and said, "This is where you live, Grandson? It is much nicer than my last residence."

That was FCI Morgantown, a minimum security federal correctional institution in West Virginia.

Looking up, White River added, "Did you leave a light on up there?"

John saw what he was looking at and said, "That's the upstairs tenant, Ms. Lipman, a retired musician."

White River smiled, "Ah, yes, so she is."

"You can hear her?" John asked.

He cocked an ear but all he could hear was a distant car horn and approaching footsteps.

"No, Grandson, I can *feel* the music in her. She's given to melancholy pieces, no?"

Surprised that the old man could know that, John was about to say yes, but the sound of the footsteps was closer now and moving with urgency. Running. Closing in fast.

John looked over a shoulder, saw a man coming straight at them.

Until Alan White River stepped back, stuck out a foot, faceplanted the guy into the sidewalk.

Metro Police Headquarters — Washington, DC

Captain Rockelle Bullard's phone rang at the end of a long day. A damn near interminable day. She'd been waiting to hear whether Mayor Arlene Tolliver was going to appoint her as the city's next chief of police. In terms of on-the-job experience, commendations and relevant education, Rockelle should have been a shoo-in. Two questions remained, however.

The first was: How would it play among the District's increasingly gentrifying, and white, voters to have *two* strong black women occupying the top positions in city government? The second question was: Could Arlene and Rockelle co-exist in a way that would be productive and make both of them look good?

Neither question had been answered so far.

The thought that the mayor might just wait Rockelle out until she lost patience and said, "Screw this," had occurred to the captain. But she hadn't reached that point yet. She'd have liked to hash out her situation with Detectives Meeker and Beemer, but they were both out of the office, using up the last of their accrued vacation time before moving on to open their own detective agency.

If things turned out the wrong way for Rockelle with the Metro PD, she thought she'd ask if she could buy a one-third interest in Meeker and Beemer's new company.

In the meantime, she answered her office phone.

Good news or bad, the sooner she knew what her future held, the better.

It wasn't Arlene, though. It was John Tall Wolf, the fed from the BIA.

She'd met him at James J. McGill's new company headquarters last year.

Trying to be polite, but still sounding terse, she asked, "Something I can do for you, Mr. Director?"

"I just made an arrest, Captain, but if this is a bad time, I can call the FBI."

Damn, Rockelle thought, had she been that obvious?

"The time isn't great, to be honest," she said, "but I haven't gone home yet. So how can I help with your arrest?"

"Well, at first glance it was a street crime and..."

Rockelle heard a shout of protest in the background, followed by a noise that sounded like someone getting slapped good and hard.

"What was that?" she asked.

John said, "My great-grandfather quieting the attacker."

"Your *great*-grandfather?"

"Yeah, he might be a hundred for all I know. He says he lost count a long time ago."

Rockelle laughed. The unexpected moment of levity felt good.

"You know, I just might like to see someone like that. Still, an attack on a federal officer is a federal crime. The FBI *would* be the ones to handle that."

"We're not sure if it was me or my great-grandfather the guy was after."

Rockelle said, "All right then, I'll be right over. Where are you?"

John gave her the address.

"Tell grandpa not to get *too* rough with the perp," Rockelle said.

"Right. He just got out of prison himself."

Rockelle laughed again. "Damn, I'll use my lights and siren."

Florida Avenue — Washington, DC

Barbara Lipman, displeased that her practice had been interrupted, opened a window and looked out at the sidewalk below. In a peevish tone, she said, "What is going on down there? If this uproar doesn't stop immediately —"

John said, "It's alright, Ms. Lipman. It's me, John, your downstairs neighbor. I had to make an arrest. I've called the police. They should be here shortly."

"Who is that with you, Mr. Tall Wolf?"

"My great-grandfather and the man we arrested."

Alan White River waved to her and smiled.

Barbara Lipman said, "Well … good work, gentlemen, but please proceed quietly, if possible. I need to get back to my cello."

"Yes, ma'am," John said.

She withdrew her head and lowered the window.

White River addressed the bruised, sullen and handcuffed man he and John held between them. "You heard what the lady said."

To John, he added, "A vision of loveliness, your upstairs neighbor."

John didn't comment on that.

He called Captain Bullard back, asked her to cancel the lights and siren.

Omaha, Nebraska

Brice Benard sat behind his desk, alone in the four stories of offices his real estate development company occupied in the commercial high-rise building on Farnam Street in downtown Omaha. Warren Buffett's Berkshire Hathaway headquarters was a ten-minute drive up the street, but to Benard it was more important that the best Chicago-style deep-dish pizza place in town was only a five-minute walk away.

Benard's most recent personal balance sheet showed he'd become a billionaire in the past quarter, not just in terms of his aggregated real estate holdings, but in cold cash, negotiable instruments, precious metals and jewels. Sure, the buildings he either owned outright, in which he held a partnership position or held an option to buy added more billions to his asset ledger, but you couldn't *spend* real estate.

You could sell it, of course, but the whims of the market or nature, say tornadoes or floods, could decide what you'd pocket for the property. You also had to work things out with buyers, lawyers, bankers and accountants. It was normally a lengthy production, to say the least. The net value of each transaction was basically an educated guess.

To Benard, money meant cash or some other form of exchange that you could spend at will in a moment of your choosing. All right, the market value of gold and gems fluctuated but you could say the same thing about one nation's currency relative to that of another country. In any case, there were always people who would take money, gold and jewels in return for something you wanted to buy.

That was the important thing.

What was equally significant to Benard was how much fun you had earning your loot.

He knew he'd never come anywhere near matching the fortunes of Warren Buffett or Bill Gates, but he felt certain he'd had more fun getting rich, at least from his point of view, than they'd had making their billions. Picking the right stocks or writing software that ran on half of the computers in the world, where was the joy in that?

Sure, both of those things must have been a blast at first. Making the breakthroughs, kicking ass, establishing dominant positions. After that, though, it was just adding to the tally sheet. You might as well be someone in a counting house wearing a green eyeshade.

The joy in making big money, Benard felt, lay in out-thinking, out-hustling and when necessary out-fighting the other guy. Then you got *victory* money, and there was no sweeter kind. You grabbed pleasure with both hands, while all the other guy got was a swift kick in the ass.

Benard had read not too long ago that Michael Jordan had become a billionaire. The man had done that on the strength of a pro basketball career in which he'd broken other teams' will and hearts on his way to six championships. Jordan had leveraged those victories to gain endorsement deals like nobody else had ever done before him.

Then Jordan had gotten too old to win any more rings. Benard didn't know the man, but he'd bet that still stung Jordan. In Benard's line of work, he could be at the top of his game for another 20-30 years, at least. When the time came that he finally slowed down, maybe he'd be so old he wouldn't give a shit any more.

If he did still care, maybe he'd build himself a pyramid right in the middle of town. Seal himself inside with all his treasure, after telling the world a curse would befall anyone who tried to break in. Some dumbasses would make attempts, of course. That always happened. So he'd have to set up some really sneaky booby-traps.

Have a good laugh at someone else's expense even after he was dead.

He looked at the Apple MacBook resting on his desk.

It didn't make him laugh, but it gave him a lot of satisfaction.

The information on the machine might make him far richer than he already was. Let Buffett and Gates know he was at least heading in their direction. Even better than that, it might let him know the satisfaction of participating in a fine old American tradition.

Stealing something valuable from Indians.

Florida Avenue — Washington, DC

The guy who had tried to attack John, or possibly his great-grandfather, wasn't talking. That made it impossible, for the moment, to determine whether his charge of attempted battery should be handled by federal or local authorities. He was now confined in the back of Rockelle's police car.

John got FBI Deputy Director Abra Benjamin on the phone, explained the situation and let Captain Rockelle Bullard take the conversation from there.

Benjamin told Rockelle, "I'll take him if you want or you can have him. Your call."

The captain knew that Benjamin's deference wasn't due to respect for the MPD.

It was Tall Wolf or someone close to him who had the clout here.

"You wouldn't mind taking him?" Rockelle asked.

"I can do that, but I'll kick the guy back to you if he was after the old man."

"Of course, but if he was targeting Director Tall Wolf —"

"Then I'll keep him."

"Sure, *that* might turn out to be a *big* case."

The deputy director came clean. "President Morrissey has her eye on Tall Wolf. So, yeah, it wouldn't hurt my career one bit to find out what's happening here and bring the hammer down, if that's what's needed."

Rockelle wondered if Abra Benjamin's ambition would stop at becoming the first female director of the FBI or the third female president. In either case, *she* couldn't blame a woman for being ambitious.

She said, "Okay, I've got the guy in the back of my car. Your people can come get him." She gave Benjamin her location.

"Thank you, Captain. I'll be sure to mention your assistance in my report."

"Appreciate it." It never hurt to get a pat on the back from the FBI.

The mope Tall Wolf had busted was cuffed to a restraining beam. Rockelle went over to take a look, make sure he hadn't tried to chew through his shackles or kick out a window. The guy's face was gashed and bruised from kissing the concrete but he wasn't bleeding on her car's upholstery or trying to make an escape.

Rockelle pivoted and saw John was alone now. She returned his phone.

"The old guy make his getaway?" she asked.

"Said he was getting tired. He went upstairs."

John could only hope White River hadn't bothered Ms. Lipman.

Asked her for an autograph or even a date.

Rockelle said, "So what was great-grandpa doing in prison? Please don't tell me, though, that he killed somebody."

John shook his head and explained.

Rockelle smiled. "That was *him*, the master train thief? I am impressed. But you're sure the two of you are related?"

John nodded. "We did the DNA test. So how are things with you, Captain?"

Rockelle clamped her jaw for a moment and then she told him her whole story. Either she became the town's top cop, and soon, or she was going to pull the pin and see if she could work in the private sector with a couple of her detectives.

John thought for a moment and said, "How'd you like to help me with a case before you move on in either direction? It's another of those hybrid situations with both local and federal dimensions."

"We don't have to tell the FBI about my participation?"

"No, I'm covering the federal side."

He told her about the robbery at Dr. Lisle's lab.

Rockelle immediately saw a possible connection.

She looked at the chump in the back of her car and then back at John.

"That guy has to be involved somehow. Even *armed* robbers don't pick on a guy your size as their first choice, and that dummy didn't even have a gun."

"Yeah, that's my thought, too. But once he refused to talk to me, I thought the Metro Police or the FBI would do a better job of getting him to open up than I would."

"Possibly," Rockelle said. "You know what, I will help you. Go out on a high note, if that's how things turn out."

A car with two FBI special agents pulled up behind Rockelle's ride.

"I'll call you tomorrow," John said.

"Yeah, do that."

She turned and went to help make the prisoner transfer.

John went inside, hoping again that Great-grandfather had gone straight to his apartment. He'd also be pleased if White River had taken the guest bedroom as John had instructed, and hadn't seized John's room for himself.

He was pleased that both his wishes had been granted. Ms. Lipman was still playing, Beethoven's Cello Sonata #3, if he had that right, giving the impression she hadn't been intruded upon, and White River was sleeping peacefully on the carpeted floor of the guest bedroom. He had a blanket wrapped tightly around him and a pillow beneath his head.

John glanced at the double bed the old man had eschewed. He saw it was more than wide enough for the old Indian but not nearly long enough. So White River had accepted the cards he'd been dealt and had played his hand as best he could. Now, he was sleeping like a baby.

Looking at him, an interesting thought occurred to John.

The President wanted another Native American as Secretary of the Interior?

How about Alan White River?

CHAPTER 2

Tuesday, January 24, 2017
Cree Indian Reserve — Alberta, Canada

Bodaway's most terrifying and frequently recurring nightmare visited him yet again in the depths of the Canadian winter's night. The images in his mind were so bone-chilling that he often woke up screaming. Other times his vocal cords were paralyzed by panic. The cabin he'd been given was a good half-mile from his nearest neighbor. Except for a narrow footpath, a dense forest of spruce and lodgepole pines also separated him from the other inhabitants of the reserve.

The distance and the profusion of trees shielded the others from the sounds of Bodaway's night terrors. That calculation must have occurred to Coyote when she chose his place of confinement. Had the Cree been able to hear his shrieks of panic, they might have fled their land. That or, more likely, killed him and disposed of his body on an enemy's property.

On that late January night his nightmare was so realistic Bodaway could hear his heart thunder as if it were seeking to burst free of his chest. Worse still, Bodaway felt Coyote's dagger- teeth seize his throat. The pain was as real as when it had first happened.

The stink of the beast's rank breath filled his nose. He would have coughed explosively, but his windpipe was being crushed. He had room for neither inhalation nor exhalation. In a moment, he would begin to suffocate. That was how the nightmare always played out.

Only this time a new element intruded.

A slimy bead of blistering hot saliva seared his skin.

The only time that had happened before was the first time … the *actual* time.

Fighting an involuntary response, Bodaway tried to keep his eyes shut, but he failed.

Coyote was there once more, fangs clamping his throat again, no longer a bad dream but an eyes-blazing, fur-standing-on-end reality, a living, breathing monster who made the worst of his nightmares pale into trifles.

As Coyote had done the first time, she growled, and beneath the deadly rumble, Bodaway clearly heard a voice speaking to him.

"I have need of you. Your time to serve me has come."

Bodaway would have nodded immediately, if he'd had the freedom of movement.

Coyote didn't require that gesture; she saw submission in Bodaway's eyes.

If he'd had a tail, it would have been between his legs.

"I have enemies who must be dealt with," Coyote said. "I need to know their strengths and weaknesses before I attack them."

Despite the desperation of his circumstance, Bodaway struggled to understand what he'd just heard. Who or what could stand up to a demon like this? Why would it need any advantage other than its simple presence in the same spot as its prey?

Before his conjecture could go further, Bodaway felt the monster's teeth pierce the skin of his throat and a first trickle of blood exit his body. Coyote wasn't about to permit any distractions. Total attention and unquestioning obedience was the price of survival.

This time, Bodaway managed the tiniest of nods and closed his eyes.

He waited without a struggle for his throat to be torn from his body.

Capitulation couldn't be any more pathetic.

Coyote was appeased for the moment.

"There are two people I want you to watch, a man and a woman. You will not speak to them, but you will watch them, observe their habits. You will learn everything you can about them short of making contact. You will come to have an understanding of them. And you will do so as quickly as possible, knowing that your miserable life and how you will spend your remaining time depends on it."

Bodaway opened his eyes. Obedience looked back at Coyote.

Within that desire to please sat a simple question.

Who were these people?

Coyote gave Bodaway the names. He recognized neither of them.

Where would he find them?

Santa Fe, New Mexico.

For just a moment, despite the agonizing grasp holding his neck, Bodaway felt a glimmer of pleasure, if not hope. New Mexico could be cold in the winter, but compared to Alberta it would be mild, possibly even warm. That alone raised his spirits.

Without daring to touch Coyote, Bodaway raised his hands and gestured to his mouth.

He needed to ask a question. Coyote let go of his throat with seeming reluctance.

After gathering himself and clearing his throat, Bodaway croaked, "How do I get there, to Santa Fe?"

Coyote told him, "Steal a car from the Cree."

"Will I be coming back here?"

The bark from Coyote might have been heard as a laugh. "Your next stop will be someplace a bit better or someplace far worse."

The consequence of failure, Bodaway understood.

Coyote added, "If you simply try to run and hide …"

The beast pulled its lips back from its fearsome teeth and snapped them once.

Bodaway had no doubt of what that meant. He would be eaten alive. His flesh rent, his bones crushed, his blood slurped.

Coyote turned and leaped through a window that Bodaway hadn't left open. He closed it quickly, knowing that wouldn't keep the monster outside, but at least the frigid wind could be held at bay.

Stealing a car would be easy, but to give himself the biggest head-start, he'd have to leave immediately in the deepest darkness of the night. Packing the few pieces of clothing he owned and odds and ends of food in the cabin didn't take long. He left the ham radio behind, but he took his MacBook.

He stole the Cree chief's black Cadillac Escalade. The ignition fob was in the car.

He needed to gas up in Edmonton and he spotted an identical Caddy on the street. There was no point in stealing another copy of the same vehicle but the chief had a toolkit in his ride and Bodaway switched license plates with the other luxury SUV. The ploy was far from a guarantee that cops wouldn't catch up with him, but it might delay things for a while, and …

There would probably be other black Escalades he could switch plates with down in the U.S. After that, if he was still on the run, and not being eaten alive, maybe he'd think of some other trick to keep going. He had to admit, it was a pleasure to be even relatively free again and using his mind in creative ways.

Looking ahead, he had to wonder: Who were these two people who had the power to scare a monster? He'd sure as hell better not get on *their* bad side. Well, he had his laptop with him. When he got too tired to drive, he'd find a Wi-Fi hotspot and google them.

Hayden Wolf and Serafina Wolf y Padilla.

He was crossing into the U.S., using an unguarded back road, when it finally hit him.

These people had to be related to John Tall Wolf, whom he'd

once tried to kill.

Tall Wolf's father and mother most likely.

And Coyote had to be afraid of them. Or she wouldn't bother using him as her spy.

Despite his fear of Coyote, Bodaway thought he had to find a way to use these people to free himself from the monster. If they had the means to kill Coyote, he'd have to see that they got the opportunity.

After that, he could see if he still wanted to kill John Tall Wolf.

Florida Avenue — Washington, DC

John knew that Rebecca was an early riser, so he took the chance of calling her at 6:30 a.m. Pacific Time. She answered on the second ring. He was pleased to hear that she didn't sound as if he'd awakened her.

"You were up before I called?" he asked.

"Yeah, for half an hour. I used to be the one who got you up, remember?"

"I do. It's just one of the things I miss."

"Me, too. You want to talk dirty to each other for ten minutes?"

"Sure. I'll record it and play it back before I go to sleep tonight."

Rebecca laughed but said, "No recording. It might fall into the wrong hands."

"Funny you should mention something like that," John said.

"What, the possibility of being either embarrassed or black-mailed?"

"No, the idea of people getting hold of something that isn't theirs. That's the core of a new case I'm working on."

"You're working a new case?" Excitement filled Rebecca's voice. "Tell me all about it. You know, if it's not government top secret or something."

"It's not like that, but please keep it to yourself anyway." He told Rebecca about Dr. Lisle's missing computer and the promising medical advance resident on it. That and the unlikely idea of three young kids being the thieves.

"Huh, that is strange," she said.

"Especially, when it doesn't seem there was any way a master thief could have pulled off the job, much less three munchkin criminals." He explained the lab's security measures. "Any overlooked solutions, on my part, that you might come up with will be gladly accepted."

"Will do. Only it might take a bit longer than usual. I hired my first employee, Emily Proctor, a former LAPD lieutenant, and she brought our first case with her."

John listened carefully to what his wife and her new partner would be investigating.

"So you have two signed contracts, each of which stipulates widely varying terms," John said, "and the signatures on each are identical."

"Right."

"And Ms. Proctor has already considered the possibility that one of the signatures was mechanically reproduced."

"We both thought of that. She's having it checked out this morning. We're inclined to think both signatures were done by hand, but only one came from our guy."

John said, "If that's the case, the other one might be a work of art."

Rebecca picked right up on that. "You're saying the other one involves an artist? We thought of that, too. We're going to look at people who've got criminal records for forgery and/or counterfeiting."

John stayed silent for a minute. Rebecca interpreted that correctly, too.

"You think we're still overlooking something," she said.

"I took a painting class in college."

"You never told me that."

"I was trying to broaden my horizons ... and there was this girl."

Rebecca laughed. "I bet there was. So you never got far with either her or your canvas."

"Right. But my point here is the instructor was a whiz. One of the things she showed us was with a keen eye, a good hand and the ability to see the reality of an object —"

"The reality?"

"The light and shadow, the curves and planes, the varying depths and shades of color: once we could see that, we should be able to paint *anything*. As an example, she had everyone in the class write his or her name in a column on this big piece of paper. Then, alongside our signatures, she *painted* duplicates with a brush. They were spot on. The trick she said was to see each letter in our signatures as an object, not part of a name. Then, if you were any good, you just knocked out a knockoff signature."

Rebecca was silent for several seconds.

"And you weren't any good at it?"

"Terrible."

"By then you knew the girl you'd had your eye on was out of reach."

"Far out of reach."

"Was anyone in class good at this exercise?"

"Four of five of the students," John said.

"Are you ratting out your old classmates or teacher here?"

"I'm just suggesting you add a fine artist to your potential list of suspects," he told her.

"Okay, that's good. Emily and I will do that. What do I owe you for the tip?"

"Call me tonight and talk dirty," John said. "Moans, groans, the works."

Rebecca laughed. "Will do. You have anything else you'd like to share?"

John told her the President wanted him to be the next Secretary of the Interior.

"*What?* Are you going to accept?"

"I'm going to suggest she nominate my great-grandfather instead."

"Isn't he still in prison?"

John explained that development, too, and both of them got a later start on their days than they had planned.

After saying goodbye to Rebecca, John showered and got dressed — short of adding his tie and donning his suit coat. He liked to dress comfortably in his own digs whenever possible. Stepping out of his bedroom, he found Alan White River at the kitchen table eating dry cornflakes and washing the cereal down with a glass of orange juice.

Great-grandfather was reading the copy of the *New York Times* that John had delivered daily. Apparently, even at his age, the old man didn't need reading glasses. John's other subscription news source, the *Washington Post,* was neatly positioned in front of John's usual place at the table.

How the old man knew which seat he favored, John couldn't guess.

Scent was the only possibility he could think of. Of course, the old guy would have to be part bloodhound to do that. Then again, maybe he was.

White River was wearing the same denim shirt, jeans and work boots he'd had on yesterday. The old Carhartt Duck Coat he'd had on yesterday was probably neatly hung in the closet of the bedroom he'd used last night, John thought.

He didn't think he'd have to worry about his guest making a mess of his apartment.

"Anything else I can get you to eat before I sit down?" John asked.

"I had my eye on that apple on the counter, but it's the last one. Didn't want to take it, if you want it."

John rinsed the apple with tap water. Set it on a napkin in front of the old man.

"Enjoy."

"Thank you." He took a sizable bite. White River apparently

had a healthy set of teeth, too.

John took two bran muffins out of the fridge, warmed them in the microwave, poured a glass of orange juice for himself and sat down opposite his great-grandfather. Before he could read the headline on the *Post,* White River said, "You are a handsome young man."

That was a compliment John had never heard when he'd visited White River at FCI Morgantown. "Thank you."

"You don't need to wear your sunglasses in your apartment?"

"No."

"You wore them when you came to see me in prison."

John smiled. "Fluorescent light is a bit harsh for me, and sometimes I wear the shades for effect."

White River nodded and grinned. "It's a good one, that effect, with the size on you."

John said, "Yeah, it can work well."

The old man continued to look at him. His stare made John think White River had something in mind but wasn't sharing it.

"What are you thinking?" he asked.

White River said, "I think your parents must be good people, and I shouldn't undo the fine work they put into you."

"What do you mean?"

"I think I may know a way to help you with your eyes. At least make you a little less dependent on your sunglasses. I thought maybe your parents might know the same thing, but maybe they thought having you learn to overcome a challenge would strengthen you."

That idea left John speechless.

"Or perhaps I just know one or two things they don't," White River added. "I'm sure many people know far more than me." He punctuated his self-deprecation with a grin and turned back to his newspaper.

Even so, John asked him, "How do you think you'd do as the Secretary of the Interior?"

White River looked up with a far broader smile. He was

amused now. "I'm sure I'd anger so many people my tenure would be very brief."

John liked that answer. "So would I."

"You've been offered the job?" White River asked lightly.

"I have, just yesterday. The President called me. She wants another Native American for the position."

"And you told her no?"

"I stalled. I'm holding out for Secretary of State."

White River laughed and slapped his knee. "That would be magnificent."

"Yeah, but I'm not going to hold my breath waiting for that offer."

"I don't see your idea coming my way either," White River said. "Not at my age, even if I knew how old I am, and not with my prison record."

"You're right," John said. He took a bite of a bran muffin. Swallowing, he said, "Maybe you could be a deputy secretary, though, the acting conscience of the department."

White River laughed again. "You're a very funny young man. Do you know of any government job title that includes the word 'conscience'?"

John didn't, but he told his great-grandfather about Margaret Sweeney becoming the chief ethics officer of James J. McGill's new investigations agency.

"Now, that is interesting," White River said. "Maybe *they'd* have a spot for me."

John said, "Okay. I understand. I don't want the job either."

"Oh, I'd want it. I just don't think it'll be available before I turn *two* hundred."

John said, "Let me talk to the President then. Maybe she can come up with an idea that won't take so long."

As if taking a cue, John's phone rang.

It wasn't the White House, though.

Cale Tucker from the NSA was calling.

Albuquerque, New Mexico

Bodaway parked the Cree chief's stolen Escalade, decked out with its third set of stolen license plates, these from Arizona, in the long-term parking lot at Albuquerque International Sunport, the town's major airport. He scoured any interior surface of the car on which he might have left a fingerprint with a HandiWipe, one of the items he'd picked up at a roadside Walmart.

He'd also purchased a cowboy hat called a Stormsnake, a pair of Panama Jack wraparound sunglasses and a disposable phone at the store. Nobody gave him a second look as he shopped, but he kept his head down anyway. Security cameras were everywhere in 21st century America. He paid cash for his purchases.

When Coyote had dumped Bodaway on the Cree Reserve in Alberta, she'd left him with his driver's license and the credit cards in his given name, Thomas Bilbray. He'd gotten a $10,000 cash advance from his credit cards. His credit rating, despite his time in the wilderness, was still excellent. He realized now that Coyote had planned ahead to a time when she'd make use of him.

The one thing she'd withheld from him was his passport. He had no doubt Coyote could have tracked him down if he'd fled the country. It just would have taken her longer and, no question, she wouldn't want to be bothered by the extra effort.

Bodaway walked away from the stolen Escalade. Even wearing his hat and shades, he kept his head down. The lot's security cameras might capture a slight angle on his chin but that would be all. From behind, all they'd see that might be of interest was his backpack. The only items inside it were his remaining stash of cash and his MacBook.

He'd thought of buying a handgun and ammunition at Walmart, but New Mexico required a permit for concealed carry. You could carry openly without a permit but Bodaway didn't think that would be a good idea. Not just yet anyway.

He caught a cab at the arrivals area of the airport and had it take him to the nearest coffee shop, a place called Epiphany

Espresso. He bought a large cafe mocha and three apple turnovers, and found a quiet table where he booted up his laptop.

The first thing he needed was an inexpensive but reliable car. He wasn't going to steal another ride. There was no need for that now. He didn't have a criminal record, insofar as he knew, and he wasn't going to acquire one unnecessarily.

Of course, John Tall Wolf would have heard he was the one who had planned to kill him, but there was no *proof* that he'd either formulated that plan or acted on it. He had tried to kill his great-grandfather and wound up shooting Marlene Flower Moon to his endless regret. There was no question in his mind, however, that Coyote had ratted him out to Tall Wolf.

Bodaway found a classified ad offering a 2002 Honda Accord with 150,000 miles on it for $2,000. The ad said, "Clean, runs great, need the money."

He called the phone number in the ad and said he was at the airport, asked how long it would take to reach the seller by taxi. Thirty minutes was the reply. Committing the address to memory, he told the woman selling the car he could be there within an hour. He'd pay in cash if the car were what she said it was.

Having already shot Coyote's human manifestation, Bodaway couldn't plead that such a thing was beyond him.

Giving him a look at his target site was apparently beyond the reach of Google's eye in the sky. The image that the app returned was a blurred view of a high desert garden. No dwelling of any kind showed up in the picture. There was what appeared to be an adobe wall around a large residential lot, but the interior space was empty.

Had the house at that street number been torn down, he wondered. If so, there were no signs of demolition. No leftover scraps of building materials that had been left behind. Not even a sign of a former foundation. Besides that, the wall around the lot looked not only intact but unblemished. If a house within its perimeter had been taken down, it should have shown either some signs of demolition damage or evidence of damage repaired.

There was neither.

Bodaway checked other houses up and down the block. Every one of them had what appeared to be an identical wall. Lot sizes varied but the walls looked to be the same in terms of both height and color. Tight zoning restrictions, Bodaway thought. Inside each of those other walls were adobe-style homes, larger or smaller, but again of a piece with the demanded traditional styles.

More to the point, each of them was clearly photographed.

Bodaway went back to his target address.

No house.

Then he remembered something he'd read in an old newspaper story. When Dick Cheney had been vice president, he'd had the pixels of Google Earth's photographs of his official residence, Number One Observatory Circle, blurred to the point where the building seemed to disappear. Was that something that had happened to the house in Santa Fe, too?

Did the residents of the house have that kind of clout?

If so, that made him a lot more leery about snooping on them.

Problem was, he didn't really have a choice. He finished his coffee and pastries, and left the caffeine bar to go buy a car.

John Tall Wolf's Office — Washington, DC

"No luck finding Dr. Lisle's laptop so far." Cale Tucker had called John Tall Wolf to give him an update.

John had tried to suppress any expectation of good news, but he was still disappointed. He'd thought if he could wrap up this hunt quickly, he might scoot out to L.A. to see Rebecca and offer to lend an unofficial helping hand with her case. Now, that idea was shot.

Being married and living apart was proving to be a challenge.

"You think it's just powered off?" John asked.

After a moment's silence, Cale said, "You didn't hear it from me, but we can work around that one."

"What?" John said. "How can you do that?"

"I wouldn't have even mentioned it if I didn't know how close you are to our new president."

"I am?" John asked.

"Yeah, she wants you bad."

John was sorry to hear that. He said, "It must be my winning personality."

"Okay. I'll use the same excuse if anyone tells me I blabbed when I shouldn't have. You remember a while back some computer companies used to provide remote controls when you bought a desktop computer. So you could turn it on without having to push a button on the machine itself. Pretty much saving steps the way a TV remote control works."

"Must've missed that," John said.

"It didn't catch on real fast, and then a lot of people realized they didn't want someone else turning on their computers. It's a lot harder to hack a machine that's shut down."

"Wait," John said, "how could someone else turn on your computer without the remote control?"

"You know there are universal remote controls for TVs, right?"

"Never gave it a moment's thought. I don't watch much television."

"Well, take it from me, there are. Same principle applies to computers, as far as turning them on. For a specific machine, you need to know its Wi-Fi code, but that's not a problem for us. You send the right signal, turn on the computer and … well, I really shouldn't get too specific with our proprietary techniques. Not until you officially become a Cabinet member, and we get a go-ahead from the Oval Office."

John mentally pushed back at the idea of being pulled in an unwelcome direction.

"That's okay, I don't need to know trade secrets. So the takeaway here is: Sorry, you can't help me."

"For the moment. We think the laptop you're looking for must be stored in some kind of secure container, maybe something that's copper sheathed. Of course, even a thick wrapping of aluminum foil can reflect radio waves."

John said, "I'll try to remember that the next time I have to thwart eavesdroppers."

"Keep a good thought, Mr. Director. I haven't said we're going to quit trying. My guess is whoever took the doctor's laptop didn't grab it just to stash it. They want to use it. So, they'll turn it on, if only to download its data to another machine. Then we'll have our chance."

"Maybe," John said.

"Yeah, maybe. I feel real bad about not being able to find this computer for you, quick and easy. Show you what geniuses we are over here in Fort Meade. So I did a little extra research on who Dr. Lisle's biggest competitors in her field are, thinking maybe one of them might have been tempted to do something naughty. You know, if their research is lagging hers. If you want, I can give you a list of their names, locations and published materials."

John appreciated Cale's initiative.

"That might help," he said. "Thank you."

"Sure. I can send the data file to your laptop right now. You want to give me your machine's password?"

"You mean you don't already have it?" John asked.

"Of course, I do," Cale said. "I was just being polite."

McGill Investigations International — Los Angeles, California

Rebecca Bramley spoke across her office desk to Emily Proctor, shortly after talking with John that morning and doing a bit of research. She told Emily of John's experience in his college painting class. Emily was skeptical at first.

"That sounds neat," Emily said, "cinematic even. Having some guy who's great with a paint brush knock off a copy of Keith Perry's signature."

Keith Perry being their first client.

Emily had called Keith from her new office, getting a highly enjoyable feeling from her new workspace and planning how she'd personalize it. Keith had not only said he'd accept the condition that he put 100 shares of his new company into the pot, he'd make it 1,000 shares.

"But is a hand-painted signature really practical?" Emily asked Rebecca. "Wouldn't it be easier just to scan Keith's own signature into a computer and print it out on the company's draft of the contract?"

"It'd be a lot easier," Rebecca agreed, "but would that stand up to expert analysis? I've never had a case involving the question, but under a microscope, so to speak, wouldn't an ink-jet rendered signature look different than one penned by hand?"

Emily said, "I don't know, maybe."

"I'm still considering a forger," Rebecca said, "but how would a businessman know somebody like that? He'd kept in touch with a childhood friend who had good penmanship but took a wrong turn in life?"

Both women laughed at the notion, but then the idea made them think.

In the same moment, they said, "A calligrapher."

They laughed again, and then Emily deferred to her new boss.

Rebecca said, "Calligraphers *are* artists. They can use brushes in their work, just like fine artists. So maybe John was on to something. You know, a person who does practical work like rendering high-end invitations or civic proclamations to pay the rent and then does his own work for artistic fulfillment."

"My dad's law office has used calligraphers for invitations," Emily said.

"Give him a call. See who his firm uses. It'll be a starting point."

Emily said, "If I give you his number, would you mind calling? Just tell his secretary you've given his little girl a new job, he'll take the call right away. He'll be so happy I'm leaving LAPD."

"Yeah, I can do that, but what will you be doing?"

"There's another angle I want to take. I want to find someone who knows Angelo Renzi's publicist."

Renzi was the owner of LifeShare and Keith Perry's former employer. LifeShare had taken the idea of personal compatibility way beyond dating and marriage. LifeShare also offered to match people to their new best platonic friends, dance partners and workout buddies. Word was, they were even developing software to put together the most successful recreational athletic teams for every sport from archery to zip-lining.

LifeShare's ad slogan was: *Why waste time meeting the wrong people?*

That rationale was taking off like a wind-driven wildfire.

Natural disasters being another thing Californians could relate to.

"How will that help us?" Rebecca asked.

"Well, just talking to you now, got me thinking about two things. You asked how would a business guy, someone like Angelo Renzi, know a forger? From what I've already found out in a quick check on him and his family, they aren't crooked in any way that shows up in police records. So a forger is probably out, but maybe a calligrapher is in."

"A good enough friend who will do something just a bit crooked," Rebecca said.

"Right. For a price. Could be money, but here's where my other idea might come in."

Rebecca held up a hand, trying to tune into Emily's wavelength.

After a moment's thought, she said, "Money transfers can be traced, even if you try to launder them, but a bundle of good will would be much harder to pin down. Let's say Angelo Renzi buys a number of his artist friend's paintings. Then Angelo hangs those paintings in his house. Anytime he entertains people with a lot of disposable income, they see those paintings."

Emily grinned, thinking it was great to work with someone who could think like her.

"Maybe they even want to curry favor with Angelo," Emily said, "They ask where they might see this brilliant new talent's other work."

Rebecca tried to play the skeptic. "Is that really how things work around here?"

"Sure is. Among a lot of other things, L.A. is Hollywood. People suck up and pony up big money all the time. If I can find out who Angelo Renzi's publicist is — and he's gotta have one — I can find someone else in the same business who hates him. That person will help me find photos of Angelo's doings. If we can find a picture of a calligrapher/painter in his entourage —"

"No, no," Rebecca said. "In any publicity release, the accomplice would be noted strictly as a fine artist. We'd have to dig up the calligraphy background. So, I'll introduce myself to your father to get a start on that."

"Great. I've got one more thing I have to do today. No, two."

"What?" Rebecca asked.

"I've got to sign my employment contract with McGill Investigations International. There's no non-compete clause in it, is there?"

Rebecca said, "If there is, I'll cross it out and initial the deletion. You can video me doing so with your phone."

"Thanks."

"So what's the other thing you have to do?" Rebecca asked.

"Hand in my resignation at LAPD headquarters."

Washington, DC

John had his sunglasses on as he and Alan White River got into his car. He looked over at his great-grandfather and said, "You know, for the time being, I'll just stick with my eyes the way they are."

White River nodded. "You seem to do all right."

John felt the presence of an unspoken note of reserve. "But?"

"But you are unhappy. You miss your wife. I saw your wedding photo. I would feel the same way. I *do* feel the same way."

John asked, "How long has it been since you lost your wife?"

"Awinita? I see her every night in my dreams." The old man smiled. "She talks to me, scolds me and soothes me. Moves me in whatever direction I need to go. Her spirit is very strong; it won't let even death separate us. But how long has it been since I held her in my arms? Seems like forever. For years now, I've considered my longevity a curse that keeps us apart. My greatest fear is I might never die."

John smiled and told White River, "I don't think I can take care of you that long."

The old man chuckled. "The condition of my parole says you need to keep an eye on me for only two years. If you're willing, that is, and *your* wife doesn't object."

"She doesn't," John told him. "We've already talked about it. Rebecca says if you're too much for me, I can ship you out to Los Angeles to live with her, though she might move back to Canada if things work out that way."

"I've always wanted to see Canada."

"Well, we can set a date to do that without too much trouble."

"Perhaps sooner rather than later? In case I'm wrong about how much time I have left."

John laughed. "Sure, and if you're still feeling vigorous after we get back, we'll have to find you a job."

"I'd like that. Something with a good retirement plan."

Laughing again, John started the car and moved into the flow of traffic.

"Let's see if you have any aptitude as an investigator," he said.

"I have endless curiosity."

"That's always helpful."

"For example," White River said, "I wonder where we are going now."

"We're going to try to solve a part of a mystery, how Dr. Lisle's computer was taken."

"Is that how you caught me," White River asked, "one step at a time?"

John nodded.

"So what do we do first?"

"We go to a place called the Newseum. Do you know it?"

"I do. It is a museum dedicated to the five freedoms of the First Amendment."

John would have said it was a place focused on the history of mass media, starting with pamphleteering, moving on to newspapers, magazines, radio, television and social media, in that approximate order.

White River continued, "The freedoms of religion, speech, press, assembly and petition."

John stopped at a red light and looked at his great-grandfather.

"I'm sorry for underestimating you."

The old man nodded. "I have been around for a long time, and my father insisted I learn how to read at an early age — so I could tell him what the white people were up to."

"A wise man," John said. "I'd like to hear about him sometime, if you'd care to tell me."

"Of course, but now we have work to do."

"Yes, we do."

"There is something or someone at the Newseum that will be helpful to you?"

The light turned green and John turned onto Pennsylvania Avenue, the street on which the museum was located. "Yes. Have you ever heard of a man named Calvin Morley?"

"No."

"He's what's known as a digital artist. He's worked on a lot of big movies and video games that feature computer-generated images. He's giving a speech at the Newseum with the title 'More Real than Reality.' It focuses on how videos purporting to be records of actual news stories can be faked from start to finish or, more subversively, be blends of real and contrived images slanted to produce a desired outcome: rage, ridicule, revenge."

White River said, "This could be a great evil."

"Yes, that's the whole point."

"But why are we going to listen to this speech?"

"To watch the examples of the fake news Morley is going to show," John said. "We're going because there's no way three young children could have gotten past the security at Dr. Lisle's laboratory, and a friend at the police department told me no children were anywhere near the lab when the computer was taken. So, the only conclusion I can reach is the children aren't real."

White River understood. "They were meant to lead us down a false path to a box canyon."

"Yes, a dead end. But if we can find out who did the computer-generated images —"

White River grew animated. "That will lead us ... perhaps not directly to the thief, if he is clever, but perhaps to another step on the true trail. How did you hear of this speaker, Morley?"

"I read about him in the *Post* last week. After I concluded the kids couldn't be real, that was when the newspaper story about Morley popped up in my memory."

"Do you hope to talk to this man when he is done speaking?"

"I called him this morning. He said he's happy to meet with us."

"Because you are an important person in the government."

John grinned as he pulled into a parking lot near the Newseum.

"No, because he wants to meet the man who stole the Super Chief."

Santa Fe, New Mexico

The old Honda was as good as advertised, clean with a smooth running engine and at least 10,000 miles of tread left on the tires. The owner, a Latina woman in her mid-30s, told Bodaway, "The only reason I'm selling my car is I got fired out of the blue. Well, not really. I should have seen it coming. You turn down the boss's son three times when he asks you out on a date, I guess bad stuff is bound to happen. But I've got great office skills. I'll have a new job inside of a month. Still, I've got rent and other bills to pay in the meantime."

Bodaway kept a dispassionate look on his face but gave her $2,500 in cash for the car, $500 above the asking price. For a moment, the woman thought the bonus was meant to purchase personal favors of the sort the boss's son had wanted. Bodaway dispelled that notion with a small shake of his head.

He said, "Hang on to the extra five hundred and maybe I'll sell the car back to you for two thousand in a month."

The woman smiled at the prospect. She neither hugged nor kissed Bodaway, but she shook his hand and said, "Thank you. That would make me very happy."

She had removed her license plates from the car, so Bodaway's first stop was the state's Motor Vehicle Division. Using valid IDs in his given name, Thomas Bilbray, he applied for and received temporary plates to put on his newly purchased vehicle.

He was told a minimum liability auto insurance policy was required in the state and he should get one right away.

"Right away," Bodaway agreed with a nod.

He even accepted a business card the clerk said was from his cousin who sold insurance policies at the best prices in town.

Bodaway stuck the card and the registration paper in the car's glove box and started up I-25 northeast to Santa Fe. Traffic was light and a news-radio station told him the outside temperature was a brisk 41 degrees. Bodaway smiled. To him, the air felt balmy, and it was good to hear someone use the Fahrenheit scale again.

Those small pleasures were almost enough to make him feel optimistic. He considered approaching John Tall Wolf's parents and portraying himself as a victim of Coyote, someone forced to pursue an evil course of action or suffer a gruesome death. All of that was true, but ...

What if Tall Wolf had told his parents that a bad dude named Bodaway had tried to kill him a couple of years ago? What if Tall Wolf had even learned of his Anglo name, Thomas Bilbray, and shared that with Mom and Dad, too? Hell, it wasn't hard to imagine but Tall Wolf's parents might be able to bring him to a more horrifying end than Coyote could.

No, a direct approach to Mr. and Mrs. Wolf would be too risky to chance.

What he had to do first off was get a look at where they lived. See if the engineer in him could figure out how they managed to keep satellites from photographing their house. It'd be too obvious to just park an unfamiliar car near their home and set up an observation post. He figured two drive-bys a day, separated by a minimum interval of four hours, would be the most he could do to scout the house.

Beyond that, he'd have to check the local newspapers and community websites to find stories about Hayden Wolf and Serafina Wolf y Padilla. He was a medical doctor, and she was a tenured professor. He'd found out that much already just by doing a cursory internet search.

People like that, they'd attract more attention locally, in a town of 70,000, than nationally. Depending on their personalities and outreach to the community, they might even be celebrities on a small scale. If that were the case, there would be a relative wealth of material on them.

The old Honda didn't have internet connectivity, but when he found a Wi-Fi hotspot in town, he'd get directions to the town's public library and do research there. Before that, though, he'd cruise downtown, see how much things might have changed in the two years since he'd last been there. After that, he'd make his first run past the Wolfs' house. Or should he call it a lair?

The city center was relatively quiet when Bodaway hit town. There were ski resorts nearby, and the snow on the mountains looked good. That would keep the daytime shopping crowds relatively thin and there would be plenty of open tables at the restaurants when he got hungry. After dark, that was when things in town would get busy, but that was a few hours off.

Bodaway pulled his car into a Starbucks parking lot, bought a coffee to go and used the store's Wi-Fi to look up Dr. Hayden Wolf's address. The local directory returned the same address

Coyote had given him and provided the directions to reach it, only a 10-minute drive, he was informed.

The Honda, old as it was, still had a holder for his coffee cup. Bodaway took a right out of the lot, driving carefully not only to avoid a moving violation but also because he felt a growing sense of trepidation. He couldn't fail to obey Coyote, not without suffering a ghastly end, but Tall Wolf's parents … the thought recurred that they might be even more vindictive.

He had no idea what kind of suffering they might visit upon him, but he continued to feel new horrors might await him on Wildflower Drive. The street name certainly made his sense of dread feel ridiculous. The target block's widely spaced, high-end adobe style houses didn't exactly convey a sense of dread either, certainly not on a sunny day.

The homes all had adobe walls, as seen from outer space by Google, but the ground-level view made clear that they also had portals for vehicles and pedestrians. So Bodaway got a quick look at the grounds of each house, which seemed to be an acre or more at a glance.

Even poking along at 15 mph, though, he could only take in general impressions. Fine detail observation would require strolling by, stopping to tie a shoelace even. Without staring like a burglar casing his next target. From his driver's seat, Bodaway didn't spot anything at the Wolfs' house that stood out from its neighbors.

Certainly not anything in the way of high-tech hardware that would interfere with Google's peeking in from high above. Bodaway wondered if people, other than Dick Cheney, could actually opt out of unwanted photographic intrusions. The answer to that was, sure you could. Provided you could bring enough political pressure to bear on a multi-billion dollar corporation.

Or simply scare the hell out of the right person.

If the Wolfs could manage that, Coyote was smart to be careful.

Then again, it would be to Bodaway's advantage to have Coyote underestimate the Wolfs.

If they did her in — if that was even possible — he'd be free.

So the way to play things would be … honesty?

Tell Coyote that the Wolfs would be way too much for anyone like him to handle, but her on the other hand, well, she was Coyote? Was there anyone or anything she couldn't overcome? Play to her ego. Get her to be less careful than she should be. Hell, even if Coyote won a battle with the Wolfs, maybe they'd hurt her enough to forget about poor old Bodaway.

Go off and lick her wounds for a century or so.

If all that happened, he'd have to go out and buy a lotto ticket.

Because that'd be the kind of odds he'd have beaten.

Still, he liked the approach to his problem: truth shaded by guile.

The Newseum — Washington, DC

"Holography," Calvin Morley told John, "that'd be one way to do it."

He spoke of how the larcenous "children" could have gotten into Dr. Lisle's lab.

John, White River and the special effects artist sat in a small private lounge at the Newseum. They'd arrived 30 minutes before Morley's scheduled presentation was to begin.

"Holography is 3-D photography?" John asked.

"It's more complicated than that. There's a fair amount of physics involved, the superposition of waves, light fields and so forth. Anyway, a holograph is a visual record, not of an image, but a light field. Think of a really big, superfine mesh screen. Behind the screen is a light source. The light field is the amount of light flowing in every direction through each tiny opening in the screen. That's not exactly accurate, but it gives you something you can, pardon the pun, picture.

"Each ray of light has considerations of direction and radiance, but cutting to the chase, holography can produce fully three-dimensional images of a subject or subjects which can be seen without the use of intermediate optics like special glasses. What you do need, though, is a suitably lit space in which to display the hologram. In a diffuse, bright light a hologram would vanish."

John said, "The lighting in question was relatively dim and, now that I think about it, the images of the children, while fairly well defined, also had a ghostly aspect to them."

White River nodded in agreement.

"Ghostly as in transparent?" Morley asked.

John shook his head. "No, not like that. More like …"

"They might blow away in a puff of wind," White River suggested.

"Exactly," John said.

Morley considered the description and then asked, "Did you notice if the figures' feet were in solid contact with the ground? Did they seem to be subject to gravity like we are? Did they seem to have any weight at all when they moved?"

John and White River looked at each other.

"I never took notice of any of that," John said.

"Nor I," White River added.

Morley said, "Okay, how about this? You know how effortlessly really good dancers move? They glide as if neither gravity nor friction exists for them. Was that how these figures moved?"

John shook his head. "No. I didn't see either Michael Jackson or Fred Astaire."

"Just kids," White River agreed. "Like they were walking to school."

The special effects artist took everything he'd heard into consideration.

"You know," he said, "this is all probably a lot simpler than holography. What I think happened here is someone got hold of the security video and added the kids in a post-production suite. Dropped in computer generated images and then put the edited video back in the original's place."

"Who could do that kind of thing?" John asked.

Morley laughed. "These days, any number of people. A little computer hacking to get into the security system and some film student to come up with the kids' images and add them to the original video."

John said, "The lab is next door to a major university. You could probably find students with all the needed skills right there. But that seems too obvious a solution."

Morley grinned. "Right. It'd be better storytelling to go with something unexpected."

He looked at his watch and said he had to start his talk in a few minutes.

"May I take you to dinner tonight, Mr. White River?" Morley asked. "You, too, Mr. Tall Wolf."

John got the feeling he'd been included as a matter of civility. He begged off.

Alan White River accepted.

"Where would you like to dine?" Morley asked the old man.

"Anywhere is fine by me. Long as it's the early bird special. I don't want to fall asleep at the dinner table." The merriment in his eyes said he was joking, somewhat.

John knew that his great-grandfather would much prefer to fall asleep listening to Barbara Lipman's cello practice. It warmed John's heart to think that a man that old could still take an interest in both culture and romance.

He hoped that he and Rebecca would have an abundance of such years.

Century City — Los Angeles, California

Leland Proctor's law offices were located in Century City, a short drive from the Westwood site of McGill Investigations International. Better yet, from Rebecca Bramley's point of view, the trip didn't involve getting on a freeway. She wasn't frightened by high-density, fast-moving traffic. She'd driven equivalent highways in and around

Toronto and Vancouver. The reputation Canadians had for being friendly, well-mannered people didn't include the times they were commuting to work or home in a rush hour.

They went after openings in traffic like opposing hockey players chasing a loose puck.

Rebecca was hesitant, at least so far, about engaging in competitive driving in the U.S. She no longer had the decisive edge an RCMP badge had given her back home if a vehicular contest escalated to road rage. More than that, she was now aware of how many Americans carried guns in their cars; John had pointed out this cultural difference to her.

Wouldn't do at all to get shot or even shot at because some dude thought you'd cut him off. So she'd decided to acclimate herself to driving on the 10 and 405 freeways by practicing at times when the automotive flow was relatively benign. She'd work up to the point where she could challenge the traffic at any hour.

The trip to Century City, and the Avenue of the Stars no less, went without incident, if you could overlook the parking fee in the office building where Leland Proctor's firm was located: $39. Attempting a bit of humor, she asked the attendant, "Is that U.S. dollars or Canadian?"

The Canadian loonie — a one-dollar coin — equaled only 79¢ U.S. at that moment.

The attendant, a young Latino, shook his head. "No Canadian, no pesos either. Who you going to see?"

"Proctor, Davidson, Wilcox, Attorneys at Law."

The attendant nodded. "They validate your parking. Charge a whole lot more up there than we do down here, too."

"The boss's daughter sent me," Rebecca told him.

"Then you cool however long you stay. *Bienvenido, señora.*"

"*Gracias.*"

John also had told her it would be helpful to learn some Spanish.

The receptionist on the 27th floor validated Rebecca's parking ticket. A moment later, a conservatively dressed and coiffed woman in her 40s stepped into the reception area and introduced herself as Leland Proctor's secretary, Nessa. She led Rebecca to the managing partner's corner office.

Proctor rose to greet Rebecca. A man in his mid-50s, she guessed, he was trim, neatly groomed and had a smile worthy of winning a screen test. His suit coat hung on a mahogany rack in a near corner. The knot in his crimson tie rested against his azure shirt an inch below an open collar. Reading the signs of relaxed formality, Rebecca carefully measured the handshake she shared with Proctor.

Strong enough to earn his respect but not enough to challenge his masculinity.

"Lee Proctor," he said. "It's a pleasure to meet you, Ms. Bramley."

He gestured Rebecca to a guest chair and retook his seat.

"Nice to meet you, sir."

"Emily told me she was going to see you today, and Nessa gave me a note that said you've hired her. So I assume she passed muster."

"Yes, she did. Even better, she brought a new client with her."

Leland Proctor understood the implication immediately. "Someone who has a problem that made her think I might be of help. There's a legal angle involved here."

"There is such a consideration, but our immediate need is artistic in nature."

Proctor flashed his brilliant smile. "Well, that's interesting. What kind of art?"

Rebecca explained the problem and the proposed avenue of investigation.

Lee Proctor listened closely and nodded. "Our calligraphy guy, Walt Wooten, does paintings. Watercolors, he told me. I've asked twice to see his work, but he's gently put me off. Says he doesn't have anything worth showing at the moment. When he gets better, he says he'll give me the first look."

"Do you believe that?" Rebecca asked.

"That he'll give me the first look? Yeah, I do. That his work isn't good enough to show? No, I don't. Walt's a very gentle guy, shy really. But he does the finest calligraphy I've ever seen. I imagine his watercolors are stunning, too. It's my considered opinion that my best chance of seeing his work is to play things his way."

"Do you think he might be willing to talk to me? Tell me if he knows any other calligrapher who also paints and maybe has sold some work to Angelo Renzi. I'd appreciate it if you'd keep that name to yourself."

"Give me a dollar," Lee Proctor said.

"Establishing a professional relationship between us? Confidentiality and all that?"

Proctor nodded.

Rebecca said, "The smallest American money I have is a twenty."

"Way too much for this transaction. A dollar is symbolic."

Rebecca thought for a moment and reluctantly dug a coin out of her pocket. Handing it over to the lawyer, she asked, "You know what that is?"

Looking at the coin, he nodded. "It's a loonie."

"My *lucky* loonie. My grandfather gave it to me. He said he carried it throughout his RCMP career, and it kept him safe. Of course, he said the same thing about the coin he gave to my dad, too."

"No reason why a man can't have two lucky loonies," Proctor said.

"Yeah. Dad said the same thing. Anyway, I'll drop off a U.S. single as soon as I can. Meanwhile, please don't lose that coin."

"I won't. Would you like me to call Walt for you now?"

"Yes, please. If Mr. Wooten agrees to see me, will he want some money for his time, and will he keep our conversation private?"

"I think Walt will see you. He won't ask for money, and he's the soul of discretion."

"How can you be sure of all that?" Rebecca asked.

Lee Proctor smiled again, this time just a sly grin.

"Walt is one of your people. He's Canadian by birth and now

American by choice. He was the first guy ever to show me a loonie. He asked if it would work in the office Coke machine."

Proctor shared a smile with Rebecca and then his expression became thoughtful.

He asked, "Have you and Emily shared any war stories yet? All the hassles and hazards women cops have to endure?"

Rebecca said, "No, sir, not yet. I'm sure that will come as we get better acquainted."

"Good, because I feel certain there are things she hasn't wanted to share with her mother or me. It'll be a help, I imagine, if both of you can talk with someone simpatico."

Rebecca had told John many of the highlights and low moments of her career in the RCMP, but there were a few things she'd held back, incidents that would be easier to share with another woman who'd worn a badge and carried a gun.

"I think you're right," she told Proctor.

"You've also made things somewhat easier for Karen and me. We hated to see Emily follow in her grandfather's footsteps and join the LAPD."

"Something you avoided," Rebecca said.

"A career choice my dad insisted upon. His boy wasn't going to be a cop. He was all for my going to law school. Of course, he thought I would become a prosecutor. My idea was if I went to school all that time, I should make a decent salary in private practice. But I mollified him somewhat by later winning a City Council seat."

"All's well that ends well?" Rebecca asked.

A look of pain shaded Proctor's face. "Almost ended well. Years after my dad had retired from the force, and we all thought we could stop worrying about him, he intervened in an armed robbery at the diner where he liked to get breakfast. He always carried his retired officer's badge and had a concealed carry permit. He shot and killed the two stick-up guys, but one of them got him."

"I'm so sorry, sir," Rebecca said.

He nodded, repressing tears from the still painful memory.

"Emily was a high school sophomore when that happened. Cops from all around the country came to the funeral. May even have been a Mountie there, for all I know. Pipers played and politicians called my dad a hero. That was when Emily decided she was going to join the LAPD. There was nothing Karen and I could do to talk her out of it."

Lee Proctor got up and took a handkerchief from his suit coat, dabbed his eyes.

He told Rebecca, "Karen and I are overjoyed that Emily is leaving the LAPD. I called her as soon as I got word from Nessa. But it's still a dangerous world out there. Both of you, please be careful."

"Yes, sir, we will."

He took his phone from a coat pocket and sat down. "I'll call Walt for you now."

National Museum of the American Indian — Washington, DC

Before John Tall Wolf had left the Newseum, Calvin Morley had invited both Alan White River and John to stay and observe his presentation of "More Real Than Reality." He promised them front-row-center seats. White River said he'd like to see the show; John had other obligations.

Morley told John, "I'll personally make sure Mr. White River gets home after we have dinner."

"You're good with that, Grandfather?" John asked.

"I promise to make no trouble," he said with a sly smile. "You are going to help Dr. Lisle?"

"Yes, after I see if I can find Marlene Flower Moon."

"Ah, that one. If you are patient, I'm sure she will find you."

"You know who she really is, don't you?"

The old man nodded. "Of course, I do. I first met her under another name long before you were born."

John found that interesting. Something he'd have to pursue

when he and White River were alone sometime. He shook Calvin Morley's hand and thanked him again for his time. Then he went to the National Museum of the American Indian to talk with Nelda Freeland, the assistant director and Marlene Flower Moon's niece.

She kept him waiting outside her office for fifteen minutes.

He parried the insult by not letting it bother him.

Once Nelda's secretary admitted him, though, Nelda kept up the assault. "What do you want, Tall Wolf? I have very little time for you."

John sat, unbidden, in one of Nelda's visitor chairs.

Nelda understood the assertion of who had more power in this room or any other.

John would stay as long as he'd like and she'd have to put up with him. After all, he was the one who'd unofficially sponsored Nelda for her current position. His contacts in the government went far above and beyond her own. She was certainly smart enough to have confirmed that for herself.

What's more, with Marlene Flower Moon having left her cabinet post, Nelda no longer had any truly powerful advocate to protect her career.

"Where's Auntie?" John asked.

Nelda's first impulse was to crack wise, but she refrained.

Her response was simply factual but satisfying nonetheless. "I don't know."

"When was the last time you saw her or heard from her?"

"We haven't spoken about official business for months. My personal conversations are none of your damn business."

John thought she was right about that. Didn't mean he couldn't throw her a curve, though. "What if Marlene's in trouble?"

Nelda's jaw dropped. Not a lot, but she'd bought the idea for a second.

Then she recovered with a mocking laugh. "I don't know anyone who could give Marlene Flower Moon trouble. Not even you. Especially not you."

"You look a lot like her, you know. The resemblance is remarkable."

That caught Nelda off guard. She knew better than to think Tall Wolf was either coming on to her or simply complimenting her. So what was he getting at?

"What's that supposed to mean?"

"Just an observation. Of course, you're a young woman, and Marlene is who knows how old. Saying Marlene is well preserved doesn't do her justice. Makes me wonder how you'll feel when you get older and she still looks the way she does now."

Nelda blinked rapidly and her cheeks turned bright red.

Apparently, she'd never thought of that and didn't find the prospect appealing.

John stood up and said, "Oh, well, we all have our problems with Marlene. Tell her I said hello and I'm thinking of her. You know, if you have a little personal chat."

John half-thought Nelda might stab him in the back with a letter opener as he walked out. She didn't, but she'd planted a conceivably valuable thought in his mind. Nelda had said she didn't know anyone who could give Auntie trouble.

That didn't mean there wasn't someone.

Only that Nelda didn't know who it might be.

So who could it be, John wondered, that might scare Coyote?

Before he got back to his car, John called his secretary, Johanna Green Eyes.

In her typically blunt fashion, she asked, "What do you need, boss?"

"It's time I know the specific conditions of my great-grandfather's parole. Check with the Bureau of Prisons and see what they are, please. I don't want him locked up again because of any negligence on my part."

"Yeah, you did that, the old guy might come back to haunt you."

Just what he'd need, John thought. Marlene lurking in the shadows and Great-Grandpa popping up and saying, "Boo!"

"Before the close of business today, please," he told Johanna.

"Sure," she said, "I'll skip my pedicure."

Prometheus Labs — Washington, DC

John had just pulled into the parking lot outside Dr. Yvette Lisle's laboratory when his laptop chimed to let him know it had received either an email or a text message. He kept such annoyances off his phone. He hoped the dispatch, in whatever form, wasn't from the President telling him she needed an immediate answer to her invitation to join her cabinet. He knew he should be honored by the prospect, but the idea itself made him cringe.

He was not now and never would be a bureaucrat.

He wouldn't even want to be Secretary of State, though he might have to accept that post, if only to appease Rebecca, his parents and great-grandfather.

He fished out his laptop from its not-so-secret hiding place under the front passenger seat. He lifted the lid and kept only one eye open in the hope that might mitigate any bad news by half. Luck was with him. He hadn't received any greetings from the President.

Cale Tucker, the NSA whiz kid, had delivered on his promise to send John a list of Dr. Lisle's most likely competitors in the race to overcome the growing scourge of antibiotic-resistant bacteria. John didn't recognize the names of any of the medical scientists involved, but he readily knew the names of the giant drug companies sponsoring their work.

So would any American whose health plan didn't cover the tab for prescription drugs provided by those companies. The prices of buying life-saving medicines these days were high enough to kill you. Wonder drugs could be godsends, but if paying for them didn't leave you any money for food, shelter and clothing, what good were they?

John would have to ask Dr. Lisle about that conundrum.

Then he saw Cale Tucker had gone the extra mile and had delivered more than he had promised. In addition to the list of Dr. Lisle's competitors and their corporate sponsors, he also provided the names, addresses and curricula vitae of the people assisting Dr.

Lisle at her own laboratory.

Cale noted: "There are external enemies and possibly internal enemies. The NSA has come to learn that second point all too painfully in recent years. It would be foolish not to look at the possibility that someone outside of Dr. Lisle's lab has subverted someone inside it.

"The motivations for such treachery are all too obvious: money, a yearning for undeserved fame and simple spite. Unlike the battalions of personnel working for the big-pharma efforts, Dr. Lisle has only a baker's dozen in her lab. No superstitious dread of the number 13 for her."

"Still, she did have her computer swiped, but I don't think one fewer or additional employee would have made a difference. Hope you find at least some of this info to be helpful. We'll keep looking for the doctor's computer. Will let you know immediately if we succeed.

"Good hunting, Cale."

John skimmed the material he'd been sent. The names, addresses, phone numbers and credentials of the big money research personnel would come close to matching a small town's phone book, if anybody still printed such things. The list for Dr. Lisle's small workforce was much easier to absorb, at least on a superficial level.

Nobody's name stood out at first glance.

John got out of his car and locked his laptop in the trunk. He armed the compartment's security feature. If someone popped the lock by force and lifted the lid, he, she or they would get sprayed from head to waist with luminescent green dye impregnated with hydrogen sulfide, the chemical that smelled exactly like rotten eggs. Any would-be thief would be both visible and sniffable at a great distance.

That would make an arrest much more likely, if more challenging, to execute.

John rang the doorbell to the lab, after being pleased to see the entrance was locked. He'd yet to count to ten before Dr. Lisle opened the door. The reason for starting to count at all was he wanted to see to what extent the people inside were absorbed by their work. It seemed to John like hardworking types with clear consciences might fail to take notice of a single distraction.

On the other hand, somebody feeling guilty, maybe even half-expecting to be hauled away by some type of cop, could be listening for heavy footsteps coming his way. Or her way, to be gender equitable. Women might not be as larcenous as men, but they had their moments.

The missing Marlene Flower Moon being a prime example.

"Director Tall Wolf," Dr. Lisle said.

A momentary gleam in her eyes expressed hope that her computer had been recovered. Then she read his expression correctly and saw that wasn't the case. She didn't even need to ask the question, only saying, "Please come in."

John stepped in, hearing Dr. Lisle close and lock the door behind him.

Looking around, he saw they were alone.

"Everyone knocked off early?" he asked.

She shook her head. "I gave the staff a day off."

"You didn't tell them —"

"That I'd been robbed? No. We frequently work six days a week here. Seven-day work weeks are not uncommon. I simply told everyone to take a well-deserved rest."

John thought about that. How the news of a day off would be received would, again, likely depend on a person's state of mind. An honest person with nothing to worry about would greet the prospect of an unexpected day of leisure with joy. Somebody who'd been up to no good might fear discovery and already be on the run.

He mentioned the latter possibility to Dr. Lisle.

The thought of having a traitor in her midst made the doctor totter. John took hold of her elbows and steadied her. "Are you all right?"

She gathered her wits, regained her balance and nodded. "I

think I should have taken the day off, too. I didn't sleep well last night. You didn't recover my laptop, did you?"

"Sorry, no."

"I'd like to sit down. Let's go to my office."

Just to be safe and make sure she didn't fall, John looped an arm through one of hers and walked her to her office, got her seated behind her desk. He took a guest chair and said, "I've got some very good people helping me to look for your computer."

"From the BIA?"

"No, the NSA."

Puzzlement etched itself on the doctor's face. "Aren't they spies?"

"In a technical way, yes. I think their term of art is electronic intelligence."

"How did they get involved?"

"I have friends in high places. Also, it's been considered that your work might have possible military aspects."

That sat the woman back in her chair. "What?"

John explained the notion that in biological warfare having only one side inoculated against a widely dispersed pathogen could be a sure path to victory.

Now, Dr. Lisle seemed to shrink before John's eyes.

She said, "That kind of attack couldn't be limited to military targets. Communicable diseases spread indiscriminately. Civilians would be affected, possibly by the millions. Small children and the elderly would be especially susceptible."

John nodded. "Not a happy prospect at all."

"I can see why the wider federal government is getting involved."

He didn't tell her that he was still carrying most of the load himself.

"Do you really think one of my people could be involved in the theft?" Dr. Lisle asked.

"It has to be considered a possibility, say someone inside working with an outside competitor. The most likely motivation for that, of course, would be money. Do you have any knowledge that one or more of your employees might be in a monetary bind? Or even be prey to some compulsive behavior like a gambling addiction?"

Feeling a need to be helpful now, Dr. Lisle sat straighter in her chair, extending her arms and legs into a forward leaning posture. She shook her head. "No, I haven't heard anything like that. If somebody here was in a financial predicament, I'd hope they would come to me and ask for help."

John thought for a moment. "In most cases, I'd never think to ask something like this, but do you have a substantial financial stake in the outcome of your research?"

She didn't flinch. "Yes, I do, but I assure you it's well earned."

"I don't doubt that. But what about your staff? Do they get a piece of the pie, too? If so, how does it compare to your slice?"

Her face tightening now, Dr. Lisle said, "The staff is included in profit sharing, at my insistence. In relative terms, their share is considerably smaller than mine. Compared to what they might get elsewhere, if they got anything at all, it's significantly larger."

John sat silent for a moment, thinking about the situation.

"Do you *really* think one of my own people might have betrayed me?" she asked.

"I don't know. I'm just thinking of how an approach might be made from one of your big competitors. The sales pitch might be something as simple as saying, 'We'll give you an amount of money equal to what all of the staff at your lab will get.' The difference for a misguided individual would be substantial, but the overall expenditure for the bad guys wouldn't be a dime more than you're willing to pay."

Now, Yvette Lisle looked as if she might weep.

"Are there really people so self-centered and uncaring of others ..."

She didn't need to complete the question, already knowing the answer.

Seeking another counter-argument, she asked, "What about those children in the security video, the ones right here in the lab?"

John told her about his visit with Calvin Morley and what the special effects artist had told him.

"Was he definitive?" Dr. Lisle asked.

"No, but he was persuasive. Still, that's one of the reasons I came here today."

"What is?"

"Children are small, supple beings. They can squeak through spaces smaller than an adult might imagine possible. I want to search this building for any nook or cranny through which a young child might slip. You can tag along and offer a second opinion if I find any possibilities."

She stood up. "I'll do that. Where should we start?"

John got to his feet. "If there's a below ground level, we'll start there and work our way up."

"I'll lead the way," Dr. Lisle said.

As they walked to the stairway leading down, John said, "My great-grandfather said you're a member of the Omaha nation."

"On my mother's side, yes."

"And your father's side is French?"

"*Oui.* Why do you ask?"

"When I drove over here today, I noticed the name of your laboratory once again: Prometheus. The fire-bringer in Greek mythology."

Dr. Lisle flipped a light-switch and they started down the stairs to the basement.

"Do you know who the fire-bringer is in Native American lore?" John asked.

She nodded. "Coyote."

Taos, New Mexico

Taos Pueblo had been occupied for an estimated 1,000 years, making it almost certainly the oldest continuously occupied community in the United States. It had been named a United

Nations World Heritage Site. About 150 people lived in the pueblo buildings year-round. Another 1,800 or so lived in modern housing most of the year, staying in the pueblo dwellings only during cooler weather. Even then, some paid only brief visits to the traditional abodes.

Contemporary comforts and conveniences exerted a powerful pull.

Marlene Flower Moon had no trouble securing space in a pueblo. She paid more than a fair price for her lodging and, as ever, she was an irresistible presence to almost everyone she met. To those who opposed her wishes … well, the foremost among them lived 70 miles south in Santa Fe.

That was where Hayden Wolf and Serafina Wolf y Padilla were domiciled.

Where John Tall Wolf also had a house.

That thought made Marlene smile. If there was to be a showdown, what better place than Tall Wolf's hometown? Before that could happen, though, Marlene needed information to stack the odds in her favor. She knew from bitter experience how formidable Tall Wolf's parents could be, and now as a grown man how capable he was, too.

She'd already considered that she might have crept too close to Tall Wolf's parents. His mother, as he'd told her many times, was a *bruja*, a witch. The modern mind scoffed at such a notion. Marlene didn't. She knew for a fact there were forces of nature that couldn't be explained by rational thought.

She *was* one of those forces.

In many communities, her energy would have stood out like a spotlight in a dark sky. Not so in the Sangre de Cristo Mountains. Magic there was more plentiful in the air than snowflakes in the winter. Whatever heightened powers of perception Tall Wolf's mother and father might have, they would not find it easy to isolate Marlene's presence.

Especially while she was lying low.

Using conventional means of communications.

She'd texted Bodaway five minutes ago, demanding to know what he'd found out about Tall Wolf's parents. She badly wanted to observe them. Take them down quickly if they were not ready for her. Show them the deadly mistake they'd made by threatening her.

But she didn't want to fall into a trap, if they'd been cunning enough to bait her.

Another minute ticked by without a reply from Bodaway and Marlene's patience ebbed like a receding tide. If Bodaway had thought he could run from her wrath … No, the smartest thing for him to do would be to ring the Wolfs' doorbell, tell them that she was hunting them and beg for their protection.

Of course, they would see through him. Would quickly learn that Bodaway had once intended to kill their son. Hardly the kind of thing to endear someone to a mother and father. Still, they might spare Bodaway long enough to use him as bait, knowing Marlene would want her vengeance against all three of them.

That desire would be all but impossible to resist.

Having had Bodaway's throat in her jaws twice now, though, she doubted if he would dare to take such a step. If he did, the next time she found him would be his last to draw a breath. As for the elder Wolfs, she would have to withdraw and lay new plans, forcing herself to be patient, no matter how much that galled her.

Then Marlene's phone chimed.

It wasn't Bodaway texting her, though, it was her niece Nelda calling.

For a moment, Marlene hesitated to answer, but she'd told Nelda to call only if she thought it would be a great mistake not to do so. Then again, the nature of what constituted a terrible error was highly subjective. In the end, it was simple but compelling curiosity that forced Marlene to answer the call.

Marlene could always scold Nelda if the young woman had made a mistake, but if she was the one who was in error …

She accepted the call and said, "What is it, Nelda?"

"Tall Wolf came to see me, right here at my office."

"What did he want?"

"You. He wants to know where you are."

"What did you tell him?"

"The truth, that I don't know. I never asked where you went and I don't want to know."

"Good girl."

The tone of that feeble compliment struck Nelda as patronizing. Or whatever the feminine equivalent of that word was.

"Is there a reason you don't want me to know where you are, Auntie?"

"Of course there's a reason, and you were wise not to ask about that either."

Hurt now, Nelda said, "I'm sorry I called. I won't do it again."

"Wait. Did Tall Wolf say why he wants to know where I am?"

"He didn't say, but when I wouldn't give him any satisfaction, he asked what if you were in trouble."

That made Marlene jerk her head back, as if avoiding a punch.

"And if I were, he'd ride to the rescue?"

"I didn't ask, and he didn't say. If he comes back, should I just ignore him and not bother you again?"

Marlene thought about that. "No, if Tall Wolf pesters you again, let me know. I truly appreciate your help and concern, Nelda."

The warmth and tenderness of that compliment eased Nelda's hurt.

"Anything for you, Auntie."

LAPD Commercial Crimes Division, Los Angeles, California

Lieutenant Emily Proctor had thought that leaving the LAPD should have been a simple matter. Maybe nothing more than dropping off a brief letter of resignation. "See ya later. No, really, I'm outta here. *Adios.* Yours truly, Emily Proctor, former lieutenant."

No such luck.

When she arrived at her office in the Commercial Crimes Division on First Street, she found three uninvited guests present: an officer from the Personnel Division named Hannah Larsen and Detectives Eloy Zapata and Wallace MacDuff of the Burglary Special Section. Everybody stood up as she entered her small workspace.

Emily said, "If I'd known I was going to have company, I'd have brought a plate of cookies."

MacDuff said, "We'd have eaten them, too."

Zapata asked, "Why the hell are you leaving?"

"Well, the divorce is final, and between you and MacDuff, I couldn't decide who I loved more. So, it's better if I move on alone."

Officer Larsen laughed and said, "You only *think* the divorce is final, Lieutenant. You've got a lot of papers to sign before you get out alive."

She plopped a thick sheaf on Emily's desk and said, "You don't have any complaints, departmental or civilian, pending against you, so there's nothing to clear up there. You're not eligible for pension payments yet, but you have to acknowledge that your recorded time in service to the department is accurate so it will be credited to you in the event you apply for reinstatement. You have to complete a health statement for consideration of any possible future worker's compensation claim."

Officer Larsen went on for another minute or two, but cops were all too aware of the paperwork that came with the job and were stoic about dealing with it. When they weren't griping, that was. Larsen concluded with, "I'll also need your department-issued Glock and your shield."

Zapata and MacDuff winced when they heard that. They were lifers. They'd either die on the job or be dragged out kicking and screaming. The word resign wasn't a part of their vocabularies.

Emily handed over her Glock and the symbol of her police powers.

Officer Larsen zipped them both in a plastic bag and said, "Last thing is doing an inventory of your locker, Lieutenant."

Zapata got to his feet, "I'll be your witness, Loo."

Emily said, "Sure." She asked MacDuff, "You coming, too?"

"I'll hold down the fort right here."

"Okay."

Emily, Zapata and Larsen went to the locker room Emily used. She opened her locker and Larsen noted the items as Emily called them out: "UCLA Hoodie and sweatpants, Nike running shoes and socks, Donna Karan Cashmere Mist Deodorant."

Officer Larsen grinned. "Gotta get me some of that."

Emily announced the few remaining items and then said, "That's it."

Larsen nodded, acknowledging that the locker was empty.

Zapata provided his initials and shield number as the witness to that fact.

The reason for taking such pains was that departmental pranksters and enemies had been known to leave either gag items or incriminating materials such as illegal drugs in the vacated lockers of departing personnel.

Doing anything like that now with Emily Proctor's locker would be thwarted by the official record. That and the miscreant knowing he'd be facing the wrath of Detectives Zapata and MacDuff. Emily felt good about that.

Then she realized that MacDuff had stayed behind to make sure nobody had left any unwelcome item in her office either. Another comforting precaution. A desk drawer could be just as useful as a locker to sabotage someone's reputation.

Larsen had no reason to suspect anyone might go to such lengths to hurt Emily, but the two detectives had a hunch about the reason for their boss's unexpected departure and took every precaution that came to mind.

That extended to walking her down to her car.

"I'm fine, guys," she told them as they completed the short trip.

Zapata said, "We know you are. You are carrying your personal weapon, right?"

Emily shook her head. "Didn't think I'd have to shoot my way out."

"A woman in your situation shouldn't take chances, Loo," MacDuff told her.

Emily stopped dead in her tracks, glared at both detectives.

"Who ratted me out?"

She had told only two women coppers about her problem: the captain for whom she'd worked and a fellow lieutenant. Both of them had sworn to keep her concerns secret. Unless she needed them to act on her behalf should things come to grief or otherwise end up in court.

"Nobody did," Zapata said. "We just figured it out, being detectives and all."

McDuff added, "Eloy asked you what happened earlier just to get confirmation we're right."

"So what do you think is going on?" she asked.

"You're leaving because Captain Adair is making unwanted moves on you," Zapata said.

Emily couldn't keep her face from turning red.

Giving the detectives all the corroboration they needed.

"How bad is it, Loo?" Zapata asked.

Dodging the question, she said, "You can call me Emily now."

Both detectives shook their heads.

"Okay," she said, "he asked me to marry him. I said no. He keeps calling me or he did until I changed my phone number and didn't have the new one listed."

"Info like that can be hacked," Zapata said.

"I used my grandmother's maiden name to get the new number."

MacDuff sighed. "So you think it's serious, too."

"Enough to quit your job," Zapata added.

"I got a new one," Emily said gamely.

"Another police department?" Zapata asked.

Emily shook her head.

"Doing gumshoe work for your father," MacDuff said.

They both knew Leland Proctor's profession.

"No, I'm working at James J. McGill's new L.A. office."

The face of both detectives tightened. They'd encountered

McGill on their home turf not that long ago, and hadn't liked how he'd big-footed his way into an investigation that they felt should have been exclusively their own. The man's damn Secret Service witch had threatened to shoot them dead if McGill had come to any harm that might be construed as their doing.

They'd never gone so far as to consider assassinating the president's husband.

Hadn't even whispered the possibility to each other.

Without saying a word, though, they both knew that accidents did happen.

Until they'd been told what the price would be for such a mishap.

"Is *he* gonna come to town again?" Zapata asked.

"He might visit, I guess, but headquarters is in Washington, DC. The woman running the L.A. office is a former Canadian Mountie."

She saw that her former subordinates weren't comforted by the thought of two women doing potentially hazardous work. Chauvinistic of them, but in a touchingly retro way.

"We'll be fine," she told them. "Rebecca told me a war story that'd make you laugh and realize how tough she is. I'll ask her if it's all right to share it with you guys."

"You still didn't *really* tell us how bad it is with Captain Adair," Zapata said.

Emily sighed. "When I told him no about getting married, I also told him I wouldn't go out with him anymore. He kept calling anyway, all hours of the night. Waking me up at three or four in the morning sometimes. That was when I changed my number."

MacDuff shook his head and said, "Guys like that —"

"Hey, Em! Emily!" a voice called out.

"Oh, shit," she muttered.

Captain Terry Adair, dressed in a Tom Ford suit and glossy loafers with tassels, was jogging their way. He grinned at Emily and cast a calculating glance at Zapata and MacDuff.

Under her breath, Emily told the detectives, "Don't go anywhere, guys."

A tough request to honor, when the captain stopped opposite Emily and said, "Give us a minute, will you, detectives?"

Emily said, "I was about to leave, Terry. I've resigned from the department."

He looked stunned. "What, just now? Oh, Jeez, Em, you didn't have to do that. Listen, the paperwork can't have gone through yet and—"

He stopped when he saw Zapata and MacDuff hadn't budged.

He said, "Guys, I've got this. Go back to work."

Neither of the detectives moved. Zapata said, "Ms. Proctor asked us to see her safely off, Captain. Now that she doesn't have a badge or a gun, you know, it's easy to feel uneasy."

Adair gave the detectives his full attention. With their size, he wasn't going to intimidate them physically. He was, however, a superior officer, and a rising star in the department, and they'd damn well better … He needed to find just the right way to word his threat.

Make it something they'd never forget but it wouldn't come back to bite him.

He was so intent on staring down Zapata and MacDuff — the bastards looking ready to take anything he might throw at them — he didn't hear Emily get in her car. He did hear the motor start and then she was on her way. For a heartbeat, it looked like he might run after her. Within seconds, though, he knew that would only make him look foolish.

He clenched his fists and ground his teeth.

Watched until she was out of sight.

Then he turned, intending to rip those two arrogant bastard detectives.

Only they were gone now, too. Back to work, no doubt. Just as he'd told them to do.

Frustrated, Adair kicked the closest car, a Porsche Boxster, thereby making four mistakes. The dent in the fender left a footprint that would perfectly match his shoe; a parking attendant saw him kick the car; a security camera recorded him doing the damage, and the car belonged to a superior officer.

A woman, to boot.

The cascade of negative consequences that ensued would make Adair furious.

With Zapata and MacDuff.

And Emily most of all.

Director Tall Wolf's Office — Washington, DC

Johanna Green Eyes, a civil servant who knew that when the clock struck five her workday was done, was just about to leave when Director Tall Wolf returned to his office.

"The President called," she said.

John grimaced as if a sudden headache had struck.

"Just kidding," Johanna told him with a grin.

John lowered his sunglasses to the tip of his nose. "There are simpler ways to resign from your job, Ms. Green Eyes."

"I love my job," she said. "You're the best boss I've ever had — and you've been around me long enough to know when I say that I'm not just sucking up."

John pushed his sunglasses up.

Johanna said, "I just think it would be cool to have a tall, good-looking dude who always wears sunglasses in the President's Cabinet, instead of just another stodgy billionaire. The thought also occurred to me that I might make more money being a bigger big-shot's secretary."

"How do you even know I'm being considered for a cabinet post? I didn't tell you."

"Us Indians, we're sneaky. Know all sorts of things."

John played a hunch. "My great-grandfather told you."

"That, too. We're respectful of old people."

"Good to know."

"I've got Mr. White River's parole conditions. You want me to read them to you?"

Johanna held up a sheet of paper. John took it from her.

He said, "Being a good boss, I don't want to keep you a minute past quitting time."

Johanna took her purse out of a desk drawer and stood. "Thanks. I wasn't kidding, though. It *would* be cool to see you up there in the White House at a Cabinet meeting. Not just another stuffed shirt. Maybe you could let your hair grow long. Make a statement."

"The sunglasses aren't enough?"

"Yeah, you're probably right. We'll save the full-native look for when you run for office."

Johanna beamed at John.

"God help us all," he said. "Go home."

She left and he went into his office, dropped the sheet of paper on his desk and sat down. He took off his sunglasses and tucked them into an inside pocket of his suit coat. Unlike many public spaces, his office didn't have fluorescent lighting. He had rose-tinted LED bulbs and an adjustable rheostat to dial up a level of illumination suitable for reading without being so bright as to cause discomfort. Under the Americans with Disabilities Act, he'd been eligible for special lighting conditions since he went to work for the federal government.

In his early days, that meant he could wear his shades indoors.

Now, he was provided with comfortable radiance.

Moving up the job ladder wasn't all a bad thing ... he just wanted to continue doing the work he found satisfying.

He picked up the sheet of paper Johanna had given him.

As he had already suspected, great-grandfather, technically, hadn't been paroled. The federal prison system had done away with paroles 30 years ago. Instead, it granted "good time," a credit counted toward early release as a benefit of "exemplary behavior."

Alan White River, his record explained, had not only followed the rules of confinement to the letter, it was acknowledged that he'd counseled other inmates at his own initiative, providing them with "a new and productive view of how to lead better lives, both within the institution and quite possibly in society at large upon their release."

Overall, he'd provided "a calming influence on the other inmates, making the jobs of the institution's correctional staff easier."

Normally, someone who'd committed a crime that had resulted in the hospitalization of innocent people would have had to serve no fewer than five years of incarceration before being considered for release. Given the inmate's greatly advanced age — estimated by the prison medical staff only as 99+ years — a singular exception was made in his case.

Two years of confinement had been considered sufficient …

Provided that: 1) He obeyed all laws; 2) Reported his place of residence; 3) Limited his travel to the contiguous 48 states of the Union; 4) Agreed to random searches of his residence or; 5) Lived with a duly sworn municipal, county, state or federal law enforcement officer; 6) Refrained from alcohol and non-prescription drug use; 7) Avoided contact with co-defendants or anyone else with a criminal record.

John considered each of the conditions to be entirely reasonable.

And he absolutely loved number five.

He was a federal law enforcement officer, but he wouldn't be if he joined the President's cabinet. Alan White River then would have to assume the burden of regularly reporting to either a Bureau of Prisons official or the clerk of the court that had ordered his release. Not a terrible burden to impose on a younger man.

But for someone 99+ … well, who knew if the obligation might not slip his mind?

It would be awful to get sent back to prison for being forgetful.

John certainly couldn't let his great-grandfather face that possibility.

He was sure the President would understand.

John Tall Wolf's Apartment — Washington, DC

"You're forgetting one thing," Byron DeWitt told John.

The former FBI deputy director had called his friend at home.

He'd mentioned with pride in his voice that he'd tapped out John's phone number himself, taking no more time to do so than using an old rotary phone would have required.

John had congratulated DeWitt on the feat and mentioned the reason he'd have to decline the President's offer of becoming Secretary of the Interior. That was when DeWitt had told him he'd committed a sin of omission.

"What did I forget?" John asked uneasily.

"The many and wondrous powers of the woman occupying the Oval Office."

John was about to say, "Such as," when he figured things out for himself.

"You mean," he said, "she could just grant clemency to great-grandfather and whisk away all those pesky bureaucratic requirements."

"Right."

"Probably wouldn't amount to any big deal politically, would it?" John asked.

"Pardon a man like Alan White River? Her approval rating would likely go *up*."

John sighed. He was still stuck for a way to bow out gracefully. DeWitt had further challenging news for him.

"I spoke with Abra Benjamin." The new FBI deputy director.

"Did she agree to help?"

"Yes, but not in a straightforward way."

"What other way is there?" John asked.

"The kind that involves the CIA."

"What?"

"After I told Abra what was going on, she said making direct requests of foreign governments to be on the lookout for a new wonder drug might backfire."

"How?" John asked.

DeWitt was silent for a moment, not due to a mental lapse on his part.

He was giving John the time to reach the answer on his own.

Which he did, "Because at the very least they'd like the prestige of pretending that the breakthrough came from one of their own people. All the money one of their companies would make would only add to the glory."

"Right on the first part. The monetary windfall part is going to be problematic."

John was about to ask why again. Instead, he thought about what the problem might be. He came up with what he thought might be an approximate answer. "The FBI and the CIA are looking at the national security implications here. There are, what, two schools of thought? Find the thieves, recover Dr. Lisle's research, take over the development of the drug and deliver the end product only to our military personnel so we'll have the unbeatable edge if, God forbid, we ever have to use a biological weapon."

DeWitt said, "Scary as hell, isn't it? The way I see it, the military would get the first supply of the drug and then mass distribution would be made available to the general public. There is, of course, a far more benevolent plan."

John had no trouble seeing that idea. "Make the new drug available to everyone worldwide for free or at a few pennies per pill. Eliminate any chance that this particular type of biological warfare could ever be used successfully."

"Also kill any chance of anyone making a fortune off the drug," DeWitt said. "It'd be a kick in capitalism's ass, but that's by far the lesser of two evils as I see it."

"Me, too," John agreed.

"Dr. Lisle could still make a tidy little sum from the Nobel Prize she'd win."

"Uh-huh. I wonder how 'tidy' and 'little' will appease her."

"I don't know the woman so I can't say, but I have talked to the President about all this. Hope you don't mind, but I felt I had to do it."

John took a deep breath and let it go. "I understand."

"She's on the side of good medicine for everyone."

"Happy to hear it."

"There's something else pertinent to you in particular."

"What?" John asked.

"Well, the CIA is already on the job outside the U.S., looking for any sign of the thieves who took Dr. Lisle's computer. Abra Benjamin desperately wants to launch a 50-state domestic investigation, supplanting your efforts."

John said, "I hope there's a 'but' lurking around the conversational corner."

"There is. The President says you've got three days to accomplish whatever you can and then the FBI will take over. Oh, and she'd like to know your decision about the Cabinet offer by then, too."

John sighed.

"You think she might grant clemency to Great-grandfather regardless of my decision?"

"I'll work on that," DeWitt told him.

McGill Investigations International — Los Angeles

Rebecca Bramley, Emily Proctor and Arcelia Martin sat in Rebecca's office drinking coffee spiked with cognac and sweetened with whipped cream and morsels of dark chocolate. It was late enough in the day to have an adult beverage, and all of them were young and fit enough not to worry about the caffeine or calorie content.

Having had no one but Arcelia to talk to for the past three weeks, Rebecca had come to value her office manager as whip-smart, bluntly honest and able to leaven her frankness with a sharp, often self-deprecating, sense of humor. Beyond that, Arcelia had a graduate degree, which neither Rebecca nor Emily possessed. Didn't mean she was any smarter than they were, but a case could be made that she was more dedicated to learning. That was nothing to be overlooked.

Anyway, Emily showed the good sense not to object when Rebecca asked Arcelia to sit in on their meeting. Emily said, "Hearing from another smart woman might be helpful."

As the head of the office, Rebecca set the agenda.

"I'll go first," she said. "I've got the feeling my day was less dramatic than Emily's."

Emily said, "Yeah, my departure from LAPD, it was a narrow escape." The other two women leaned forward, the better to hear the details, but Emily offered a thin smile and said, "That was my cliff-hanger. How'd your meeting with my dad go, Rebecca?"

Emily and Arcelia's attention shifted to her. Rebecca played along and said, "I stayed on surface streets to get to Mr. Proctor's office, discovered how outrageous the parking fees in this town can be, and met a very nice man."

Emily smiled. "Dad is a sweetheart. Generous to a fault. A hard-ass only in court or when a situation calls for it."

Arcelia nodded in approval. "Can't ask for better than that."

Rebecca continued, "We had a pleasant meeting. He told me a little bit about Emily and he gave me the name and phone number of the calligrapher his firm uses, a Mr. Walt Wooten, who also headed south from Canada. I phoned Mr. Wooten, who told me to call him Walt and said he'd be available to see me tomorrow. End of story — except I got on the 405 for a few minutes coming back to the office and lived to talk about it."

Arcelia smiled derisively and raised her cup to Rebecca.

"Captain Courageous," she said.

"Captains, plural, if you're borrowing from Kipling," Rebecca said.

Arcelia nodded approvingly. She looked at Emily and said, "Can't slip a fudged cultural reference past that one."

"You can fool me," Emily replied. "I was a criminal justice major."

"Okay, enough chitchat," Rebecca said, "let's hear about this narrow escape."

Emily told them the story of Terry Adair making a surprise appearance and Detectives Zapata and MacDuff distracting him long enough for her to jump in her car and drive off. Emily filled in Arcelia on the backstory she'd shared with Rebecca earlier.

Arcelia thought about the account.

Then she said, "This is real nosy, what I'm going to ask, and tell me to get lost if you want, but did you go to bed with this guy?"

Rebecca hadn't been forward enough to ask, but she'd wondered the same thing.

Emily's long sigh was answer enough, but she didn't back away from the truth. "Yes, I did. You could count the number of times on one hand. It wasn't bad, it wasn't great, it wasn't decisive. All the things he did when we were both dressed mattered a lot more. He's a micro-manager, a control freak."

"He never tried to get rough, did he?" Rebecca asked.

Emily shook her head. "We were both cops, always had our guns close to hand."

Arcelia said, "That had to be both comforting *and* scary for you, didn't it? Not so much at first, but down the road a bit … you worried about what you might do to him. Maybe he'd tell you to do something and exactly *how* to do it for the tenth time, all in the same day and, bang, you'd just shoot him."

Both Emily and Rebecca stared at Arcelia.

"How did you know?" Emily asked.

Arcelia shrugged. "Heard of it happening before. An aunt on my mom's side did that to my uncle, except she used a knife not a gun."

"Killed him?" Emily asked.

"Stuck him so many times he could've had a cat's nine lives and that wouldn't have been enough."

All three women took a hit from their cognac-supplemented coffee.

"Okay," Rebecca said, "Emily showed good judgment ending the relationship but it looks like this guy — a police captain —

doesn't want to take no for an answer. Other than homicide, what's the most effective way of dealing with the situation? Is there an appropriate office in the LAPD to act on a complaint like this?"

Emily said, "The police department's final word comes from the Police Commission. It sets policy and oversees operations. Five civilians make up the Commission's board. You need a majority vote to make any big change."

Rebecca asked intuitively, "Is one of the board members more equal than the others?"

Emily nodded. "There's an executive director."

Rebecca followed up, "Among other things, is he responsible for discipline in the ranks?"

"Yeah," Emily said.

"Fine," Rebecca told her. "I'll phone him first thing in the morning. If he doesn't take my call, I'll ask Jim McGill to get his attention."

Arcelia asked, "You can really do that?"

"Why not?" Rebecca said. "He's the big boss and if one of his people is being messed with, or worse, seriously threatened, shouldn't he know? Wouldn't he want to deal with it?"

Emily held up a hand. "You don't have to go that far. My dad knows the executive director. They're old friends, in fact."

Rebecca and Arcelia sat back and looked at Emily.

Arcelia gave voice to the subtext of the silence. "You don't want to go to your father or his friend. Have either of them think you can't manage, sorry for the pun, your own affairs."

"Is that right?" Rebecca asked.

Emily nodded. "Yes."

"But you know guys like this, they never quit," Rebecca said.

"Never," Arcelia agreed.

"So I should have shot him?" Emily asked.

"No."

"Then what's the answer?"

"Take things one step at a time," Rebecca said. "Maybe we're wrong and he can be ... persuaded. Or intimidated. Maybe he loves his job more than he thinks he loves you."

"He might," Emily conceded.

"So you will talk to your father, tonight?" Arcelia asked.

Emily sighed. She nodded, but the gesture was half-hearted.

Rebecca wrote a 10-digit number on a slip of paper and handed it to Emily.

"What's this?" she asked.

"That's *my* father's mobile phone number. He answers it any time of day or night. In case something awful might have happened to me. Call him, if you like. Tell him you work for me, and would like to know just who I am, embarrassing stuff and all. He'll call me to verify, but I'll give him the word and then he'll talk to you quite frankly."

"You're saying if you can swallow your pride, I should be able to do the same?" Emily asked.

Rebecca shook her head. "I'm saying if you don't tell your father what's going on, I will."

Florida Avenue — Washington, DC

John arrived home before Alan White River returned. He thought about ordering Chinese food, but he didn't know what Great-grandfather might enjoy. John hadn't thought to ask him about his food preferences, if any. John had lived alone long enough that he hadn't needed to consider anyone else's favorite meals. He was still learning Rebecca's preferences in that area and many others. He felt a sudden yen to talk with her.

Adolescent as the notion was, he hoped she would call and talk dirty to him.

He decided to go with sesame chicken. Had to be one of the most popular Chinese dishes in the country. He confirmed that when he placed his order. A young woman's voice speaking perfect American English said, "Sure, that's popular with just about everyone."

"There are exceptions?" John asked.

"Doesn't work for vegans."

"Of course not." He ordered two servings.

He seriously doubted Great-grandfather was an herbivore.

The young woman spoke to someone in the restaurant in Chinese and a demanding tone.

She came back to John, got his address and said, "Twenty minutes. Tip is included in the tab."

"Efficient," John said, but the young woman was already gone. Handling her next transaction, no doubt.

No sooner had he clicked off than his phone chimed. Rebecca, he hoped. In vain, it turned out. The caller ID display showed Metro Police. Captain Bullard, he assumed, correctly.

"I just heard from Abra Benjamin at the FBI, Mr. Director," she said.

John hoped he wasn't going to be called out. "I just ordered dinner, and I'm waiting for my great-grandfather to return home. I also thought about calling my wife out in L.A."

Rockelle said, "You're telling me you don't want to be dragged out into the night? Don't worry, it's not like that. The FBI says other than getting the name and home address of the creep who bothered you and Great-grandpa last night, there's nothing to find in the way of a criminal record. No fingerprints in AFIS. So she doesn't feel like holding the guy and making a federal case out of a failed mugging, if that's what it was. She asked me if I want to take custody of him. I said I'd consult you first. She gave me one hour. If I don't get back to her by then, she'll cut him loose. So how do you want to play it?"

Before John could reply, Rockelle added, "I got the feeling Deputy Director Benjamin is clearing her decks because something big has come up. Not that she cared to share it with me."

John thought for a second. "What's the guy's name, the one Great-grandfather tripped, and where does he live?"

"Wilbur Rosewell, Omaha, Nebraska." She gave him a street address.

John said, "Huh."

"Something click for you, Mr. Director?"

"Dr. Lisle, whose computer got stolen, is a member of the Omaha tribe, comes from the same location, more or less."

"There's an Omaha tribe?"

"That's how the town got its name. It's a corruption of the original word, of course. And I bet you don't like coincidences any more than I do."

"Don't like them at all. So should I take custody of Wilbur?"

"No. If you don't mind, please ask a couple of your best detectives or undercover people to follow Mr. Rosewell surreptitiously to wherever he goes next."

"Within the limits of our jurisdiction, I can do that."

"Can you enlist help from the Virginia or Maryland state police, if you need to?"

"Yes, I have friends I can call on. Are you going to let the FBI in on what we're going to do?"

"I don't see why," John said. "They don't seem interested in Mr. Rosewell."

Rockelle laughed. "I like the way you think, Mr. Director."

"Not everyone does. Would you like to know what has the FBI preoccupied right now?"

"You are *not* your average federal officer, are you?" Rockelle asked.

"I've heard as much. I'll confide in you, but it can't go any farther."

"Deal."

John told her about the possible national security implications of his case.

"Good God," Rockelle said.

"Yeah. I'll have to ask the FBI for copies of the fingerprints they took from Mr. Rosewell eventually. They might not be in AFIS, but they might be on Dr. Lisle's laptop or in her lab."

Articulating his thoughts that way gave John another idea.

"Captain, would it be possible for you to access video from

public closed-circuit cameras around the American University campus? Dr. Lisle's lab is adjacent to the school."

"I can get the feeds from District cameras; you'd have to go after the federal databases."

"Right. I'll need everything you can get for the past 48 hours within a mile radius of the laboratory. Every face the cameras have recorded. If necessary, we'll subpoena the university and private business security videos."

"Who are we looking for?"

"Everyone working in Dr. Lisle's lab. See if any of them made an unscheduled visit."

"Ah, an inside job," Rockelle said.

A classic for anyone involved in police investigations.

John added, "I'll check their personnel files in the meantime."

Rockelle knew just where he was going. "See if there's someone else from Omaha involved."

"Exactly," John said.

"Thank you, Mr. Director."

"For what?"

"For trusting me with what you know, and giving me the chance to exit the MPD on a high note, if that's what it comes to."

"How would you like to become Secretary of the Interior?" John asked.

"Um, thanks, but I don't think so."

John thought it was getting harder to dodge that damn job with every passing second.

The Chinese food delivery was every bit as efficient as the woman who took the order. John understood the implication. That lady on the phone was no one you'd want to displease. He added an extra 15% to the tip-included tab, paying in cash.

Let the delivery guy decide whether he wanted to pocket the extra money.

If he even *dared* to.

Great-grandfather came home early enough to sit down with John while the food was still hot. John said, "I know Mr. Morley said he was going to buy you dinner, but I ordered extra food in case you were still hungry."

"Do you think I'm underweight, Grandson?"

White River picked up the plastic fork that came with his meal and addressed it to the portion of rice that came with his meal.

"Depends on your future fitness plans," John told him. "For track and field, you're fine; for Greco-Roman wrestling, you'd need to bulk up."

"I'd want a freezer full of buffalo steaks, if I was going to grapple." He popped the forkful of rice into his mouth and chewed contentedly. "Very good. Might I have something to drink?"

"San Pellegrino sparkling water, bottled spring water or straight from the tap."

"The Italian stuff, please."

John fetched two bottles and two glasses. He took the twist caps off the bottles.

"I could have done that, you know," White River said, accepting his bottle and glass.

"Okay, I'll remember. How was your time with Mr. Morley?"

The old man smiled. "Wonderful. He asked me to tell him about myself, and he was such a good listener I told him things I've not shared with many people. I told him about Awinita, how her spirit still lives within me. How I cannot wait to see her again when I, too, am a spirit."

All John wanted at the moment was a phone call from Rebecca. But he could see one day wanting what Great-grandfather did. That or Rebecca wanting to be with him again.

White River tried the chicken and gave that a nod of approval. He told John, "Mr. Morley is going to give me a great gift."

"What's that?"

"He's going to do a painting of Awinita for me. He did a pencil sketch under my direction and the likeness was so true to my memory it brought tears to my eyes. The painting will be in oils and that might cause more longing for me than I can bear. The man is a great artist and his talent with his computer images is truly magical."

More real than reality, John remembered.

Only now the idea of magic brought another subject to mind.

"Grandfather, how well do you know Marlene Flower Moon?"

White River took a sip of his sparkling water and set the bottle down.

He hadn't bothered with his glass.

Looking John in the eye, he asked, "Are you asking if I know she is Coyote? Yes, of course, I do. We have met many times over the course of all my years."

John found that very interesting. Maybe Coyote was interested in more than just him. Maybe there was a familial link, a dance of generations in play here. John asked, "Has she ever threatened you?"

"Many times." White River chuckled. "Not so much anymore. The closer my time comes to passing on from this life the less fearful any threat becomes … and I've told Coyote she will have to deal with Awinita's angry spirit if she causes me too much trouble. Coyote didn't like that idea at all."

The old man returned to eating his chicken and rice. John looked at him without speaking. To be at peace with yourself at White River's age was a great gift. John was glad now that Great-grandfather had stolen the Super Chief. Pouring the laments and sorrows of an overwhelmed people into an icon of the new age had been an act of both courage and genius.

Awinita's spirit surely must have been proud.

She may even have looked upon John with favor because that was when he had an epiphany. If the spirit of one strong woman might stand up to Coyote, why couldn't the spirit of another strong woman do the same? John wasn't thinking of his own wife. Rebecca certainly had the courage, but the idea of dealing with otherworldly challenges would be hard for her to accept, much less rise to the fight.

His mother, however — and his father, to be fair — would have no trouble going against Coyote in whatever plane of being either side chose. They'd already saved his life when he was a newborn. But why would they renew the battle now?

If that was indeed what was happening.

In his bones, he felt it was.

Marlene had gone into hiding because of something his parents had done.

He'd have to find out exactly what was going on, but not tonight.

"Very good food," White River said.

He'd finished eating before John had.

John said, "Would you like me to ask President Morrissey to grant you clemency? Remove any conditions from your release or your freedom of movement."

The old man smiled. John thought he even saw Great-grandfather's eyes misting.

"Will you still let me live with you?"

"Always. Right up until the end. Yours or mine, whichever comes first."

White River laughed. "We'll both pray mine does. Yes, I would like clemency. It is another magical thing that my grandson is so close to the person who can do such things." He got to his feet. "And now I must have my rest."

"You're okay sleeping on the floor?"

White River nodded. "The carpet is deep pile and nicely padded, quite comfortable with the quilt and pillow."

"Say hello to Awinita for me," John said.

The old man smiled. "Your grandmother is proud of you, too."

John was cleaning up the kitchen when his phone rang.

It was Rebecca. She said, "Guess what I'm wearing."

"What?"

"Nothing at all."

CHAPTER 3

Wednesday, January 25, 2017
Florida Avenue — Washington, DC

John rose early that morning. He silently looked in on Great-grandfather, supposing that would be a daily obligation from now on. Making sure the old guy was still present and accounted for, hadn't left to rejoin a mate that even death hadn't been able to take from him. White River's eyes danced beneath their lids; he was dreaming. The corners of his mouth turned up as if he had good reason to smile. John eased out and closed the door soundlessly.

Great-grandfather's resting happiness brought to mind John's phone conversation with Rebecca. She'd made believe he'd never seen her nude before. He'd played along, oohed and aahed at appropriate points of the narrative. It was all good, silly fun. They'd laughed and promised to find time together as soon as possible, and John slept soundly the whole night through.

He couldn't remember having any dreams, but he woke with a spring in his step and a feeling that everything would work out, if not perfectly at least to his general satisfaction. As a sign that he was not just being foolishly optimistic, he'd awakened with an idea that might help him solve one of his problems.

After eating breakfast and waiting as long as his patience

allowed, he called Cale Tucker at the NSA. Maybe a young guy like him was a go-getter and would be at his desk first thing in the morning. Of course, if Cale had a girlfriend who wasn't on the other side of the country ...

The NSA whiz kid answered on the first ring. "Director Tall Wolf, wish I had some good news."

"So nothing yet," John said.

"Sorry, no ... and word came down that this matter is now the FBI's case exclusively. So I was told to butt out until and unless otherwise advised."

"It's not the FBI's case until Saturday. That's the word I got from the White House."

"Yeah? Who at the White House gave you that word?"

"Byron DeWitt. You know who he is?"

"Oh, yeah. So you know the President's husband."

"We're buds."

The NSA kid was silent for a moment, evaluating John's claim.

Then he said, "I don't suppose you could ask him to give me a call."

"Verifying what I just told you? I can do that. Might not be for an hour or two. Wouldn't want to wake him up or pull him out of a therapy session. So why don't I tell you what kind of help I need, and you can get a head start while awaiting confirmation."

"I ... suppose I could do that quietly, but I would need official word before I could get back to you."

"Understandable. I wouldn't want you to lose your job."

"Glad you understand my position. What do you need?"

"The deputy director of the National Museum of the American Indian is a woman named Nelda Freeland. I'd like to know the names and phone numbers of anyone she called either from her office phone or personal phone from, say, three p.m. until midnight yesterday."

John had the thought that his visit to Nelda might well have provoked her to call Aunt Marlene. If the NSA could pinpoint where Marlene had taken the call, if one had been made, that might be helpful to John's understanding of what devilry she was planning.

"This is related to the case we discussed?" Cale asked.

"No." John didn't want to lie to the kid. "It has to do with another case, but regarding the missing item we discussed, I do have a possible suspect. His name is Wilbur Rosewell. He lives in Omaha, Nebraska." He gave Cale the man's street address.

"How'd you find this guy?" the kid asked.

"He took a run at my Great-grandfather and me. Tried to assault us."

"Wow. So what happened, you got his info but let him get away?"

"No, we turned him over to the MPD. They handed him to the FBI. They cut him loose."

"Because?"

"They think it's possible he's just a screw-loose street criminal."

"But you think otherwise?"

"Dr. Lisle is also from Omaha. The native half of her family has been there for hundreds of years. You think it was just a coincidence someone else from Omaha decided to take a run at me?"

Cale said, "You put it that way, no."

"You know what, something else I should have thought of earlier, can you check the phone records of everyone who works in Dr. Lisle's lab?"

"We can, yeah, but you'll need some real juice to get that approved."

John sighed. "I suppose I'll have to call the President then."

Cale asked, "She'll take your call?"

"No doubt," John told him. "She's waiting for it."

Then he added, "Let me know about Nelda Freeland as soon as you can, okay?"

"An assistant museum director? Sure, I'm authorized to snoop someone like that."

John had just clicked off when his phone rang. Cale calling back with a question he'd forgotten to ask, he thought. But his caller ID said Metro Police. Had to be Captain Rockelle Bullard, and it was.

"Good morning, Mr. Director," she said.

"Captain."

"Just following up on Mr. Wilbur Rosewell. Two of my people, independent types, figured that since they weren't being asked to make an arrest or otherwise assert their police powers, they could drive across jurisdictional lines like any other citizens. They followed Mr. Rosewell to Dulles Airport. They saw him purchase a first-class seat to Omaha, making a connection in Chicago along the way."

"That's some fine eyesight your people have," John said.

"Yes, well, they got that information from a ticket agent. They didn't have to show their badges or claim they were working on official business."

John got the picture. "Your people look like cops and they talk like cops. The airline person understood the situation implicitly and exactly."

"Uh-huh. They did give their names and badge numbers when they called the Chicago PD. Officers from that department working at O'Hare Airport confirmed seeing a man matching Rosewell's description exit the flight from Dulles and board the one to Omaha."

"I bet your people called the Omaha cops, too," John said.

"They did. Gotta give them points for follow-through. Omaha officers saw Rosewell deplane there and followed him to the address he gave to the FBI. Being thorough types themselves, the Omaha police followed Rosewell to their city's downtown business district this morning and saw him enter a commercial high-rise."

"That was where their collegiality ended?" John asked.

"As far as surveillance, yes, but they gave my people some background on Mr. Rosewell. He once wore a badge in Omaha himself. Then he went into private investigations."

John said, "Quite a few people doing that."

"Sure are," Rockelle agreed. "Anyway, Rosewell seems to have done well. Commands some serious money for his services. Serious for Omaha, anyway."

John thought for a moment. "Someone with police experience, how would he explain taking a run at me? Makes me wonder what kind of story he gave the FBI. I'll have to call Deputy Director Benjamin."

Rockelle said, "No need. I've heard his story from her already. Rosewell said he was minding his own business, walking down the street, when he remembered an appointment. He saw he'd be late if he didn't hurry, started to jog and your Great-grandpa stuck out a foot and tripped him. The fall left him dazed and by the time he pulled himself together the FBI had him in custody."

John said, "All a big misunderstanding, huh? That wasn't the way Great-grandfather and I saw it but it would be hard to argue with his story nonetheless."

"One other thing," Rockelle said. "Rosewell left the Omaha cops after killing two people. The first was an on-duty shooting deemed to be self-defense. The second was an off-duty bar fight. Words were exchanged and a much bigger guy pulled a knife on Rosewell. He not only took the knife away from the guy, he used it to slash both of the big guy's arms in just the right places and he bled out. That was when Rosewell moved to the private sector."

"How long ago was that, the knife fight?" John asked.

"Just a second. Okay, here it is. Eight years ago. What're you thinking, he's slowed down some?"

"Can't say," John said, "but we know he still has no fear of larger opponents. Something to keep in mind. Thank you, Captain."

"Happy to help. Let me know if there's anything else I can do."

John was sitting at the breakfast table drinking a cup of green tea with honey and thinking about his conversations of that morning when White River appeared. John had set out a cup for him and poured some tea.

"Still hot," he told the old man.

"Thank you." White River took his tea straight. "Very nice."

John only nodded.

"Something is bothering you, Grandson?"

"The man who tried to attack us the other night, did he strike you as … dangerous?"

"His intent was serious."

"But what about his ability?"

"We can't say. I did something unexpected, and he was focused on you. Had I let him pass, as he expected I would, he might have had some trick to use against you. And then he might have come back to attack me."

That made sense to John. In Rosewell's position, he probably wouldn't have expected a man of White River's age to intervene, and if Rosewell hadn't wanted to leave a witness, he *would* have gone back to dispose of the old man.

"Thank you for sticking your foot out, Grandfather," John said.

The old man chuckled. "It was the least I could do, also the most. I spoke with Awinita again last night."

"That's good."

"Yes. She said you have powerful forces watching over you."

"Including the two of you?"

"Of course, but others also."

"Would you care to tell me who?"

"You will see," White River said.

Just what John needed: another puzzle.

Farnam Street — Omaha, Nebraska

"You did *what?*" Brice Benard asked Wilbur Rosewell.

The Midwestern real estate titan and the cop-turned-PI sat in Benard's office, separated by a desk that reminded Rosewell of the flight deck of the aircraft carrier on which he'd once served: a place from which engines of destruction might be launched at a moment's notice.

Himself being one of them these days.

"Got arrested, just for a little bit," Rosewell said.

"What the hell does that mean?" Benard asked. "The cops were full up and they didn't have room for you?"

Rosewell laughed. "No, if it comes to that, they always make room. What I mean is no one came to any harm, and I denied doing anything wrong, which in this case is the truth because I was stopped short."

"Start at the beginning and go slow," Benard told Rosewell.

"I followed these two big Indians, the ones your friend in D.C. said might be trouble. They were tall but not bulked up. Sort of lean, both of them. One was older than original sin; the other looked like he might play a mean game of darts. Well, maybe, he might land a good punch, if you let him have the first shot, but I didn't intend to do that."

Benard saw fresh abrasions on Rosewell's forehead, nose and chin.

"Somebody besides you got in the first lick," he said.

"The *old* bastard, he moved faster than I ever thought possible. He stuck out his foot and tripped me. I got my hands up in time to keep from breaking any bones in my face, but ..."

He shrugged.

"What the hell did you *hope* to do?" Benard asked.

"Lower my shoulder, slam it into the young guy's sternum, knock him on his ass, maybe step hard on an ankle and be on my way."

"Figuring he would be smart enough to learn his lesson right off?" Benard asked.

"Yeah. You said you didn't want anyone sticking his nose into this deal of yours."

Rosewell had known better than to ask just what Benard's deal was.

The less he knew, the smaller his area of legal exposure would be.

"So the cops let you go because they had nothing more than two Indians' word that you *tried* to cause trouble?" Benard asked.

Rosewell shook his head. "The younger guy, the one your friend in D.C. is worried about, he's a fed with the Bureau of Indian Affairs, the director of their Office of Justice Services. The Indians' top cop. The local cops turned me over to the FBI."

"Jesus," Benard said.

"Yeah, exactly, but they were busy with other stuff, and, like I said, I hadn't actually hurt anyone except myself. The feds offered to give me back to the local cops, but they weren't interested either. I caught the first plane out and here I am."

"Nobody followed you?"

Rosewell thought about that. "No police cruisers. An unmarked car?" He shrugged. "What was there to see? I already gave the FBI my right name and address. Maybe some cop saw me board a flight to Chicago. The trail might end there or they could've checked my ticket and saw I was flying on to Omaha. If they did that, so what? I went home. What could be more innocent?"

Benard wanted to argue that point but didn't see a flaw in Rosewell's logic.

Instead, he asked, "If you'd been successful, knocked the big young Indian on his ass, but he still didn't get scared off, what did you have in mind then?"

"Nothing specific. Just take advantage of an opportunity to make it seem like genuine misfortune. Maybe set up an auto accident involving a tree, a body of water or a sixteen-wheeler. Something fatal but impossible to prove malice aforethought."

Cops, especially one who'd already put two guys down, understood the legal liability of taking a life. Murder-for-hire could get you the death penalty in Nebraska. A 50-year sentence was another possibility, but not if the victim was a federal agent. Even if he was an Indian.

"I might need you to do that," Benard said, "run this big Indian into a tree."

Rosewell shook his head. "Unh-uh. I turn up anywhere near this guy again and he gets killed, there'd be no explaining that away. They'd execute me and not even bother about giving me a final meal."

"Well, what the hell am I supposed to do if I need help?" Benard asked.

"You're talking *serious* money for a job like this."

"I know. Hell, I can pay in gold, if that'd make a difference."

For just a second, Rosewell looked as if he might reconsider, but then he shook his head again. He got up and walked toward the door, upsetting Benard no end. Tycoons weren't used to being abandoned in a moment of need.

"That's it?" Benard yelled. "You're leaving me high and dry?"

Rosewell stopped in the office's doorway.

He looked back and said, "Just make sure you pay your phone bill."

Benard would have to figure out for himself that he might be getting a call.

While Rosewell wondered just *how much* gold Benard had.

That and how to get his hands on it. Some of it, at a minimum.

Los Angeles, California

Rebecca Bramley called Arcelia Martin early, waking her.

"Sorry for disturbing you," Rebecca said.

"Only an hour before I usually roll out. I'll take a lunch-time nap. Your office sofa has a hide-a-bed."

"It does?"

"I asked for that when I ordered it. Thought you might need it sometime. You won't mind if I use it, will you?"

"No, not at all."

"Then we're even on the lost sleep. What can I do for you?"

"By any chance, do you have a handgun?"

"I do."

"With a permit?"

"You mean concealed carry? Yeah, I've got that, too."

"Don't you have to—"

"Have a 'good cause for issuance?' Because you or someone in your family is in immediate danger? That and have 'a good moral character.' Yeah, you need both those things, and there are also residency requirements."

Rebecca asked, "Are you in immediate danger? I don't remember you mentioning that during your employment interview."

"Must've slipped my mind," Arcelia said. "I actually was in danger up in Northern California. There was this street gang that decided an initiation requirement would be that the wannabe badass had to grab a woman off the street and rape her until he couldn't get it up anymore. Then he could either let her go with a threat to kill her if she went to the cops or just kill her if he thought a threat wouldn't work."

Rebecca said, "Jesus ... Were you —"

"No, the dumbass who tried to pull me off the sidewalk and into a car only grabbed one arm. I stuck my right thumb into his left eye, broke the nail right off. Didn't do his eye any good either. Then I stamped a high heel into his foot and kneed him in the balls. He was bent over, bleeding and crying inside of five seconds. His pals in the car apparently thought he wasn't made of the right stuff for their outfit and they took off."

"Did you run, too?" Rebecca asked.

"Hell, no. I stayed right there and called the cops. They came, I told my story, and the creep confessed. Once the name of the gang came out, *they* had to run and change their name, public outrage was so great. I doubt if they're even still in business. Even so, I thought I'd better get a gun, in case somebody had payback in mind, and my application sailed right through."

"I don't have any horror story like that," Rebecca said, "to justify carrying a weapon."

"You don't? What about the shootout on Wisconsin Avenue back there in Washington, DC? The McGill PIs versus the forces of evil. I read you were a part of that."

"You did?" Rebecca asked.

"Yeah. You don't think I'd apply to work at a private investigations agency without checking it out first, do you? I read all the newspaper stories I could find online. Saw some photos of you and your colleagues at the scene."

Rebecca said, "I ... I'd never done anything like that before. It was pretty damn scary, people firing automatic weapons in the middle of a big city."

Arcelia replied, "I bet. So you use that story in your application. If anyone tries to give you a hard time about getting a concealed carry permit, you say you work in a dangerous profession and you've got the media coverage to prove it."

"I guess so."

"So are you thinking things might be getting iffy again?"

Rebecca said, "Very iffy, if a certain LAPD captain were to confront Emily again. I keep thinking he might try something when she first steps out her front door this morning. But if there were three of us there he might be more reluctant to do something stupid."

Arcelia laughed. "With some guys, stupidity is a way of life."

Rebecca nodded. "I know. That's why I asked if you carry a gun."

Prometheus Laboratory — Washington, DC

John had just pulled into the parking lot outside Dr. Lisle's lab when his phone chimed. He'd left Alan White River at his apartment. Great-grandfather had asked John whether it would be all right if he introduced himself to their upstairs neighbor, Barbara Lipman. His motivation, he said, was strictly neighborly.

He had told John, "I should let her know I'm staying with you now. Wouldn't want her to think I was an intruder or something."

John repressed a laugh. He doubted if there was a burglar anywhere in the world within 20 years of Alan White River's age.

"Very considerate of you," he said.

"Do you doubt me, Grandson?"

"I was just wondering what Awinita might think."

"Her only concern is my happiness."

"Very open-minded of her. If she feels that way, who am I to object? My only suggestion is to plan your visit for a time when you don't hear Ms. Lipman practicing her instrument."

"Of course," White River said. Indian warriors knew when to make their moves.

John had estimated Ms. Lipman to be in her mid-70s, decades younger than Great-grandfather, but after gray hair prevailed he supposed there was no longer any such thing as cradle-robbing. He found it encouraging that elderly — and even ancient — people might take emotional interests in one another.

Beyond that generalization, he chose not to ponder.

He only hoped his ringing phone call wasn't news of a family embarrassment.

It wasn't. Byron DeWitt was calling.

"A little too soon to be asking for a progress report, isn't it?" John asked.

DeWitt chuckled. "You say that only because you've never worked in the White House or been married to someone who does. Immediately is already too late for getting the word on something important. Yesterday, last week or even a year ago would be much better."

"How do people survive conditions like that?" John asked.

"Just barely while aging rapidly," DeWitt said. "Take me for example, and I was only a deputy director at the FBI."

John winced and was glad they weren't doing FaceTime.

"Sorry about that, Byron."

"No worries. I'm mending and I *will* surf again."

Unable to restrain himself, John asked, "Are there such things as novices' beaches?"

DeWitt laughed. "Yes, in fact, there are, as you will learn when you ride those meek, little waves alongside me."

"Oh, no," John said. "Not unless my hair turns blonde and my eyes go blue."

"If not you, then your dear bride. I'm sure she has the courage."

John had to admit, "I'm sure she does."

"All right then, moving along to substantive matters. A young fellow named Cale Tucker from the NSA called me. I admitted to knowing you and confirmed that the President has given you until Saturday at high noon to conclude your investigation before the FBI claws it away. Young Tucker patched me through to the NSA director and I gave him the word, too."

"Thank you, Byron."

"I'm not done delivering glad tidings yet."

"Great-grandfather?" John asked.

"Yes. Jean says that pending a pro forma review of his life and times she will grant him clemency. Remove any and all legal shackles on him."

John was delighted to hear that and felt like an ingrate for the thought that occurred to him. Happily, DeWitt relieved him of the necessity of asking the question that had come to mind.

He said, "If this awkward silence that's preceding what should be a sincere 'thank you' means you have something to say that you'd rather not, let me add the following. Your great-grandfather's clemency is not dependent on you accepting a certain Cabinet post. I made sure of that."

"Thanks again, Byron. Even if I don't go out with you, I'll wax your surfboard."

DeWitt laughed. "We better not let the media hear about that."

John's face grew hot, but he laughed, too. "You know what I mean."

"I do. You just usually express yourself better."

"Okay, how's this: I really don't want to be Secretary of the Interior, but if it's important to the President, I'll do it. Only for one term, though."

"I'm sure that would be enough."

John added, "But hold off saying anything until Saturday, okay? I'll tell her in person."

"That's a deal. I'll tell Abra to back off until Saturday. You have any leads on the case yet?"

"Maybe one," John said.

John got buzzed into the laboratory. The young woman at the

reception desk, identified by a nameplate as Kirsten, looked up from reading a volume so dense with pages and blocky paragraphs that it had to be a textbook. She assessed John's appearance and said, "You've got to be the government guy."

"What gave me away?" John asked.

"Dr. Lisle described you to the staff as 'tall, dark glasses and handsome.' Not many people in DC wear shades in January. You know, unless they're visiting from Hollywood."

"My wife lives and works in L.A., but she's from Canada."

"Does she wear sunglasses whenever she goes out?"

John didn't know, and that bothered him a little. Losing touch even on small matters.

"I don't know. I'll have to ask."

The receptionist nodded as if that would be a good idea. "You're here to see Dr. Lisle?"

"If she's not in the middle of something important, yes."

Kirsten, quaintly, looked at a wristwatch to find the time and then at her phone to consult what John assumed to be Dr. Lisle's schedule. "She should be back in her office in about five minutes."

"Just wrapping up some work or a meeting?" he asked.

Kirsten responded with a blush, as if he'd asked an embarrassing question. Rather than answer aloud, she jotted a response on a Post-It note: *Potty break.* As soon as she saw he'd read the message, she crumpled and tossed it into her wastebasket.

John didn't consider a need to answer nature's call to be a reason for sheepishness, but he did find it interesting that Dr. Lisle's visit to the ladies' room was something a receptionist would know about. He asked, "Does Dr. Lisle keep a tightly organized schedule?"

"Right down to the minute," Kirsten said. "She says that's how she gets the most from her day. It could be hard working for someone like that, but she cuts the rest of us a little slack. Maybe five to ten minutes before she starts getting antsy and snaps us back into line."

John thought about people who hewed to compulsive behavior for a moment.

"Does she also like to organize her workspace just so? A place for everything and everything in its place?'

Kirsten smiled and nodded. "Exactly. She says that way she never has to look for anything; she knows right where everything is."

The young woman looked at her watch again. "Two minutes to go." She looked back at John and asked, "So what are you?"

"I beg your pardon."

"Sorry, should have been more specific. What nation, tribe or band do your ancestors hail from?"

"Oh. Apache and Navajo."

"Full-blooded Native American?"

"Yes, but raised mostly mainstream Anglo."

"Interesting. I'm Danish, Portuguese, Irish and Choctaw. Not necessarily in that order."

John momentarily lowered his glasses and took a closer look at Kirsten.

"You're one-quarter Native American?"

She nodded. "Most people can't guess my background."

"You are artfully blended. My compliments to all your forebears."

The young woman smiled. "Thanks."

A question occurred to John.

"Are there other people working here who have Native blood?"

He hadn't noticed any obvious names on the printout of staff personnel he'd seen.

But Kirsten nodded and said, "That would be *all* of us."

Los Angeles, California

Emily Proctor lived in the Carthay neighborhood of the city between Olympic Boulevard and Pico Boulevard. She owned, outright, a Spanish Colonial home with four bedrooms and good sized, landscaped yards front and back. The house's appraised value was $1.8 million. Her father had made home ownership possible, not that he'd simply bought the place for her.

What Lee Proctor had done was match the payments Emily had made in her first year there 1:1. The agreement was that he'd make the contribution each month Emily wasn't injured on the job due to criminal violence. In the second year, he'd make a 2:1 contribution. Each year of uninterrupted good health increased the level of the subsidy accordingly.

Money couldn't buy good fortune, of course, but it did serve as a regular reminder to Emily not to take any foolish chances with her well-being. Not that she'd ever conceded that point to anyone, especially another cop, but there were times when her father's deal did give her pause, might well have kept her from stepping in front of a runaway truck.

Metaphorically speaking.

By the time she'd had 10 years on the job and made lieutenant, she owned the place free and clear. She'd wanted a nice, big place because she'd thought it likely she'd get married someday and have a kid or two, but her career path hadn't allowed for such domesticity. She was still young enough to get married, of course, and even have a baby if she hurried.

Only she doubted, starting out on a new job now, that she'd find time for much else besides her work.

Especially now that she had to think of a way to get rid of Captain Terry Adair permanently. Short of killing him, she hoped. So she thought maybe it was time she sold her centrally located home and moved somewhere nice out in the boonies. Anyone who grew up in the sprawling expanse of Los Angeles knew that "geographic undesirability" had foiled many a would-be relationship.

Men and women alike had been known to utter the words, "Baby, I love you, but there's no way I can make this drive every day."

Emily was sure Terry would feel the same way and fixate on someone new.

The only problem with that logic, though, was that *she* would have to make nightmare commutes to and from work every morning and night. Inside a year, she'd look so frazzled nobody would want her and any chance of motherhood would be long gone.

While doing her morning, post-yoga meditation, the thought came to Emily that maybe her dad would go half with her on the cost of a hitman to get rid of Terry. She was still laughing at the facetious idea when the front doorbell rang and it occurred to her that it might be Terry calling on her right now.

Obsession knew no regard for phoning before dropping in.

Emily silently scurried to her bedroom and got her gun. She'd turned in her service weapon, but no cop had just one firearm. She'd have to get a concealed carry permit for her new job, but she had the right to keep a weapon in her house. True, it was only a Ladysmith .38 holding five rounds, but it was better than yelling for help.

The doorbell rang again as Emily reentered the living room. The curtains were still drawn so she couldn't see who was outside and he — if it was Terry — couldn't see her. But she was able to hear a woman's voice and then a second woman respond. The second voice she recognized as belonging to Rebecca Bramley. That helped her place the first one, Arcelia Martin.

Her new colleagues had stopped by.

Emily called out, "Coming! Just a second!"

She considered hiding her gun under a sofa cushion and usher the ladies into the kitchen. Only if she forgot leaving the gun there and somebody came along and sat down later … She didn't know if someone might get shot in the ass, but a visitor would certainly feel the lump under her backside. Explaining what the weapon was doing there would be more embarrassing than …

Emily opened the door with her gun in hand.

Rebecca and Arcelia looked at Emily and then at each other.

All three of them turned to look when they heard Terry Adair's car pull up to the curb in front of Emily's house.

Downtown Santa Fe, New Mexico

The temperature in Santa Fe, elevation 7,000 feet, that morning was 10° Fahrenheit. Nonetheless Marlene Flower Moon and Bodaway, aka Thomas Bilbray, were sitting at a table outside the Plaza Café. The predicted high temperature for the day was a relatively mild 45°, but the pale sun rising in the sky was going to have to put in some hard work before that level of warmth was reached.

Bodaway felt almost as chilled as he'd been in Canada. He didn't dare complain, though, because Coyote would only scorn him. She would take pleasure in his discomfort as she lounged comfortably with her silver fox coat open and her scarlet minidress revealing a daring slope of cleavage and a long stretch of toned thighs.

All that exposed flesh revealed not even the hint of a goosebump.

Then again, Coyote wasn't subject to human frailty. Bodaway, wearing a parka, sipped continuously at the hot cocoa he'd ordered. He was trying to use the cup he held to warm both his hands and his insides. He wasn't sure if he consumed all the cocoa that Marlene would allow him to have a refill. Even so, he felt compelled to finish his drink before it grew cold.

Marlene turned her head from watching the sparse traffic, pedestrian and automotive, pass by and turned her gaze on Bodaway. She said, "Tall Wolf is looking for me."

"Why?" Bodaway would be hugely grateful if Coyote forgot about him.

"Because he's noticed I've left Washington and didn't say goodbye."

Bodaway couldn't stop himself from saying, "He was expecting a fond farewell?"

He immediately regretted his words. It wasn't wise to get snarky with Coyote.

To his great relief, she only smiled, but even that revealed her terrible canine teeth.

"We're not friends, Tall Wolf and me," she said, "but we have become something in the way of companions. Co-dependent perhaps."

Marlene took a sip of the black coffee she'd ordered.

She'd decided that morning not to pursue a stealthy approach to Tall Wolf's parents. They'd likely not be taken by surprise anyway. So she chose to make plain her presence in their town. Let them come to her. Her appearance in Santa Fe wouldn't be headline news in their morning newspaper, but they'd sense her proximity and find her.

Once again yielding to impulse, Bodaway asked, "Do you miss Tall Wolf?"

Rather than snap at him, figuratively or literally, Marlene said, "That's a good question. He makes a point of irritating me, even challenging me, but ..."

"What?"

"We keep each other alert," Marlene said, "aware of the world and its dangers."

"There are risks even for you?" Bodaway asked with a hint of bitterness. "Why couldn't you do to Tall Wolf what you did to me? Seize his throat in your teeth and piss on him?"

Marlene's eyes flared, were no longer human in appearance, but had grown huge and canine. Worse, they showed rage and malice. Bodaway felt a new chill, deeper than what the weather had inflicted. He thought she might finally do him in right there.

Only a man's voice said, "Long time, no see."

Marlene's head whipped around and standing in front of her she saw Hayden Wolf.

At his side stood Serafina Wolf y Padilla.

Tall Wolf's mother and father.

Marlene turned to Bodaway. "Wait for me in the car."

He left without a moment's hesitation, glad to escape, even if only temporarily.

Marlene looked back at Hayden and Serafina, the white man and the brown woman. Regardless of skin tones, she had not the slightest doubt that these people were Tall Wolf's true parents.

That only confirmed to Marlene that there were higher powers at work here. For all the legendary wiles and shape-shifting deceits she called her own, Marlene knew these people were not to be underestimated.

There had to be a reason they'd saved an Indian infant's life all those years ago.

Even if neither they nor she knew exactly what it was. Not yet anyway.

A young waitress stepped out of the café. Sensing the tension in the air, she asked Hayden and Serafina, "Would you like to come inside or have something out here?"

Serafina, her voice as cold as the temperature, asked Marlene, "May we join you?"

"I was waiting for you," Marlene replied with a nod.

Hayden told the waitress, "Another round of whatever she's having."

Prometheus Laboratory — Washington, DC

Kirsten, the receptionist, showed John into Dr. Lisle's office. The head of the lab had returned to her workspace within seconds of the predicted time. Dr. Lisle looked up at John with an expression that featured both hope and anxiety.

Before addressing what was foremost on her mind, she thanked and excused Kirsten, closed the door to her office and offered John a seat. While still standing behind her desk, she said, "Please tell me you have some good news."

John gestured to Dr. Lisle to take her seat.

She took that as a sign that any news he might have wasn't good.

Disappointment made sitting a necessity.

"You haven't been completely forthcoming with me, Doctor," John said.

She took that as an affront and stiffened. "What do you mean?"

"I'm just guessing now, but I'd be willing to bet a month's pay that your laptop was not only stolen, it was also replaced by an identical model. Probably one that had all the same scientific data, inferences and future plans on it as the one you claimed was stolen."

Anger flashed in Dr. Lisle's eyes. "It *was* stolen, goddamn it."

Unruffled, John said, "And it was also replaced, wasn't it?"

The doctor looked away and didn't say a word.

"I'll take that as a yes," John said.

She looked back at him, tears starting to form in her eyes.

"How do you know ... about the replacement?"

"We both searched this building, remember? Neither of us found a hole or even a gap in the mortar big enough for a mouse to pass through. So how could three children get in and out of the facility and take a computer with them? Did a starship beam them down and back up?"

A frown of disapproval was the doctor's only reply.

"Didn't think you'd like that explanation," John said.

"I hope you have a better one."

"I think I do. Holograms, how's that sound? You know what they are, right?"

Still feeling defensive, she snapped, "Yes, I know what they are. But who could have produced holograms in my lab?"

"The same person who swapped out a substitute laptop for your own."

"But how could they have copied all the —" Dr. Lisle bit her tongue, realizing she'd just admitted John was right. There had been a decoy computer left behind. She also understood that she'd just been duped.

She said, "How did you know about the decoy?"

He didn't rub it in, only said, "You knew that the roof has weight sensors. As I believe you put it, 'anything heavier than a chihuahua up there, you'd think an air-raid siren was going off.' Then we searched this building together. I was sure then that you knew there weren't any secret entrances.

"So, after more time than it should have taken, I could think of only one reason why you weren't completely forthcoming about all the details of the theft from the start, why *you* didn't debunk the idea of small children stealing your laptop, and didn't mention the existence of a substitute at all. You had something besides your medical research on your computer, something you didn't want anyone else to know. The only question is whether that information is personal or criminal."

Lowering her eyes, Dr. Lisle whispered, "Personal."

"But not criminal?"

"No."

"And you knew that the switch had been made when you tried to open your personal file and couldn't find it?"

"Yes."

"Is the personal file password protected?"

"Yes, you get only two tries before the file is deleted." She gave a flat laugh. "It's more secure than all my research."

"How long ago did you realize the switch had been made?"

"The day before I reported it."

"That must have been a hard day for you, worrying that both your professional and personal lives were in jeopardy, wondering what you could do to make things right."

Looking haggard now, she said, "It was."

"How did you hear about my great-grandfather?"

"I read about him in *The Washington Post*. When he stole the Super Chief, I began writing to him. He told me when he would be released and that he was coming to Washington. I thought he could sympathize with my situation, and if he was smart enough to steal a train, maybe he could help me. I didn't know about you, but when he suggested having you help, I didn't think I could turn the idea down without it looking suspicious."

Dr. Lisle took a tissue from a desk drawer and blew her nose.

She continued, "I didn't know you'd be as smart as you turned out to be. I imagined you'd be just smart enough to get my laptop back and not go any further."

John smiled. "That would have been asking for a lot."

Despite her dismay, Dr. Lisle had to laugh. "A girl can hope, can't she?"

"Sure."

"You have more bad news, don't you?"

"Good and bad," John said. "The theft had to be, at least in part, an inside job. That's the bad news. The good news is the suspect pool is now a whole lot smaller."

Emily's House — Los Angeles, California

"You ladies want to excuse the lieutenant and me?" Terry Adair said.

The LAPD captain had approached to within ten feet of Emily, Rebecca and Arcelia. The inflection in his voice turned his question into a statement. The look on his face was also telling Rebecca and Arcelia to get lost.

They stayed put. Rebecca took out her phone. She started a video recording, showing Adair, Emily, Arcelia and herself. The captain understood that his presence was being documented in the world's most popular medium: moving pictures with sound.

He wasn't pleased, and was foolish enough to let his displeasure show on his face.

Worse, he vocalized his feelings. "Put that damn thing away."

Rebecca said, "Emily?"

"Keep the video going."

Nicely put, Rebecca thought. "Keep shooting," might have been intentionally misconstrued, and things could've gotten ugly fast.

"There's no need for that, Em," Adair said, his anger now tinged with the note of a plaintive whine. "You can send your friends inside or we can go in and they can stay out here. Whatever you want."

Emily took a step forward and said evenly, "What I'd really like, Terry, is for you to understand that I no longer want to see you. Leaving the LAPD means I no longer have to do that professionally.

In personal terms, I don't want you to come to my house. I don't want you to call, text or email me. No snail mail either. I don't want you to follow me while I'm driving. I don't want you to harass me in any way. When I told you we were through, I meant it. Now and forever, amen."

The captain's face contorted and went red. He looked as if he wanted to rebut what he'd heard, to explain to the damn woman that she, in fact, loved him as much as he loved her. She just hadn't realized it yet, but she would soon. Perhaps right after he roughed her up a little.

Only he couldn't do that with two witnesses watching and a video being made.

So he lashed out verbally. "You sure put out for me enough."

Emily nodded. "More than enough. Once was one time too many."

Arcelia laughed, involuntarily but aloud.

Adair scowled at her, might have said something insulting or even threatening, only Rebecca wasn't going to let that happen. She laughed at the captain, too.

Adair's head swiveled from Arcelia to Rebecca and back.

"You two bitches just bought yourselves a world of trouble."

Arcelia stuck out her tongue at Adair.

Rebecca thumbed her nose at him.

The captain clenched his fists but didn't raise them.

He told Emily, "We're not done, you and me."

"You're done around here, buddy," a voice called out.

Everyone turned to look. A hard-faced middle-aged woman with short gray hair stood on the front lawn next door. She was a commanding presence all by herself, but the AR-15 semi-auto rifle she carried easily also drew a good deal of attention.

"Is that SOB bothering you, Emily?" she asked.

"He's trying not to take no for an answer, Colonel. That and making none-too-subtle threats to my friends here."

"Hit the road, shitbird," the colonel told Adair.

"LAPD, you old bitch. Put that weapon down before I shoot you."

"USMC, sonny. If things get real around here, it won't be me going down."

For Adair's benefit, Emily added, "The colonel is an Operation Desert Shield veteran, won a Bronze Star and a Purple Heart. Besides all that, her family has money."

"And the video is still running," Rebecca said.

Arcelia said, "And on top of the rest of that stuff, I just called 911. We ought to be hearing sirens real soon. You know, coming from cops who don't have a misplaced crush on anyone."

Adair looked at all of the women, naked hatred in his eyes, finishing with the colonel.

Her weapon wasn't pointing at him, but she had it right.

She'd drop him if he went for his gun.

He turned on his heel and started for his car, breaking into a run for the last few strides. He was gone before the patrol cops could arrive, but their siren was now audible and closing in fast.

Emily turned and waved to her neighbor. "Thank you, Colonel."

"You're welcome, neighbor. You really quit the cops?"

"Yes."

"You have another job?"

"Private investigator. Working with Rebecca and Arcelia here."

"Good. But, Emily, you know my family isn't rich. We're reasonably successful working people, that's all."

"Psychological warfare, Colonel."

The older woman grinned and gave a salute.

She was back inside her home when the LAPD black-and-white pulled up at the curb.

Emily asked Rebecca, "Can you back up your video?"

"The file's already on the cloud."

Omaha Indian Reservation — Nebraska

The Omaha Tribe of Northeastern Nebraska originally lived in the Ohio River Valley, until it was displaced by the Iroquois

Confederacy: the Mohawk, Oneida, Onondaga, Cayuga, Seneca and Tuscarora tribes. These six tribes took many other native people into their cultures by means of warfare, adoption of the children of vanquished combatants, and by extending shelter to other displaced native peoples.

The Omaha chose to move west rather than fight or be absorbed by the Iroquois. The Omaha also never fought against the United States military, but they did assist the Union during the Civil War. In a scant measure of gratitude, the government established a reservation for the Omaha that was but a small fraction of the size of the lands they traditionally claimed.

Perhaps inspired by that heavy-handed swindle, many newly arrived 19th-century white settlers followed suit and made further inroads into Omaha land by buying individual properties from Native landholders, paying pennies on the dollar in value. It was all perfectly legal in Western terms, and utterly without conscience.

That was the legacy real estate tycoon Brice Benard tried to extend into the 21st century when he and a soil scientist in his employ, Darnell Elston, Ph.D., went to see the Omaha's Chief of Tribal Administration, Thomas Emmett. The three of them met in Emmett's office.

He offered his guests coffee, which they both declined.

He helped himself to a cup of Colombian blend.

Then Emmett listened closely to the story his white visitors had come to tell him. Unlike the illiterate tribespeople of the 19th century who'd sometimes sold their land for a wagonload of whiskey, Emmett was a graduate of Creighton University. True, he'd won a football scholarship to the school and was one of those big lugs who played the offensive line, but he was nobody's fool and had kept up with all his classes, graduating *cum laude.*

He told his visitors, "I read the letter Dr. Elston sent me. It says, Mr. Benard, that in looking for land to develop on either side of the Omaha Reservation, the doctor's people found ..." He paused to pick up the sheet of paper on his desk and put on a pair of reading glasses. "I better read this from the source, so I get it right.

"'Inputs from sources such as the deposition of long-distance, atmospherically-transported aerosol particles from fossil fuel combustion and other sources such as the contaminants in fertilizers were found in such significant amounts as to be hazardous to human health.' Is that right, Dr. Elston?"

"It is," Elston said with a nod.

"It's even more than that," Benard added.

"It is?" Emmett asked.

Benard said, "The most recent tests showed frightening amounts of arsenic."

Emmett took his glasses off and laid them on his desk. "Arsenic? That certainly is frightening. Where'd that come from?"

"The common sources in this country are the residues from burning coal and mining gold," Benard said. "Haven't heard of anybody hitting a bonanza lately, but people around here burned coal for quite a while."

"So the contamination could be widespread," Emmett said.

Dr. Elston replied, "It undoubtedly is."

Benard added, "But I'm only interested in the areas adjacent to your tribe's land, Mr. Emmett."

The chief said, "According to Dr. Elston's letter, Mr. Benard, you also have an interest of sorts in the Omaha tribe's land as well. You're offering to do a ..." Emmett put his glasses back on and looked back at the letter. "A bioremediation of our land for as long as it takes to clean up the soil, or technical words to that effect."

"That's right," Benard said.

"Pardon me for asking, sir, but wouldn't that be a fairly expensive, time-consuming task?"

"The cost would run seven figures at a minimum and more likely eight figures."

"So, we're talking millions and millions of dollars."

Benard said, "Yes, we are."

Emmett leaned back in his chair and rested his hands on what had once been a substantial middle. His wife had forced him to go on a diet centered on fruits and vegetables. He got to like it, and he lost a lot of useless weight. Felt halfway young again.

Thing was, he felt right this moment like he had at the *start* of his diet, about to go down a road he wouldn't have chosen for himself. Only this time he had even greater doubts about the outcome. Didn't think he'd like the result at all.

"How come you want to be so generous to us, Mr. Benard? Just feeling charitable?"

The tycoon laughed. "I've got two reasons, Mr. Emmett, neither of them selfless. One is making sure the thousands of acres I plan to buy adjacent to your reservation hold their value, aren't harmed by run-off from the toxins in your soil. The other is I've done exceedingly well lately and I could use a tax write-off, a great big charitable contribution. Now that I think of it, lending a helping hand to your people would also be good public relations. So, that's three reasons."

Benard got to his feet; Elston followed.

Benard said, "Thank you for your time, Mr. Emmett. If you could get back to me in a week with your decision, I'd appreciate it. I tend to be an impatient guy. When things get gummed up, I just move on to my next project."

"I'll take that under advisement," Emmett said.

Neither man made an effort to shake the other's hand.

Maxine's Tap — Omaha, Nebraska

State law in Nebraska allowed beverages containing alcohol to be served between the hours of six a.m. and two a.m. Maxine's Tap, shamelessly advertising itself as having the coldest beer and the cheapest booze in town, had patrons on hand *every* hour of the day. More than a few paid a five-dollar nap-time fee to snooze in place during the brief respite from imbibing.

When this convenience was introduced, the police department sought to have the premises cleared during non-drinking hours. A lawyer for the establishment took the cops to court and argued reasonably that the *good* citizens in town would be better served if Maxine's habitués were not out in public peeing and puking on their lawns or, worse, driving on their streets.

Police officers would be welcome to stop by every 30 minutes to get a free cup of java and see that only coffee would be served during the hours of alcohol abstinence. The court added a requirement that 911 be called for any patron who no longer seemed to be breathing or was otherwise in distress, and Maxine's was allowed to remain open around the clock.

Private investigator Wilbur Rosewell — who had confronted John Tall Wolf in Washington, DC — and a sinister looking fellow who made do with only one name, Petrovich, arrived at Maxine's just after nine in the morning. The productive people in town were already at their jobs or in their classrooms, and many of the overnighters in the bar were still taking their beauty rest. Maxine's policy allowed them to snooze until ten. Then they had to have at least an eye-opener or management would turn them loose on the public.

Rosewell and Petrovich sat near the rear exit. To get the top of their table wiped clean, they ordered drinks. Rosewell had a bottle of Moosehead he insisted on uncapping himself; Petrovich had a cup of black coffee he spiked with a shot of Stolichnaya from a flask he carried in a coat pocket. He paid for his drink as if the coffee had been topped with a shot of the house swill. Maxine's considered that to be an acceptable arrangement.

Getting down to business, the Russian immigrant asked Rosewell, "How do you know this man's talk of gold is real? People often exaggerate. Especially about money and women."

"Yeah, they do," Rosewell said. "So I did some checking."

He took his phone out and pulled up a story he'd found online in *My Omaha* magazine. An article headlined *Midwest Midas* showed a picture of a smiling Brice Benard sitting on a throne-like chair with a table stacked with gold bars on either side of him. Rosewell handed the phone to Petrovich.

As the Russian took in the image, Rosewell added, "I know a guy who used to sell ad space for that magazine. He remembered that story and told me the photographer had wanted Benard to wear a crown, but he's very vain about his hair and nixed the crown. But the ad guy says the gold was real. Benard had four armed guards on hand to make sure none of it got swiped."

Petrovich looked up and handed Rosewell's phone back to him. "This story's date of publication was 2001."

"Yeah, so?" Rosewell asked.

"The price of gold was down that year. Let me see exactly." He took out his own phone. "The average price was under $400 per ounce. Now ..." He checked another screen. "The price is $1,348.70 per ounce."

Rosewell whistled softly. "That's some big increase."

"Would you say this man is shrewd or lucky in his investments?"

"Well, shit, does it matter? If I had to guess, probably a little of both."

"There is a difference," Petrovich said. "If he was only lucky, he might have known this was the chance of a lifetime to cash in. He may well have sold all his gold as soon as the price doubled, and now curses himself that it has more than tripled. On the other hand, if he is shrewd, he may have continued to buy when the price was low and now holds a true hoard of wealth."

Rosewell thought about that. "I know he's supposed to be a big real estate hotshot but, hell, who knows how many buildings he actually owns outright, not just holds monster loans on, maybe scrambling to make his nut every month."

"This is a possibility, yes," Petrovich said. "It is good you are aware of it."

He added more Stoli to his coffee. Put out a few more dollars for the house.

"If he does have money trouble," Rosewell said, "he sure the hell hides it well. Lives like a freaking king who never worries about tomorrow."

Petrovich sat back and asked, "Have you ever dined out with him?"

"A couple times, yeah."

"He picked up the check, both times?"

"Yeah."

"How did he pay?"

"Credit card. One of those black ones, the kind most people can't get. But you know what? Both times he tipped in cash, big money. Big enough that both waitresses didn't say boo when he copped a little feel."

"The man is a swine," Petrovich said.

"What do bad manners have to do with anything?"

"Quite a lot. If he had offended either woman, or anyone else he meets, as he goes about his day, he will buy them off with cash, too."

Rosewell laughed. "Yeah, you can't get off the hook for being an asshole with a credit card, no matter how fancy it is."

"This is true," Petrovich said. "It also speaks to his fondness for real wealth, tangible currency, not just a symbol of how deeply in debt he is permitted to go."

"So you think he might really be sitting on a ton of gold?" Rosewell asked.

Petrovich said, "One more question first, my friend. Has this man ever been late in paying you for the work you've done for him?"

"Never. I complete a job, he gives me a check the same day. I go straight to the bank it's drawn on and cash it. Always get my greenbacks with a smile."

"That is very good. People with money difficulties either try to delay paying what they owe or accuse a third party, say their bank, of causing problems with the payment."

"Never had to deal with anything like that. So are you interested in going for a score here?"

"You can pluck a goose only once," Petrovich cautioned.

"That's okay by me, provided you think we're talking *big* money here."

The Russian said, "The gold in the picture on your phone,

those are called standard bars. Just one of them holds from 350 to 430 ounces of gold. You remember what I told you *one* ounce is worth at today's price?"

Rosewell had a good memory. "One thousand three hundred and forty-eight dollars and change."

"Seventy cents," Petrovich said. He pulled up the calculator on his phone. "That means each bar is worth between $472,045 and … $579,941. Yes, my friend, I think you've brought me a very interesting proposition today. From what you tell me, the man is likely to keep at least a few bars close to hand, either at home or work, possibly both. He does this so he can either buy his way out of big trouble in an emergency or just to enjoy the physical sensation of touching his wealth."

"We've got to get *our* hands on some of that," Rosewell said.

"I will bring a truck," Petrovich told him.

Plaza Cafe — Santa Fe, New Mexico

The young waitress brought a round of coffee to Serafina, Hayden and Marlene. Hayden paid the tab and tip and said, "If we want anything else, I'll step inside and find you."

"Deal," she said, wanting neither to go out into the cold nor to overhear whatever these three people had to say to each other. A vibe coming off all three of them said, "Steer clear."

She went inside, leaving the trio to themselves.

Serafina validated the young woman's uneasy feelings by starting the conversation with a pointed question to Marlene: "Eat any babies lately?"

Without batting an eye, Marlene replied, "Not the human variety."

"Other species are fair game?" Hayden asked.

"We all need our protein," Marlene told him.

Hayden said, "I suppose nuts and seeds won't do for you."

Marlene only pulled her lips back in a feral smile, revealing her pointed incisors.

That was usually enough to make most people retreat in horror. But Hayden and Serafina were anything but your average Mom and Pop. The pupils of Serafina's eyes elongated vertically, became slits like those of a cat; Hayden's eyes maintained their normal shape and blue color but seemed to crystallize to a diamond hardness and gleam.

"You don't scare us," Serafina said. "You never have; you never will."

"No matter what shape you may take," Hayden added.

Marlene sat back, relaxed, evaluated the situation and smiled.

"I believe you," she said. "There is no way I can intimidate you, not when it comes to Tall Wolf's well-being. Both of you would rather die than see him suffer."

Serafina leaned forward. "It's a good thing you understand that."

"My wife regrets that I didn't shoot you all those years ago," Hayden said.

Marlene looked at him. "That wasn't me; that was a *part* of me. If you had shot that coyote, we'd have had our confrontation long ago. I wouldn't have been nearly so patient as I am now."

Now, Serafina leaned back, let her eyes assume their normal shape.

"I see what you're thinking," she said. "You feel patience is your ultimate weapon."

"There's no doubt I will outlive you both. You are mortal; I am not."

"My sympathy," Hayden said.

She turned her head to look at him. "What?"

"You've just admitted that you'll never know what it is to rest, to be at peace. How many times have you already satisfied your pleasures, outwitted your foes, eluded their snares, seen them fall away while you continue on? What lies ahead for you but endless repetition? Even if you never die, the satisfaction you take from your triumphs will wither and turn to ash."

Marlene scowled, not caring at all for Hayden's appraisal of her future.

Serafina added to Marlene's discomfort.

"It is true my husband and I will die, but there is one thing that will live on long after us: the curse I have placed upon you. You don't sleep well lately, do you? Terrible dreams come to you every night, horrors so vivid and embedded in your mind you have trouble separating them from what you experience with your eyes open."

Marlene drew her lips back again and even snarled.

Her voice hoarse and no longer entirely human, she growled, "Maybe we'll finish this matter here and now, and no matter what else afflicts me or pales in memory, I will always relish what I do to you. As to what I have planned for Tall Wolf —"

Serafina and Hayden saw Coyote start to change shape, becoming a beast of enormous proportions when … her phone chimed. Marlene glanced at her phone on the café table. The caller ID said: JOHN TALL WOLF.

Unable to resist the temptation, Marlene resumed her human form and hit the answer button.

Tall Wolf said, "You didn't really think you could get away without saying goodbye to me, did you? You had to know I'd find you."

Serafina and Hayden Wolf heard their son's words and looked at each other.

"How did you find me?" Marlene asked.

"What, you think you're the only one with wiles? Knowing you're in New Mexico, I wouldn't be surprised if my parents are with you."

Being a good mother, Serafina called out, "John, are you all right?"

"Fine, Mom. Hi, Dad. I assume you're there, too?"

"I am, Son."

Marlene grew irritated at the turn of the conversation.

"What do you want, Tall Wolf?" she demanded.

"I'm working a case and thought you might be of help, if you're interested."

"In other words, you want me to do some of *your* work again."

John said, "I think this one could be right up your alley. Might even have a nice element of spite to it, and I know how you enjoy that."

Marlene definitely was in a mood for lashing out.

Having Tall Wolf's parents hear him asking for her help only made things sweeter.

"Where are you?" she asked.

"DC, but I'll be leaving for Omaha soon." He gave Marlene the name of his hotel there.

Marlene stood up, put a $50 bill under the salt and pepper shakers as an added tip.

She was sure Hayden hadn't been that generous.

Tall Wolf said, "Marlene?"

"What?"

"Put me on speaker for a minute so none of us has to shout, okay?"

Marlene did so. John heard the beep and said, "Mom, Dad, you guys are the best. You saved my life, you raised me better than I probably deserve, and I know you still look out for me. But, really, I've got things covered. Marlene keeps me on my toes, but she really can be of help at times. Strange as it may sound, I'd hate to lose her."

Serafina and Hayden looked at each other. Marlene looked at the phone in her hand.

She replayed Tall Wolf's words in her head, listening for a note of deceit. She couldn't find one. Her problem was, she didn't know what to do with honest affection, even if it came only in a small dollop.

John added, "I mention all that in case the three of you weren't sitting around playing pinochle."

The Wolfs called out their goodbyes.

Marlene said, "I'll meet you in Omaha."

Los Angeles, California

Emily knew one of the two patrol cops who had answered Arcelia's 911 call. His name was Jack Beacher. He'd labored under the lifelong burden of almost everyone in Southern California telling him he had the perfect name for a surfer. His standard reply was, "I don't care for sharks or skin cancer." His game was squash. Sometimes tennis, if it was played indoors. He had a fair complexion and kept it blemish and melanoma free.

He'd worked for Emily when she'd been a sergeant and appreciated the way she handled her patrol officers, including never once making a joke about his name.

His partner was a Latino officer named Alonso Beltran whose main sporting activity was watching fútbol. Emily explained to both officers what had happened, including the fact that she'd resigned from the LAPD. Both men listened closely, occasionally sparing glances at Rebecca to invite her to comment.

She remained silent and watchful.

Arcelia had left to open the office just before the cops arrived.

Hearing everything Emily had to say, Beacher responded, "So you only want us to make official note of the reason why your friend called for help?"

"Yeah. As my dad might say, we're laying the predicate for possible future legal action or criminal charges."

"Laying what?" Officer Beltran asked.

"Ms. Proctor's father is a lawyer," Beacher told him.

Beltran nodded as if that explained everything. Captain Adair, he figured, was being set up to have his ass nailed to a wall. In either criminal or civil court.

Beacher asked, "You want to make a copy of this video you told us about, Ms. Proctor? Include it in our report?"

"Let me know if someone well up the food-chain needs to see it."

"How about you let us take a look?" Beltran asked. "So we have a better understanding of things when we write our report."

"That would be helpful," Beacher added.

Emily looked at Rebecca and she nodded. The cops bracketed her as she brought out her phone and played the video. Neither Beacher nor Beltran said anything as they watched, but they shared a look when it was done. Both of them were uneasy.

Beacher told Emily, "Being fair about it, I never met Captain Adair, but I think your neighbor was right."

"About stepping outside to help?"

"About bringing an assault rifle to the party," Beltran said.

Beacher nodded. "Alonso's right. Cop or not, I wouldn't trust Captain Adair. I have a bad feeling he's going to come back."

"With his own amped-up firepower," Beltran said.

"So what's your advice?" Emily asked.

"I don't see you hiding out indefinitely," Beacher replied, "but do your best to be inconspicuous. Don't keep regular hours. Maybe rent an unfamiliar car for a while. Get a throwaway phone in case he knows someone who can let him listen in on yours."

"Maybe ask your neighbor if she knows a Division of Marines who can camp out in your house a while," Beltran said. "Let him know what he's up against and he's never gonna win."

Knowing Emily would be able to read between the lines, Beacher added, "Nobody will think it's wrong if you drop First Street on this guy's head."

"Some people will," Beltran said, "but they're all assholes anyway."

"First Street?" Rebecca asked.

"That's where the Police Commission has its offices," Emily explained.

"If you haven't already, get your concealed carry permit," Beacher advised.

As a final gesture, both cops gave Emily and Rebecca their business cards, the ones bearing their direct phone numbers. 911 might still be faster, but Beacher and Beltran promised to take a personal interest when they responded.

After hearing all that, Rebecca pulled rank and said she and

Emily would do their rounds together that day rather than work separately. Emily put her car in the garage and made sure her home security system was on.

Rebecca steeled herself for the freeway trip to see Walt Wooten, Lee Proctor's calligrapher.

35,000 Feet Over Ohio

John thought anyone as old as his great-grandfather shouldn't have to put up with the hassles of commercial air travel. At six-foot-four Alan White River was also way too tall even to consider trying to wedge himself into a coach-class seat. John's status as a minor poobah in the federal government qualified him to travel business class, but he'd have to fill out reams of paperwork to cover Alan White River's travel on the government's dime, and he didn't have time to do that.

He could have picked up the tab out of pocket, but he didn't think that was fair since he intended to use Alan White River's wealth of knowledge of Native Americans to help him with his case. And then there were Dr. Lisle's travel expenses. As a researcher, she didn't command the hefty salary a physician in private practice might reap. So John would feel compelled to cover her tab, too.

Unless he figured out a way to access his preferred means of long-distance travel: an executive jet. Preferably one equipped with a crack crew and a respectable number of creature comforts. All of which would come out of somebody else's budget.

With those considerations in mind, John turned to someone who, at first glance, wouldn't be inclined to help him at all: FBI Deputy Director Abra Benjamin.

She did, however, answer his call without delay.

"Director Tall Wolf, are you calling to relinquish responsibility for the investigation of the theft of Dr. Yvette Lisle's computer? If so, I'd be happy to have you brief me immediately on the progress you've made so far."

John said, "That's not quite why I'm calling."

"You know the President has said the case will belong to the FBI as of this Friday."

"Saturday, actually. At noon. But I have to give you credit for eagerness."

A note of frost entered the deputy director's voice. "What can I do for you, Mr. Director, in the short time you have remaining on this case?"

John said, "I'd like to borrow one of the FBI's airplanes. An executive jet. Nicely crewed and outfitted. Recently washed, if possible. And safety inspected within the past 30 days, of course."

"Would you like cocktails and meal service, too?" the deputy director asked dryly.

"I don't think anyone in my party drinks alcohol, but snacks would be nice."

"And you understand the FBI will bill the Bureau of Indian Affairs for the aircraft, crew, fuel and incidental expenses?"

John said, "You could do that or you could pick up the cost yourself."

"And why would I want to do that?"

"Well, I think I'm getting close, or at least closer, to wrapping up my investigation. If you want me to incur the overhead, I'll reluctantly have to take the credit, too. If you choose to bear the financial burden, I'll step into the background and let you and the FBI have the limelight. Your choice."

The perpetually ambitious deputy director thought about that for a heartbeat. "Where do you want to fly?"

"To a domestic destination."

"That being?" she asked.

"That being somewhere you'll learn once I'm aloft and well en route."

"You sound like you don't trust me, Mr. Director," a distinct chill in Abra's voice now.

"Just relying on what Byron DeWitt has told me, Ms. Deputy Director."

For just a second, John thought Abra had ended the call.

Then she asked, "How do I know you'll let me claim credit?"

"Byron can tell you how self-effacing I am, and you can chastise him for talking about you. But maybe you shouldn't be critical, his being married to the President and all. Madam President also wants me to be the next Secretary of the Interior. Do you think I should take that job?"

Abra Benjamin didn't offer an opinion, but now she certainly understood that John had a lot more clout than she'd ever suspected. "Please hold while I speak with Mr. DeWitt."

The conversation must have been terse.

Would John yield credit? Yes, he would.

And she was back on the line with John. A plane would be waiting at Dulles as soon as he could get there. She would expect another call from John as soon as the plane was well on its way to its destination.

"Will do," John promised.

All in all, the exercise of securing an FBI executive jet had turned out to be easier than finding and booking a commercial flight.

Santa Monica, California

Rebecca and Emily looked on as Walt Wooten examined each of their signatures under a large magnifying glass attached to a double-hinged extension arm with a rotating ball-socket base. He hummed along with a recording of Billie Holiday singing "God Bless the Child" that was playing through the speakers in the studio of his Santa Monica house.

A naturalized American citizen of African-English-French-Canadian origin, Wooten was an immigrant who had made good in the United States. It helped, of course, that he'd been born with natural artistic talent and had refined and disciplined his gifts at the Ottawa School of Art. Drawn to the larger realm of artistic possibilities in the U.S., but contrarian in nature, he eschewed New York and moved to L.A.

The weather in Los Angeles also appealed more than New York's.

At that moment, mellow Mediterranean-like light flooded through a north-facing skylight. God bless the child that's got his own.

Walt hadn't arrived with much money in the bank or even in his pockets. He hadn't gone hungry after hitting L.A., but he had to apply his talents to commercial tasks to get his financial foothold in his new country. He designed logos for start-up businesses; he drew storyboards for both ad agencies and movie studios, back in the days before such tasks fell to computers; and he did calligraphy for well-heeled businesses and charitable organizations.

These days, his oil paintings sold for mid-five to low-six figures. Approaching 60 years old, he felt the market had accurately assessed his gifts, though he did think the sales prices of his work would appreciate after his death. As much for sentimental value as artistic worth.

The artist himself thought he was pretty damn good but not great.

Watching him duplicate their signatures with a keen eye and a deftly fluid brush in hand, Rebecca and Emily might have said he was underestimating himself.

What they did say was, "That's amazing." And "Scary, too."

So commented Rebecca and Emily respectively.

Walt turned to look at his guests and chuckled. He said, "Thank you, and what's so frightening?"

Emily said, "Well, just what we came here for — somebody creating a fake signature on an important document that could make the difference between who gets to walk off with the next big business idea and piles of money."

The artist thought about that, nodded and smiled appreciatively.

"You're right, scary," he said. "I guess I lack the larcenous spirit to think like that, but in a way, it's nice to know that someone besides a geek sitting at his computer could pull off a modern caper. With far more elegant simplicity, too."

"We haven't corrupted you, have we?" Rebecca asked.

"Possibly if you both offered to pose nude," Walt said with a sly grin. "No, no, I'm too old for that sort of stuff now."

Emily undid a button on her blouse to tease back, and the artist blushed.

Then she said, "Do you know any artist who might be seduced by sex, money or something else to do a dead-bang knock-off of someone's signature?"

When Rebecca and Emily had arrived, they'd explained the nature of the case they were working on without revealing the names of the people involved. That was when Emily had asked to see a demonstration of the skill at copying signatures that John had described to Rebecca.

Now, they'd both seen what could be done. What Walt had done.

The artist steepled his fingers and thought. "Sex and money *are* terrific motives ... but I think *prestige* would be even more seductive. Something that an artist might receive from a boost in both critical and popular acclaim."

Rebecca and Emily hadn't told Walt that they'd had the same idea.

"How could something like that happen?" Emily asked. "It can't be as simple as people just opening their eyes wider and suddenly noticing how wonderful somebody's work is."

Walt laughed. "No, epiphanies are few and far between, and critical consciousness doesn't get raised from the bottom up. On the other hand ..." Walt sighed. "I can't begin to tell you the extent to which art has been influenced by the tastes of royalty and nobility. The preferences of kings, queens and archdukes must have some value, *n'est-ce pas?*"

"You're saying the bourgeois figured they'd better fall in line?" Rebecca asked.

Walt nodded.

Emily said, "But blue-bloods are more figureheads than rulers these days."

"Which leaves room for billionaires and mega-celebrities," Rebecca countered. "They're the ones with influence these days."

"Exactly," Walt said. "You get people with big money and social cachet to say something is wonderful, it will be the rare critic who contradicts them. Most of them will fall in line or even pretend they were leading the parade all along."

Emily asked, "So you know anyone who's shooting up the art-charts these days, Walt? Someone who might knock off a forged signature or two in his spare time?"

He gave them a name.

Telling Emily, "I do this for your father. He was one of the kind souls who kept me from becoming a cliché: the starving artist. That's why I still do work for him. But I really don't want this to trace back to me."

"Mum's the word," Emily said.

Rebecca mimed locking her lips.

"Thank you," Walt said, "and do stop by again. We won't have to do nudes; sitting for a portrait would be fine."

35,000 feet over Illinois

Peering out a window of the FBI executive jet, Alan White River told his great-grandson, "I've never done this before, looked down on clouds."

John said, "You've never flown before?"

"Not in an airplane."

For a moment White River had left John puzzled. Then he understood.

"You're talking about stepping outside of your body," he said.

"Yes."

Dr. Lisle, sitting opposite John in a conversation cluster of seats, asked the old man, "Do you use peyote to aid your spiritual experiences, Alan?"

He gave a small shake of his head. "I don't criticize those who do, but I have never felt the need. I've always been able to release my spirit, my consciousness, from my body without any outside help."

Dr. Lisle nodded. "The functioning of the brain is still largely a medical mystery. The National Institutes of Health spend $4.5 billion a year on brain research, but no one knows how information is encoded and transferred from cell to cell. Nobody knows if information is encoded differently in various parts of the brain. It would be as likely as not to think that different people's minds function differently in substantive ways."

John chose to focus on a different question. "If you separate your mind from your body, how do you bring them back together?"

"There is a point of fastening," White River said, "like a helium balloon grasped in a child's hand."

John looked at Dr. Lisle for her opinion of that simile.

She only shrugged as if to say, "Why not?"

John pushed the point further. "A child can let go of the helium balloon, and off it goes, hardly ever gets retrieved. Would the same thing apply to your spirit, Grandfather?"

He smiled serenely and said, "I've been trying to master the skill of letting go. So far, I've had no luck. I don't worry about drifting on the wind. There is someone waiting to catch me."

Awinita, John knew.

White River looked out at the clouds again. Sunlight was painting them with shades of gold. "This is all so beautiful. I would never have seen it without you, Grandson."

"My pleasure," John said.

The old man said, "I wonder how different our lives would have been if the white man had invented airplanes before trains. He might have ignored large stretches of our lands that did not appeal to him. We might have managed to live next to one another with a bit less bloodshed."

The musing was rhetorical and neither John nor Dr. Lisle

responded to White River as he continued to stare at the sky outside the speeding aircraft.

In a quiet voice, John told Dr. Lisle, "I have to make a phone call. When I'm done, I'd appreciate it if you'd join me over there."

He pointed to a cluster of seats on the other side of the aircraft.

She nodded, but with reluctance.

Tall Wolf was anything but a bad cop, but she correctly feared an interrogation.

Interstate 25 Southbound — New Mexico

"You're letting me go?" Bodaway asked.

He was behind the wheel of his recently purchased Honda, taking Marlene to Albuquerque.

"Never," Marlene told him.

"But you're not saying I have to go back to the Cree? Not after I stole their chief's Cadillac SUV." He deeply hoped that wasn't the case.

Marlene looked at him with a bleak smile. "Keep your eyes on the road."

Bodaway obeyed without hesitation.

Marlene said,"No, I'm not sending you back to the Cree, though that is an amusing idea. They have very severe customs concerning people who have wronged them, even if those punishments haven't been practiced for many years."

Bodaway's heart started to slow to a normal pace. He knew he should just shut up, but he couldn't keep himself from asking. "What are you going to have me do, after I drop you at the airport?"

"I haven't decided."

"So I should just stay in Albuquerque?"

"If you choose."

Bodaway squeezed the steering wheel, while continuing to watch traffic. Anxiety and uncertainty were amping up his adrenaline once more. "I don't understand. How can I choose to do anything if you're not freeing me?"

Marlene explained, "You will always be my creature. You will come when I summon you. If you don't come, it will be because you are dead or you will soon wish you were. You may travel the country as you wish, and I will always know where you are. I will be able to smell your dread of me and your hate for me at any distance. Now, do you understand?"

Bodaway nodded, not wanting to say anything he might regret.

Marlene sensed his apprehension and approved of it.

"You fear me now, as you always should. With time and distance, though, you will come to despise your weakness. You will think you're stronger than you are, and I am weaker. You will know that isn't true, but you will tell yourself it is. So, really, what I'm doing to you is much crueler than sending you back to the Cree, and you're beginning to understand that already."

Marlene didn't have to look at him to know this.

She could hear his teeth grinding.

"Well, let me make things even worse for you. If there's one thing you should *never* attempt again, it would be trying to do any harm to Tall Wolf. I've told you he is mine, and you will leave his fate to me."

Bodaway didn't say a word, but his teeth would soon crack if he didn't ease the pressure.

Tormenting the fool had made Marlene feel just a bit better.

Tall Wolf's implicit praise of her had thrown her off balance in a way she could not remember ever having experienced. She had long tried to seduce him with sexual allure and had failed every time. That he might have beguiled her with a bit of simple flattery was unnerving.

Of course, the difference was that her intent had been malicious while Tall Wolf's words still echoed in her mind as being honest.

She'd have to figure out a way to deal with that, somehow turning it to her advantage.

She was still working on the problem when Bodaway dropped her at the airport.

25,000 feet over Iowa

The pilot had announced that the aircraft was beginning its descent into Omaha a moment before John's call to FBI Deputy Director Abra Benjamin went through. "You certainly took your time getting back to me," she said.

"I had to make sure your employees in the cockpit weren't taking me to Disney World," John told her.

Despite her adversarial position, the deputy director laughed. "And how did you determine that?"

"I saw fallow cornfields below not orange groves."

"You can't make that kind of a distinction from a cruising airplane."

"Eyes like an eagle," John said.

There was a pause just long enough to indicate uncertainty before Abra said, "Bullshit."

"Yeah," John confessed. "Truth is, I didn't think you'd want to mess with the next Secretary of the Interior."

"You're really being nominated for that job?" Cynicism was infectious.

"I am, but I'll swap places with you if you're interested."

"No, thanks. How about we get down to business?"

"Okay, it turns out Wilbur Rosewell, the guy your people let go after he tried to attack my great-grandfather and me, lives in Omaha. That's also where Dr. Yvette Lisle was born and raised. I don't think that's a coincidence."

"It could be," Abra said.

"Is that the way you'd be investigating this?"

"No."

"Me neither. Anyway, after a heart-to-heart conversation, the good doctor told me the thieves not only stole her computer, they left her a substitute laptop that holds all the same data that was on the one that was taken."

Abra asked, "How did she know…" And then she answered her own question. "She had a file on her machine that the thieves didn't know about. So they couldn't duplicate it in advance. Damn, how long did she hold out before admitting the theft?"

"Three weeks. Then she told Great-Grandfather. He brought me into the situation."

"What about these kids on the security video?"

John said, "My best guess is that the little so-called rascals were holograms. You see what that leaves, don't you?"

Abra knew immediately. "It was an inside job. Someone on Dr. Lisle's staff was suborned to aid in the plan, be the hands-on thief." The deputy director made a further leap of logic. "That person might even have a knowledge of holograms."

"Just what I was thinking," John said. "That person might also have roots in Omaha, if we want to think how our bow might be very neatly tied."

"You don't have any evidence to indicate that, do you?"

"No," John said, "just a feeling. If it's not a hometown thing, then I think there will be some other sort of intersection between the thief and Dr. Lisle."

Abra said, "I can buy that. Unless you're talking about random violence at the hands of a sociopath, there's usually some sort of incestuous angle to wounding people physically, emotionally or financially."

John sighed. "If only we could all evolve a bit faster."

"Yeah. So I take it you've shared this information with me so my people can find the inside man or woman here in Washington."

"If that person isn't already on the run, yes."

"And you're going to tell me what you'll be doing in Omaha, right?"

"All in good time," John said.

Abra told him, "I'll want my plane back soon."

"Saturday," John said, and they left things there.

The pilot told his passengers to buckle up. They were coming in for a landing.

John waved Dr. Lisle forward, indicating she should sit next to him.

She told him, without being asked, what her secret file contained.

Having had the time to stew about it while John talked to the FBI.

Marriott Hotel — Omaha, Nebraska

John booked a suite for himself and Alan White River, and a room for Dr. Lisle at the Omaha Marriott Downtown, the most expensive hotel in town that he could find on short notice. He thought maybe if he painted himself as a free-spending, high-maintenance character, that wouldn't go over well at his Senate confirmation hearing, and he'd be voted down as the nominee for Secretary of the Interior.

Besides all that, when you were six-foot-four-plus, as he and Alan White River were, your chances of finding a comfortable hotel bed were better at the top of the hospitality pyramid. That was certainly where NBA players stayed, and they were the experts at finding mattresses that best accommodated the long of leg.

White River marveled at their lodgings. "I have never known such luxury, Grandson. Your apartment in Washington, the private airplane, this hotel. I fear I might become used to such extravagance and then it will be taken away from me."

"Grandfather, if you'd like, I can set you up with a speaker's agency. You can give public talks and make more money in one night than most people make in a year."

The old man took a step back as if retreating from a precipice. "How can this be?"

John said, "You don't think Calvin Morley gave his talk on movie magic at the Newseum for free, do you?"

White River nodded. "Yes, I did, until just now."

"Mr. Morley took you to an expensive restaurant, didn't he?"

"Yes, but I thought the money for that came from his movie work."

John said, "I'm sure he makes quite a bit from doing that, but he also earns money from public speaking, too."

White River lowered himself into a plump armchair. John sat on a sofa opposite him.

In a gentle tone, John told his great-grandfather, "If you can draw an audience on a consistent basis, you have a marketable skill or talent. The larger your audience, the greater the fee you can command. Alan White River would likely do quite well on both ends of that equation, I think."

The old man shook his head. "I do not need to be rich; I do not want to be."

John said, "Nothing says you'd have to keep all the money you'd receive. You could set up your own charitable organization. Help people you feel are worthy."

That idea brightened the old man's eyes. "Will you help me, Grandson?"

"Of course, and not only because I'd like to ask you for help."

"Anything you need, I will do. If I can, of course."

"The first thing I need is a promise you'll keep what I tell you to yourself."

White River nodded, his expression solemn.

"Okay, Dr. Lisle confided to me that she is engaged to be married … to another woman. In some segments of American society that would no longer cause anyone to bat an eye; in other parts, it still causes family rifts, to say the least. What I'm wondering is whether you know how it would be received by the Omaha tribe."

White River paused to reflect. Then he said, "Some of the Omaha were among the earliest of Native Americans to assimilate into white society. They were the first in this part of the country to forsake their tepees for wooden houses. You might think this was simply a matter of adopting a more comfortable dwelling, but the traditionalist members of the tribe called the grouping of new wooden houses 'The Village of Make-Believe White Men.'"

John laughed. "No pun intended, but that must have ruffled a few feathers."

White River smiled. "It did. Some of the hard-core nativists thought it was even a bad idea to learn to read and write the white man's language … until they saw that literacy made it harder for the white men to swindle them out of their land. The value of being able to read a bill of sale before you put your mark on it soon became obvious. The benefit of a general education followed quickly, inspired among the Omaha by the likes of Susan La Flesche."

"Who was she?" John asked.

"She was the first woman Indian doctor of Western medicine in this country. Some of the conservative members of the Omaha at first refused to be treated by what were then modern methods. That changed when people saw her medicine saved more lives than theirs did."

John said, "The name La Flesche sounds French to me. As does that of Dr. Yvette Lisle."

White River nodded. "French fur traders were the first whites to meet the Omaha, in the early nineteenth century, if I remember right."

"You weren't around back then?" John asked with a straight face.

The old man grinned. "No, but my father may have been."

John laughed, and then he had an idea. "With all the criticism and struggle of adapting to new ways, how did the Omaha feel about members of their tribe marrying white people? For all I know, Dr. Lisle's fiancée might be white and that's what concerns her."

White River gave the question some thought and after a moment he frowned.

"You think that's it?" John asked.

"It may be, but what came to my mind was what if this other woman is a member of another Native American tribe, a former enemy of the Omaha?"

That notion gave John pause. "You mean bygones still aren't bygones for some people?"

"Only when both sides face a common enemy."

"White people?" John asked.

"To some extent the white people themselves. More often the

government. But while the shedding of blood between tribes has stopped, for the most part, a sense of rivalry still lives. To some extent anyway. That is the case with *all* tribes everywhere, I think, not just ours."

John had no problem accepting that idea.

He also couldn't argue when Great-grandfather told him, "You have much to learn about us Indians, John Tall Wolf."

John only nodded.

Even though Marlene Flower Moon hadn't been present to hear that evaluation, John was sure she was laughing at him somewhere.

After his great-grandfather had gone to his bedroom, John called Rebecca to let her know he'd taken his show on the road. They talked about their respective cases. Didn't bother at all with phone sex. That stuff had paled quickly.

CHAPTER 4

Thursday, January 26, 2017
L.A./Beverly Hills, California

Meeting at the Westwood offices of McGill Investigations International that morning, Rebecca and Emily each received gifts from Arcelia: a can of police-grade pepper spray and a tactical palm-sized flashlight. The spray was clearly legal; the flashlight came with a caveat.

Arcelia addressed the precaution specifically to Rebecca.

She said, "Emily, with all her time on LAPD, has to know all about this, but you're new to the country and this state, Rebecca, so here's the drill. If your spray doesn't stop an attacker, and we won't mention any names here, you can temporarily blind him with your flashlight." She turned to Emily, "There's no law against that, right?"

"You can't use a laser light," Emily said. "A strobing, high-lumen light is kind of a gray area, but if you use it on someone who has epilepsy and that person has a seizure, you'll probably be looking at a civil suit at a minimum."

Arcelia said, "No laser, no strobe in these babies, and they're way too small to be considered a billy club."

"That's important because?" Rebecca asked.

"Billy clubs and switch-blade knives are illegal to carry in California," Emily said.

"You want to give her the main talking point on flashlights, Emily, or should I?" Arcelia asked.

Emily said, "I'll do it." She turned to Rebecca, "If you carry a tactical flashlight and a cop ever stops you and asks what you use it for, there's only one response to give: 'I use it to see in dark places, Officer.' If you say you carry it for self-defense, you'll be admitting that you're carrying a weapon, and that could very easily work against you, if you go to court."

"You understand what Emily just said, right?" Arcelia asked.

Rebecca nodded, suddenly thinking she'd come to a very strange country.

"There's no amendment in your Constitution, then, that provides a right to bear flashlights?" she asked.

"Unh-uh," Emily said. "The Founders didn't anticipate electrically powered weapons, but you'd probably be good sticking a flaming torch in someone's eye. You know, as long as you had been using the torch to see in the dark."

All three women laughed.

Arcelia said she'd hold down the fort. Rebecca and Emily headed for the Beverly Hills office of Angelo Renzi's publicist. They didn't have an appointment, but that might not matter. Just getting in the front door might be good enough.

The firm called itself AdvanTech and was located on a small tree-shaded north-south street between Wilshire Boulevard and Burton Way. There was metered parking in front of the modern low-rise office building, and Emily pulled over to the curb. Rebecca paid for an hour's toll and the two women went inside.

AdvanTech was on the top floor. An elevator took them up in the company of a young woman who looked dewy enough to be a recent college graduate. She smiled at them and asked, "You ladies have your own start-up?"

Rebecca and Emily glanced at each other, understanding how to play this opportunity intuitively.

Rebecca said, "Indeed, we do."

The young woman's smile broadened. "My name's Mira. I handle new accounts, if you're looking for a public relations firm."

The elevator arrived at its destination and the door opened. The three women stepped out.

"Which I assume you are," Mira said, "since that's what we do here."

Emily gestured to Rebecca to take the lead.

She said, "Yes, we are, but even before that, we're looking for some art to hang in our offices."

Emily added, "We heard from a discerning friend that you have some very exciting pieces from a fantastic new artist. What was his name again, Becky?"

Thrown for just a second by the use of her name's diminutive, Rebecca said, "I don't recall, Em, but I know Angelo Renzi was the one who recommended both him and AdvanTech when we're ready for PR help."

Hearing the name of a client who obviously carried some weight, Mira was happy to provide the artist's name. "Jack Murtagh."

The same name Walt Wooten had given them. One box checked off.

"That's it," Emily said, smiling.

Rebecca asked, "Would you mind if we take a real quick look at any of the pieces you've chosen for your company?"

Emily segued, "Then if you have some literature about your services, we'd be happy to take them with us, too."

"Well ..." Mira had been hoping for instant gratification, landing a new client, but she didn't want to blow an opportunity for future business. "I have to tell you that I didn't pick out the art. Don't get me wrong. I think it's great but I can't take you into our partner's offices. Would it be okay if I just showed you what we have hanging in the common areas? And my office, too, of course."

"That would be great," Rebecca said.

Emily nodded.

"Okay," Mira said, "one nickel-tour coming up."

In the interior design fashion of the time, the company's major offices and the conference rooms had glass walls and doors, giving the place something of a fishbowl effect. But AdvanTech had taken the next step in the theme. Each of the glassed-in spaces had at least one square or rectangular area that was opaquely black.

Emily pointed at a darkened space and asked, "Is that polarizing glass?"

Mira grinned. "I don't know that it's glass exactly, but you can do what we call 'drawing the curtains' when you need a little privacy. It's sort of a way of saying, 'I need a little space right now.' When the glass is clear, the welcome mat is out."

Rebecca said, "But every office has at least one partially darkened area." And then she made the leap. "That's where you hang the art."

Mira nodded. "Cool, isn't it? The paintings aren't really hung. No nails and hooks or anything like that. They're just sort of stuck to the wall, but not with an adhesive. I think it's some kind of magnetism or an electrical charge or something. Your business doesn't involve a lot of hard science, does it?"

"More like social science," Rebecca said.

"Figuring out what makes people tick," Emily added.

Mira smiled. "Oh, good, that's my specialty."

She showed them the Jack Murtagh paintings in her office and three common areas. The son-of-a-gun was a real draftsman, used a technique called photo-realism, only he made people and structures a bit more heroic in stature. Or a bit less, depending on who or what was being favored or disfavored. Which put a narrative slant on each picture. His color sense worked the same way. If he liked a figure, he or she was flawless and godlike. If he didn't care for another figure, that character looked shrunken and sneaky at best. He'd actually painted a street scene in which a pickpocket had a hand in a woman's purse as she was busy picking up a toddler from a stroller.

One thing that was consistent in each painting was the artist's signature. Each letter of both of his names was almost mechanically identical in size, spacing and color density. Both Rebecca and Emily found that interesting.

They sat with Mira for a ten-minute pitch on what AdvanTech could do to help any modern business. They accepted a thumb-drive that went into even greater detail. And, at their request, Mira produced an old-fashioned business card for Jack Murtagh to take with them.

As soon as they were back in Emily's car, Rebecca took out her iPad to see what the Internet had to say about Mr. Murtagh.

Keeping her eyes on the road as Rebecca cyber-surfed, Emily said, "You know what? After seeing that guy's paintings, I bet he's got some kind of criminal record."

Marriott Hotel — Omaha, Nebraska

Dr. Yvette Lisle joined John and White River for breakfast in their suite. Room service brought crepes, whole grain cereals, rye toast, fruit cups, coffee, tea, orange juice and skim milk. The hotel expressed its regret that their kitchen would be unable to provide White River with either baked turnips or rabbit of any sort.

The old man had grinned at his younger companions after the order had been placed.

"I do that as a joke mostly, ask for traditional tribal foods. I think I might die of shock if a white waiter ever told me, 'Very good, sir. May I suggest a wine to pair with that?'"

John told him, "Be careful if someone takes you to a trendy French restaurant. They can be pretty daring with their menus."

Dr. Lisle nodded. "New age places would probably try to obtain any plant food you might suggest. Animal protein would be another matter."

White River smiled. "My horizons widen even as my light dims."

Dr. Lisle responded with professional concern. "You're not

feeling well?"

The old man patted her hand. "I can't have more than 10 to 20 years left."

John chuckled. Dr. Lisle frowned at the old man, until she gave in and smiled.

Taking advantage of the good humor around the table, John asked, "Should I wait until we finish eating or would it be all right to discuss some business now?"

"Can we avoid it until we've had lunch and possibly dinner?" Dr. Lisle asked.

"I don't think so," John said. "I'm working under tight time constraints already."

The doctor chewed and swallowed a bite of crepe and said, "Okay, go ahead."

"You have to know by now," John told her, "that one or more of the people in your DC lab was in on the theft of your computer. Once we eliminated the make-believe child thieves, that left only your staff. I wouldn't be surprised if the thief or thieves are already getting anxious that suspicion hasn't fallen upon them after three weeks, especially now that I'm looking into things. So what I'm wondering is this: Has anyone in your lab recently given notice, either that he or she will be leaving for a new job or has requested a few weeks of vacation time?"

Lowering her eyes, Dr. Lisle nodded. "Two people. Just yester-day. Both say they've been recruited by a lab in Texas that's owned by a Swiss pharmaceutical company."

"Are these people simply colleagues or are they a couple?" John asked. "My guess is the latter."

"They are a couple, a straight pair. Recently married. How did you know?"

John said, "To do something like this, two people would need to have a lot of trust in each other. If they're both moving from one workplace to another, you can bet that was part of their negotiations. Two people lacking any bonds of personal affection would probably think it was smarter to go their separate ways."

Of course, John thought ironically, he and Rebecca loved each other and still managed to work on opposite sides of the country.

John moved on to his next question: "Of this pair, which one is the alpha? In conversation, who talks first and most? Who tends to finish the sentences the other one starts? If you've socialized with them, who decides when to call it a night?"

"She's the top dog, and while I'm not an expert on their type of relationship, I think he likes it that way."

"May I have their names, please?"

"You're going to question them when we get back to Washington?"

John shook his head. "I'm going to let the FBI have that pleasure."

Dr. Lisle speared a strawberry with her fork and chewed on it longer than needed.

Then she asked John, "May I see your eyes, please?"

He took off his sunglasses. The lighting in the room was borderline bright for John, causing him to blink a bit at first. The nictation provided the moisture his eyes needed to hold his gaze steady.

"See anything you like?" he asked. "The warmth of a gentle soul?"

"What I don't see is any cruelty. That's what I was curious about." She gave John the names he wanted. "I know you have another question to ask, so go ahead and get to it. You can put your glasses back on first, if you want."

John did. He asked, "Who's the boss in your relationship with the woman you love?"

"In the lab, I am."

"And everywhere else?"

"She is."

"At the lab, is your significant other a superior to the couple looking to leave?"

Dr. Lisle nodded.

"So they were the couriers, but your special friend, I'm fairly certain, she's the one who switched computers on you because she had the greatest, least suspicious access to it."

Yvette Lisle hung her head.

Alan White River placed a compassionate hand on her back.

John, however, wasn't done. "You were reluctant to say anything about losing your computer because you knew your lover was the most likely suspect. You tried to persuade yourself that couldn't be what happened, but denial lasts only so long. So you turned to Grandfather ... hoping, what, he could work some magic for you?"

Tears fell from her eyes as she nodded.

"But then he brought me in and you were stuck."

She sobbed and White River put his arm around her.

John continued in a soft voice, "But either your lover or one of the other two put in a call to someone, and that was when a former Omaha cop turned private investigator named Wilbur Rosewell showed up in Washington and took a run at Grandfather and me."

"I'm sorry," the doctor mumbled through her tears.

John sighed and said, "You made a mistake of the heart. The others broke the law. But now that we're here in Omaha, I'll find Mr. Rosewell and we'll make things as right as we can."

The doctor looked up. "There's another reason I came to Omaha." Yvette Lisle wiped the tears from her eyes and firmed her jaw. "I know how to stop these miserable bastards dead in their tracks."

John smiled and said, "Good. Tell me all about it."

Brice Benard's Office — Omaha, Nebraska

Rich as hell or not, Brice Benard had gotten damn nervous since Wilbur Rosewell had abandoned him yesterday, the cur. Not that Benard had anything against mixed blood mutts. But, goddamnit, he could feel things starting to come apart around him. He was sitting on the cusp of an opportunity to make the kind of money the Pentagon spent in a year: billions, billions and more billions.

He just needed someone who could scare the hell out of the

Omaha tribe's chief of tribal administration, Thomas Emmett, and get rid of that other damn Indian, the tall one working for the Bureau of Indian Affairs. He could be real trouble. Worse than just losing a wet-dream of a business opportunity. That sonofabitch could put him in a federal prison for a long, long time.

That kind of thing hadn't happened to someone with his money since ... ever.

Jesus, he thought, what if his getting locked up started a trend, putting rich bastards away for all the evil, sneaky shit they pulled? The feds might put all the greed-merchants in one vile, steaming sinkhole. Everybody there would blame him for all their suffering. He might wind up getting shanked by a former investment banker from Wall Street.

That idea didn't stretch credulity much farther than the nightmare he'd woken up from that morning. A war party of Indians, the two tall ones from Washington, Dr. Lisle, and Thomas Emmett from right there in Omaha were chasing him through a forest, brandishing war axes and knives, howling for blood and intending to scalp him.

Benard remembered reading a newspaper story about who invented scalping, white men or red men. Each side blamed the other. What was clear, though, both sides had been enthusiastic participants. The European arrivals, however, were definitely the ones who had married capitalism to barbarism: They'd paid bounties for scalps.

As Benard fled through his hell-scape nightmare forest, a new pursuer appeared from behind every tree he passed. All of them howled for his blood and the bounty money they'd get for his scalp. A battalion of hands reached out and seized him from his neck to his ankles.

He screamed and ... that was what woke him up.

The sound of his own terror.

His third wife had left him the year before. He had no one in bed beside him to apologize to for his REM panic. He also had no one to comfort him, and tell him it was nothing more than a bad dream. That wouldn't have helped anyway. The horror might have been imaginary, but the basis for it was real as a tax audit.

He'd committed a federal offense by setting the theft of Dr. Lisle's computer in motion.

It had been all Benard could do to get showered, dressed and out the door to go to his office. He'd thought of asking his chauffeur if he might like to take on a new task. He just couldn't squeeze the topic — *How would you like to become a killer?* — past his sense of better judgment.

Benard managed to get himself all the way into his office without exhibiting any erratic behavior. He closed the door and used the intercom to tell his secretary not to let anyone bother him. The only calls he'd take would be on his private line.

The one that rang only inside his office.

Wilbur Rosewell's parting words from yesterday echoed in Benard's mind.

"Just make sure you pay your phone bill."

The implication being he might get a call.

One that might solve all his problems.

So he stared at his phone for hours, thinking at first and muttering later: Ring … ring … ring, goddamnit. He'd long since lost count of his pleadings by the time it finally did. He picked up the phone and didn't even dare to say hello.

"Hey, Mr. Benard, you there?"

It *was* Rosewell.

"Yes, I'm here."

"Good. You still need some help with your problem?"

"Yes."

"Okay, then," Rosewell said. "You remember what you said about paying in gold? I've got someone who's interested."

Interstate 29 — En route to Omaha Reservation

John's original thought, after having breakfast, was to go to the Omaha cops and ask for help dealing with Wilbur Rosewell, but then Yvette Lisle reminded him she had an idea for finding her purloined laptop, and she volunteered to do the driving that would be required.

John rented a Chevy Impala with enough leg-room, front and back, for himself and Great-grandfather, and they were on the road as soon as the morning rush hour ended.

Dr. Lisle told her story as she did a steady 70 miles per hour in the right-hand lane.

"The Omaha Nation is sitting on a natural resource of great value. They just don't know it yet."

Alan White River chuckled softly and said, "That is a very old Indian story."

John said to Dr. Lisle, "You intend to tell tribal officials as soon as we arrive?"

She nodded. "Yes. After my computer was taken, I thought to do so, but I hesitated. Now, I'm afraid I might have waited too long. But I've been reading the *Omaha World-Herald* online to watch for any announcement of a big business deal involving the tribe. So far, I haven't seen any such news."

John gave her a dubious look, but she kept her eyes on the road. He said, "Many business deals get announced only when the terms are finalized."

"Yes, I know," Dr. Lisle said softly. "I kept hoping my computer would be returned. I was foolish. But I'm praying no news is good news."

"There might already be an agreement in principle," John said, "while the paperwork is being massaged by the respective legal teams."

She finally spared John a glance. "Would *any* kind of a deal stand up in court if one party had an illegally obtained advantage?"

"Good question," John said. "Not being a lawyer, I can't answer with any certainty. Doesn't seem, though, like the interests of justice would rest with the bad guys."

White River laughed louder than before. "Our people don't have a great record in American courts, historically speaking ...

and as of this morning."

"I'm going to tell the President that I'll serve as her Secretary of the Interior," John said.

Yvette Lisle looked at him again. "What?"

"She asked me to help out. I've been trying to put her off without being off-putting."

Her eyes back on the road, Dr. Lisle asked, "You don't want the job?"

"I don't aspire to lead a bureaucracy, but I think as a Cabinet member, I could help balance the scales of justice in any court proceeding involving the Omaha."

For the first time that he could recall, John saw Yvette Lisle smile.

"Maybe you could help," she said.

"So what's the treasure on the Omaha Nation's land," John asked. "Gold?"

"Even better: microbes."

"That was going to be my next guess," he told her.

Once again, the old man in the back seat laughed.

John said, "It's been a long time since I was in a high school biology class, but aren't there any number of microbes in any handful of dirt you might pick up anywhere?"

"There are, indeed," Dr. Lisle said, "and 99.9% of them have never been examined. The problem was isolating one strain of bacteria from the next. Then two years ago a biotech firm in Massachusetts solved that problem. My lab was the first to license their process. By capturing single cells, you can cultivate microorganisms that never existed before."

"Mightn't that produce a Frankenstein monster?" John asked.

Yvette Lisle gave a small nod. "Potentially, yes. In terms of biological warfare, if you were specifically looking to create a killer pathogen, it wouldn't be beyond imagining. But the Biological Weapons Convention of 1972 banned bacteriological weapons. One hundred and seventy-eight nations are signatories. The only hold-outs are in Africa, three non-signatory nations. They're not scientifically advanced places, but if terrorists were to set up shop in any of them and got financing and people with the right educations ..."

A small shudder passed through Yvette Lisle.

"We'll table that nightmare for the moment," John said. "Meanwhile, back on the rez."

Dr. Lisle nodded. "On a much smaller scale, one strain of bacteria can be as competitive and hostile to other strains of bacteria as one group of people can be aggressive to another group."

White River said, "That does not surprise me."

"Such is the nature of nature?" John asked Great-grandfather.

The old man nodded. He let his chin fall to his chest and closed his eyes.

Dr. Lisle continued John's education. "Anyway, antibiotics are devised to kill other microbes. For example, the microorganisms from mold that make penicillin kill the bacteria that cause pneumonia, ear and throat infections and —"

"And then they stop working when the bad bugs adapt to the medicine," John said.

"Exactly. That's why we'll always need new antibiotics."

"And you found the microbes to create a new cure on the Omaha Reservation?" John asked.

Dr. Lisle nodded. "Yes, I think so. I found them in my grandmother's backyard, but logic tells me other nearby patches of earth should hold the same strains of bacteria."

Alan White River raised his head.

John continued his questioning, asking Dr. Lisle, "The same might hold true for any other number of other places around the world, right?"

"Maybe, given a similar topography, climatic conditions and related kinds of soil, water and maybe even air pollution. But how would you know exactly where to look? The time you'd need for exploration might be longer than what you'd require to develop the antibiotic."

Yvette Lisle took the highway exit to the reservation.

Alan White River asked, "Your grandmother, is she as pretty as you?"

Albuquerque International Sunport
— Albuquerque, New Mexico

Marlene Flower Moon was in a vile mood. She'd been unable to find a single seducible business executive or celebrity she might prevail upon for a free ride in a private jet to Omaha. It wasn't that either her beauty or her wiles had slipped, she simply hadn't been able to find a warm-blooded male of any age who had his own Gulfstream, Dassault or Cessna luxury aircraft.

What was the country coming to, she wondered angrily.

That left her with only the distasteful option of chartering a flight paid out of her own purse. Coyote did not fly commercial, not even in first class. Her aggravation only heightened when she found out there was not even an executive jet available for hire. The only reason she didn't go on a rampage was that the leasing agent at the general aviation terminal took note of her building exasperation.

He said, "I can get you an aircraft from Colorado Springs within the hour."

"What kind?"

"Beechcraft jet, room for 12 passengers. Two thousand mile range."

"Cabin steward?"

"Sure, if you'd like. Full bar. Snacks on board. Take longer if you want to order a chef-prepared meal."

"I'll go with the bar and snacks. How much?"

The agent told her.

For a moment, she thought to haggle but decided not to. If the guy dug in about the price, she might snap off his head, literally. That wouldn't do in a public place. Coyote preferred to be wily, not obvious. She handed over her Amex Centurion Card.

The agent said, "I'll just run your card and be right back. May I bring you a drink when I return?"

"A Bloody Mary, heavy on the blood."

The agent grinned, thought to return the quip. Then he looked at Marlene's eyes. All he said was, "Yes, ma'am. Right away, exactly as you like it."

Marlene took a lounge chair that looked out on airport arrivals and departures.

In a moment of bitter self-recrimination, she thought Tall Wolf would have gotten an executive jet for free somehow. That galled her: the idea that he might have become more cunning than she was. His intercession on her behalf with his parents still left her unsettled. It clearly would have better served his interests to let them attack her with every means at their command.

Marlene knew that Serafina Wolf y Padilla by herself couldn't have tormented Marlene's dreams indefinitely. What she could do, though, would be to have the curse of nightmares handed down from one generation of *brujas* to the next to continue her work. And who knew what sort of dark hell Hayden Wolf might inflict upon her? That and how many generations of accomplices might continue his attacks indefinitely.

The combined damage those two forces might do to her was horrible to contemplate.

And Tall Wolf had spared her all that.

It seemed impossible to her that *anyone* would do that. Tall Wolf knew who and what she really was. He'd seen that immediately the first time he'd met her as a young man. He'd had no doubt that she'd meant to bend him to her will, before she consumed him, figuratively and literally.

So why, why, why had he interceded on her behalf?

There had to be some ulterior motive.

The only smart thing to do would be to play along with whatever his game was, come to understand it, then get him looking the other way and ...

Try as she might, she couldn't deny the idea that in some perverse way she and Tall Wolf had become friends. She'd never had a friend before. The notion made her uneasy. Friends had to be taken into account when you made decisions, and she'd never thought of anyone but herself.

The leasing agent returned with a smile and her drink order.

He returned her Centurion card and handed her the drink.

"Your aircraft will be here in 45 minutes, Ms. Flower Moon. Your drink has been made just the way you like it. I tapped a vein in a junior staffer to top it off."

That image pleased Marlene enough to make her smile.

The agent said, "Happy to be of service. Let me know if there's anything else I can do."

She gave him a nod of approval and he left.

The agent was wearing a wedding ring, but she knew she could have had him with a wink.

There was the answer for her. For the moment anyway.

Even if Tall Wolf was beyond her reach for the time being, she could still indulge her wiles, hunger and rage on other targets. Since she'd be on her way to Omaha soon, she saw no reason why she couldn't start there. The idea perked her up.

Once Bodaway had dropped Marlene off at the airport, it was all he could do not to speed away. Reason overcame impulse, though, and he managed to keep to the speed limit. He had a full tank of gas and his list of possible destinations was as long as both continents of the Americas. He could take the Alaska-Canadian highway all the way to Fairbanks. From there, he could hire a bush pilot to take him into deep wilderness at any point of the compass.

Only Bodaway had no desire to go anywhere that might be even colder than Canada.

That still left him with the choice to turn south and get on the Pan-American Highway. That network of roads ran from Prudhoe Bay, Alaska all the way to Ushuaia, Argentina: 30,000 miles of what was described as "motorable road." There had to be plenty of places to hide out along that enormous stretch of pavement. Warm places. Agreeable locations for both living and hiding.

Try as he might, though, Bodaway couldn't persuade himself that there was any place he might hide that Coyote wouldn't be able to find him, should she take up the hunt. To escape her completely, he'd have to leave the planet. Even that might not be a sure bet.

As he approached Interstate 40, he had the choice of turning east or west. He wasn't sure if one direction might be better than the other for his purposes. With his education and experience in civil engineering, he was sure he could find work pretty much in any big city. After all, he was a military veteran — employers liked well-educated vets, especially those who'd been officers — and thanks to Great-grandfather, he had no criminal record in connection with the theft of the Super Chief.

Alan White River had refused absolutely to implicate any accomplices in that crime. Bodaway had scoured the internet, while in Canada, to make sure he hadn't been charged in the matter. It warmed his heart that the old man hadn't cut a deal with the government to reduce his time in prison in return for naming other participants. In Mafia parlance, Great-grandfather had proven himself to be a stand-up guy.

Bodaway wondered if the old man was still in prison. Still alive, for that matter. He'd have to find out. See if he could think of a way to see the old man without being noticed, assuming Great-grandfather had been turned loose and was still drawing breath.

Thinking of Alan White River led Bodaway to wonder about John Tall Wolf. That bastard was the one who'd proven himself to be the old man's favorite. By all rights, Tall Wolf should be dead. He should have ridden around the bend of that New Mexico mountain on his motorbike and sailed right off the collapsed road and into oblivion.

Only somehow that bitch he'd been with must have overtaken him and stopped both of them from taking the plunge. That and collapse the canopy of his parachute with a rifle shot. He was sure she had been the one to do it because Tall Wolf wasn't that ruthless.

He'd learned that much about his cousin from internet study.

Still, he wanted to settle matters with the woman who shot him out of the sky and Tall Wolf, before Coyote eventually returned and finished him off. He was sure that was her ultimate plan and …

It came to him in an epiphany. Thinking of Tall Wolf, led him to recall the encounter between Tall Wolf's adoptive parents and Coyote. She had chased him away from the café table where he'd sat with her, but he hadn't gone far. He hadn't been close enough to hear their conversation but he'd been able to see all of them clearly.

Tall Wolf's parents hadn't feared Coyote. If anything, their body-language was aggressive. For all he knew, they might have been threatening Coyote verbally. How could they do that? How did they dare to confront her?

He knew from his more recent research of Serafina and Hayden Wolf that they were supposed to have mystical powers. He'd mentally scoffed at the notion. Of course, he'd done the same when Great-grandfather had told him of Coyote … right up to the time she'd had his throat in her teeth.

So, maybe Tall Wolf's parents did know something he didn't.

Something he might learn that would allow *him* to challenge Coyote.

Bodaway bypassed the entrance ramps to I-40 east and west.

He wouldn't head south either.

He stayed on I-25 and headed north, back to Santa Fe.

By being careful and as close to invisible as he could manage, he would learn everything he could about Serafina and Hayden Wolf. Gain as much knowledge as he could about whatever means they had to stand up to Coyote. Master those skills for himself.

Then he would best both Coyote and Tall Wolf.

He would live up to the meaning of his name, Bodaway.

Fire-maker.

Reduce anyone who got in his way to ashes.

Omaha Reservation — Nebraska

Omaha Chief of Tribal Administration Thomas Emmett greeted John, Dr. Lisle and, most effusively, Alan White River in his office. He had his entire staff with him. He pleaded with White

River to spend a night or two on the reservation so that all the Omaha people there, and those who lived within a day's drive, might come to hear him talk of stealing the Super Chief.

John whispered in Great-grandfather's ear, "See what I mean about a public-speaking career?"

"I still do not wish to be rich," White River quietly replied, "but I take your point that I might raise money for good causes."

He accepted Chief Emmett's invitation of hospitality.

It didn't hurt that Dr. Lisle had told him she did indeed get her good looks *and* her smarts from her grandmother.

After several photos were taken of White River and his smiling hosts, the staff left the office and the remaining guests took seats in front of Emmett's desk. They got down to business without the benefits of coffee, water or light snacks.

John took the lead by informing Emmett that Dr. Lisle's laptop computer had been stolen from her laboratory in Washington and that it held data regarding a possible medical breakthrough of the sort that would be worthy of a Nobel Prize.

Emmett momentarily disregarded the crime that had been mentioned and looked at Dr. Lisle with a regard befitting a proud parent.

"I remember you when you were a schoolgirl, Yvette. Always top of your class. You made everyone here so proud."

Dr. Lisle blushed, lowered her head for a moment and then looked back at Emmett. "Thank you, sir. I've always tried hard, but I'm not without my faults. Ones I regret right now. I obviously trusted someone I shouldn't have, and I didn't report the theft as quickly as I should have."

Emmet turned to John for further explanation.

"She turned to Great-grandfather, who then came to me," he said. Turning to Dr. Lisle, he said, "Tell the chief the idea you shared with me this morning."

She nodded and said to Emmett, "I know this sounds far-fetched, incredible really, but has anyone recently tried to buy any of the reservation's land?"

That was indeed a touchy subject for a people who had lost much of their land to governmental coercion and opportunistic swindlers. From the way Emmett's face darkened and his mouth tightened, the question had clearly struck a nerve.

John took notice and said, "Someone did try to buy tribal land?"

Emmett shook his head.

White River was the one who intuitively understood the situation. "Someone came to you saying he would do the tribe a favor. He was so generous he even would pay for the privilege of helping you."

Emmett nodded.

"Exactly what kind of a con game was this person trying to sell?" John asked.

The chief said, "It was just yesterday. A Mr. Brice Benard and a soil scientist, Dr. Darnell Elston, came to see me. Mr. Benard said he is looking to buy land adjacent to the reservation, and Dr. Elston found that the land Mr. Benard has his eye on has arsenic contamination caused by airborne contaminants from coal burning. Mr. Benard is willing to pay for bioremediation for both the land he wants to buy and Omaha land so he won't be building next to a toxic waste site."

John asked, "Did he say how much he'd be willing to spend to help out the Omaha people?"

"He said it could be ten million dollars or more."

John looked at Dr. Lisle. "That would be far more than he'd need to collect the microbes he'd need, wouldn't it?"

"Microbes?" Emmett asked.

Dr. Lisle gave Emmett the layman's explanation of her work to develop antibiotics that would kill bacteria that had become immune to the present generation of medicines.

Emmett sat back and rested his hands on his midsection. "Damn, we've got something really valuable. Thanks to you, Yvette, we now also know it. What's your plan here?"

She said, "To get my computer back, to get my data from any other machine or server onto which it might have been uploaded.

To work as hard as I can to reach my goals. To make any new antibiotic I come up with available to the Omaha and other native peoples first, and then to make it universally available at the cost of production with no profit mark-up."

John smiled and White River nodded his approval.

Emmett said, "Maybe we could make just a modest profit to benefit the tribe."

When he saw resistance to that notion in Dr. Lisle's eyes, Emmett added, "You would have the final say on any expenditure, of course."

"Very well," Dr. Lisle conceded. "But think of basic things: a library not a football stadium."

The chief looked momentarily disappointed, but he said, "As you wish."

John asked him, "Did Dr. Elston mention where he got his doctorate?"

Emmett said, "It was in the letter Benard sent to me. Michigan State."

"Give me a second here," John told the others.

He took out his phone and started Googling. "Well, Michigan State is very highly ranked in soil sciences and ..." He searched further. "Dr. Darnell Elston was the head of a department there, but it was the English Department. The good doctor specialized in Elizabethan poetry, and he died in 1976."

White River said dryly, "Maybe he's back from the Great Beyond."

"Or somebody thought the local folks wouldn't check all that deeply," Emmett said.

John asked the chief, "Did Mr. Benard leave you a business card? Presumably, he'd want to give you at least a working phone number you could call."

Emmett handed John a card. "Came with his letter. He told me yesterday his offer would be good only for a week."

John said, "I'll contact the FBI and maybe the local police. We'll find Mr. Benard and have a long talk with him. See if he knows anything about a missing computer … and if by chance he's acquainted with a fellow named Wilbur Rosewell."

John got to his feet and shook Chief Emmett's hand.

Dr. Lisle said she'd stay and introduce White River to her grandmother.

John headed back to the town of Omaha by himself.

Melrose Avenue — Los Angeles, California

After Rebecca and Emily made a quick stop at Fred Segal to pick up a pair of ridiculously priced black jeans for each of them and, more important, the Segal label bags dangling from their hands to show off their affluence, they stepped into Daisy Jane's Pictures, by its own reckoning the cutting-edge art gallery in town.

Rebecca's internet search had revealed the gallery was where Jack Murtagh exhibited his work. Confirming Emily's hunch about the artist's criminal tendencies, Rebecca also found a *Boston Globe* story online saying that Murtagh had been arrested in connection with an art-fraud charge. A Boston-area art gallery owner had sold one of Murtagh's paintings by representing it as a Jamie Wyeth work. The painting was a likeness of a boy just hitting his teens. He was reaching into a dresser drawer with one hand while keeping a sharp eye on a nearby door that was open just a crack.

The overt impression was the kid was about to filch something that didn't belong to him. Maybe it was his father's dresser. Maybe the kid was grabbing some money, car keys or a condom. The painting had fetched $25,000. Shortly afterward, the credulous buyer had been informed by a more knowledgable friend that a *bargain* Wyeth oil painting would sell for ten times the price he'd paid. Also, to the friend's knowledge, Wyeth hadn't painted any juvenile sneak-thieves.

The buyer had been further informed that the feeling of the faux Wyeth was more in the spirit of a combination of Norman Rockwell and *Mad Magazine*. The kid in the painting did bear a certain resemblance to Alfred E. Neuman. All of which led the bamboozled buyer to go to his lawyer and then to the police.

The cops arrested the owner of the gallery that sold the painting and hauled in the artist, Jack Murtagh, too. At the time of his arrest, Murtagh had been seventeen. He told the cops and the Suffolk County assistant district attorney that when he'd sold the painting to the art dealer it was signed: "After Jamie Wyeth by Jack Murtagh."

After being the art world's way of saying "in the style of," he told the authorities.

Young Murtagh also pointed out how crude the brushwork around Jamie Wyeth's name was compared to the rest of the painting.

"I'll bet you," he said, "that guy covered up my name."

He pointed to the dumbfounded gallery owner, a recent immigrant from Portugal.

Murtagh told the assistant D.A., "You get a good art restorer to remove that sloppy paint, you'll see what I'm telling you is true."

The authorities did just that and found exactly what Murtagh had described to them. The gallery owner, who claimed he was new to the art business as well as the country, insisted to the end that he was innocent. He asserted that Murtagh had told him he could make a bundle on the painting, and had paid Murtagh $2,500 for it.

The problem for the novice art dealer was that Murtagh was just a kid, and he had no criminal record. Why would someone like that lie? How would he even come up with such a devious scam? All the gallery owner could tell the authorities and later the judge, was, "That boy is evil."

The court found the gallery owner guilty of grand larceny, and ruled Jack could keep the $2,500 he'd received as there was no evidence he'd done anything wrong.

When Rebecca and Emily, who'd agreed to call themselves Becky and Em in public, entered Daisy Jane's gallery, they spotted Jack Murtagh himself, twenty years on from Suffolk County, and a woman they guessed to be Daisy Jane at the rear of the shop. The proprietor and the artist eyed them across the length of the gallery. Daisy Jane's eyes went first to their Segal bags, then to their shoes and finally to their bracelets and Rebecca's wedding ring — a tasteful item for which John Tall Wolf had spent a small fortune.

Murtagh looked at the drape of their blouses over their boobs, their legs and their faces, in that order. The corners of his mouth turned up, forming more of a leer than a smile. Daisy Jane was already on her way to greet the new arrivals. Her smile was genuine.

Motivated by the fact that she thought she might have a couple of live ones here.

"Good morning, ladies. Would you like a guided tour of the shop or just browse?"

Rebecca and Emily looked at each other and responded intuitively and simultaneously.

Rebecca said, "Guided."

Emily said, "Browse."

They looked at each other and giggled.

Daisy Jane renewed her smile. If she couldn't make a big sale to these two ninnies …

Emily didn't wait for further conversation. She walked off to look at the shop's paintings. Well, she focused on the art, but out of the corner of her eye, she could see Murtagh watching her. He hadn't aged badly, going by the online photo and what she saw now, but in person, she could see a predatory gleam in his eyes that the old picture hadn't captured.

Rebecca took a more direct approach with Daisy Jane. "Who's the guy back there? He looks like he might steal something."

The question made the gallery owner blink, before she laughed with real humor.

"He's no thief," she said. "That's Jack Murtagh. He's my 'Featured Artist of the Moment.'"

"The *moment?*" Rebecca said. "Fame is fleeting, huh?"

"In this town, you bet it is," Daisy Jane said, "but cool lasts forever. And buying something when it's hot is as cool as it gets."

Or as foolish as you could get, Rebecca thought, but she didn't want to seem too argumentative. Instead, she pursued another line of conversation. "So what about the guy back there? Has he painted something that will be cool beyond the next moment or two?"

She noticed that Murtagh was sidling over to Emily.

Leaving one of them unattended was working the way they'd hoped.

Daisy Jane told Rebecca, "Why don't we take a look around? Maybe you'll see something you'll like longer than this year's hairstyles."

That made Rebecca laugh. "Okay, let's do that."

As they started their tour, she saw Murtagh had just struck up a conversation with Emily. Turning her attention to the art on the walls, Rebecca was hit by conflicting feelings. Murtagh had real gifts. His draftsmanship, composition, color sense, and use of light and shadow were all first rate. Maybe not quite in the class of modern masters, but in the neighborhood.

The thing that spoiled all those fine qualities for Rebecca was that Murtagh insisted on putting someone or something discordant or even downright creepy in every last painting: a group of laughing young kids danced around a sunlit Maypole while a lecherous troll-like figure in the distance kept time with a tapping foot and clapping hands; a teenage couple sitting on a sofa, seen from behind, shared what might be a first kiss while the TV in front of them showed Thelma and Louise driving off a cliff; an elderly man held the hand of an old woman lying in a hospital bed, perhaps to say a final farewell, only he was glancing at his watch as if being kept from something more important.

"This guy's a million laughs, eh?" Rebecca said.

"Some people find the juxtapositions funny," Daisy Jane said. "Others think they're edgy. Good art allows for a range of interpretations."

Rebecca actually agreed with the last point, but she wouldn't have any of this guy's work hanging anywhere she ever lived. Wouldn't like it if the neighbors hung any of Murtagh's stuff either.

"You know," she said, "I think this guy has real talent, but the things I see here don't grab me. Any chance he might do a piece on commission?"

"I know he's done some work on that basis in the past. Can't say if he'd still be willing to do something like that. It'd be a sure bet, though, a commissioned piece would cost more than anything we have here. Possibly a good deal more."

Rebecca knew immediately Daisy Jane was figuring in a hefty commission for herself.

She said, "I've got the money for him, you and a whole lot more."

The gallery owner was pleased they understood one another.

"What kind of a painting do you have in mind?"

"A nude."

Daisy Jane did another frank appraisal of Rebecca, concentrating more on physical attributes this time. She nodded and said, "Let's go ask Jack how he'd feel about the idea."

The artist and Emily were now standing next to a counter at the back of the shop. There was nothing so gauche as a cash register there, but it gave the feeling of a place where a painting might be exchanged for a check with the right number of zeros. Emily gave Rebecca a grin while Murtagh was already undressing her in his mind, without even hearing about painting a nude.

Daisy Jane saw the same thing and quickly voiced the subject.

Murtagh nodded, stared at Rebecca some more and asked, "Would this be a painting for someone in particular?"

"Yes," Rebecca said.

"What about the pose?" Murtagh asked. "Are you thinking of standing, sitting or reclining?"

"Reclining, definitely."

Emily watched Rebecca work with keen interest.

Daisy Jane looked as if *she* was getting a bit worked up.

"Are there any other particular details that interest you?" the artist inquired. "An indoor setting or outdoors?"

Rebecca told him, "I'll leave that to you, but I would have a couple of requirements."

"What?" Murtagh asked.

"I have a tattoo on my right thigh. I'd want you to remove it in the painting. I want to remember what my leg used to look like."

Murtagh nodded. "I can do that. What else?"

"I'd like to see how my breasts would look a bit bigger, a cup size, maybe two. I've thought about getting that kind of surgery. It strikes me as a good idea to see what I'd look like first."

Murtagh laughed. He turned to Daisy Jane and said, "I think I just found my new specialty."

Covering the side of her face so only Rebecca could see her, Emily rolled her eyes.

After a bit of haggling, the two sides settled on a fee of $100,000.

Then Daisy Jane said, "We'll need half down to get started."

Rebecca said, "Really? A canvas and some paints cost that much?"

Getting just a bit frosty, Daisy Jane said, "There is the artist's time to consider."

"How about twenty-five grand?" Rebecca countered.

For his part, Murtagh was happy just to see the two women contend with each other.

"I'm sorry, but we have business practices to maintain," Daisy Jane said.

"You know what?" Rebecca told her. "I think I'd better take a look at some nudes Mr. Murtagh has done before I pay you *any* money."

Giving a sigh of exasperation, Daisy Jane said, "We don't have any here."

Emily decided it was time for her to intervene.

She said, "We should go, Becky. This is getting to be too hard. And then there's that other problem you have, with your hand."

Murtagh looked at Rebecca. "I don't see anything wrong with her hands."

"Tell him, Beck," Emily said.

Rebecca gave Emily a cross look, but then told Murtagh, "The guy I'm divorcing? We got into it the night I left. That was six weeks ago now."

"A physical fight?" Murtagh loved that idea. "Did he hurt you?"

"Are you kidding? I was the one teaching him Krav Maga. I ducked the sucker punch he threw and hit him with two shots to the head. Put him down for the count, but I broke bones in both hands. The swelling and the bruising are gone, and after six weeks the doctor told me the bones have knit — but not to hit anyone else for a while."

Murtagh liked that, too.

Emily picked up the story, certain of where Rebecca was going.

"I took Becky out shopping to celebrate, but I had to put our stuff on my card because her hands still tingle and she can't sign her name for anything."

Rebecca said, "I try to write my name, it looks like something a little kid might do with a crayon. My doctor says I've got another month or two before I get my fine motor skills back. I was thinking that was when you could do the painting."

Murtagh thought about things for a moment before he said, "Do you have an exemplar?"

"A what?" Rebecca asked.

"An example of your signature. You have one on your driver's license, don't you?"

"Yeah, I do."

Daisy Jane shook her head. "Don't do that, Jack."

Emily asked, "Do what?"

Murtagh waved Daisy Jane off and said, "With your permission, and we'll make the check out for $10,000 and —"

"Jack!"

Murtagh whirled and jabbed a finger at the gallery owner's nose, giving the clear impression that he might stick it in her eye next.

"*I'm* the artist, remember?"

Emily stepped to Rebecca's side so they stood shoulder to shoulder.

That sign of solidarity might have told Murtagh something, but he missed it.

"We don't want to cause any trouble," Rebecca said softly.

She and Emily took a step back as if it were choreographed.

Murtagh held both hands up to placate them. Getting himself under control, he said in a reasonable tone. "I'm sorry if I scared you. I've had some troubles of my own recently. Here's what I was trying to say: If it's all right with you, I'll sign your check for $10,000, and I'll make it look exactly like yours. No one will ever doubt that it's your signature. Is that all right with you?"

Rebecca made a show of thinking about the idea, for a count of three.

"Okay, but can you make the rest of the check look like my writing, too?"

"I think so, yes."

"All right. Let's do it then: ten thousand."

She made a show of being clumsy opening her purse and getting the checkbook out. Murtagh took it gently from her hand and asked, "You gave the guy you're divorcing some kind of beating, huh?"

Rebecca nodded.

Emily added, "I've seen the pictures."

"I'd like to see them, too."

Daisy Jane had heard enough and retreated to a back room.

"Do a great job with the painting and I'll show you," Rebecca said.

"Deal," Murtagh said.

Emily grinned. "This is all so cool. Can I ask a favor?"

"You want to be painted nude, too?" the artist asked.

"Maybe later. What I'm wondering is, can I video you while you work? I mean, this is going to be a piece of performance art, isn't it, you writing out Becky's check."

Daisy Jane would've screamed bloody murder, but she wasn't around.

Murtagh said, "Sure, why not?"

In a matter of minutes, the transaction was completed ... and visually recorded.

Rebecca and Emily walked out of the gallery working hard not to burst out laughing.

They were aided in their restraint by the first thing they saw outdoors.

LAPD Captain Terry Adair, in uniform, was sitting on the back end of a patrol car parked two buildings up the street, waiting for them. The sonofabitch was still stalking Emily. They'd expected that, but not the explicit show of his police powers.

Be my love or I'll throw your ass in jail.

He said, "Emily, we've got to get right with each other. We've just got to."

U.S. Interstate 29 — Approaching Omaha, Nebraska

A bread truck versus SUV versus Greyhound bus collision reduced the highway approach to the city to one lane. Traffic still should have proceeded at a crawl, but for some reason John Tall Wolf was unable to see, things had ground to a complete halt. Hoping to make good use of the unforeseen delay, John took out his phone and made a call to Cale Tucker at the National Security Agency in Fort Meade, Maryland.

The young cyber-snoop answered the call with a glum tone. "Mr. Director, I'm sorry, but I don't have anything for you yet."

"Your bosses have you working your normal duties, don't they?"

After a two-beat hesitation, Tucker admitted, "Yeah, they do, but I've been working through my lunch hour and staying late to help with your investigation. That's no BS. I just haven't been able to find that damn computer yet. It's starting to make me doubt the powers of technology, and for me that's like a preacher losing his religion."

"Be of good faith," John told him. "I've got a strong lead."

"You do?"

John said, "I'd have been happy if you'd come up with the

answer, but this way I feel good there's still room for doing things in the classical fashion."

"Retro can be cool, too," Tucker said. "So what have you found out?"

"A real estate mogul named Brice Benard, working out of Omaha is trying to pull a fast one on a tribe of Indians also called the Omaha."

"Bet the Indians had the name first."

"They did indeed," John confirmed. "Anyway, it's not absolutely certain, but close to it, that Benard had someone steal Dr. Lisle's computer for him."

Tucker would assemble the pieces with commendable speed, John thought.

The young security wizard said, "Dr. Lisle has an affiliation with the Omaha tribe, probably a kinship relation. The tribe has some natural resource that's essential to Dr. Lisle's plan to formulate a new antibiotic. Benard's trying to fleece the Indians and use the information on the computer he stole from a member of the tribe to make huge piles of money."

"Exactly," John said. "A very neat summary."

"Got a question for you, though, Mr. Director."

"What's that?"

"How'd this Benard guy hear about Dr. Lisle's work in the first place? I hadn't known about it before I talked with you, and checking on things since then, Dr. Lisle's work isn't secret, but it's very low profile. Brief, generalized mentions in highly specialized publications."

John thought about that and said, "Good point. At the moment, I'm certain Benard had to have help from an insider at Dr. Lisle's lab to steal the computer. Addressing your question, that's the likely source for the news of Dr. Lisle's work reaching Benard, too."

"Okay, I can see that," Tucker said. "Now, I'm wondering something else."

"What?"

"Well, if Dr. Lisle is Native American, and the Indian reservation has a natural resource that's essential to creating the new antibiotic, is there anyone else involved who's one of your kind of people?"

"Tall, dark and handsome?" John asked.

Tucker laughed. "Yeah, that, too. But I was thinking more of other Native Americans being in on the scheme."

John said, "I was told everybody in Dr. Lisle's lab has some measure of native blood."

"That's really interesting. I'm not big on anthropology or gene-alogy, but Brice Benard doesn't sound like an Indian name to me. Wouldn't it make more sense to take the stolen goods to somebody with money who's part of your tribe, so to speak?"

"The chief of the Omaha is named Thomas Emmett," John told Tucker.

"No kidding? Well then, maybe Brice Benard's family was a real early arrival in this country, too, don't you think?"

"I hadn't until you just mentioned it," John said. "Thanks for the notion."

"About time I was a little help."

John saw the line of vehicles ahead of him was starting to inch forward.

He said, "Maybe you can do a bit more. Do you have the ability to listen in on Brice Benard's phones? Not just tap them when he's on the line, but overhear what he says in his office or home when he's not using his phones?"

Tucker hesitated, then said, "I'm really not cleared to tell anyone what we can do."

"How about the President?"

"Well, yeah, she can know anything she wants ... I think."

"Okay, well, call Byron DeWitt and sum up our conversation for him."

"Or I can just replay it."

"I should have known," John said. "Do that and say I suggest he gets the President involved at this point. Then replay the whole thing for FBI Deputy Director Abra Benjamin, too. Can you do that for me?"

"Right away. You'll recommend me for another job, if I lose mine?"

"Absolutely, but don't worry. You'll be doing the right thing."

"Sure hope that's enough," Tucker said, "but I'm on it."

"Oh, hey, if you do get the go-ahead to listen in on Benard and things get hairy at any point while I'm visiting him, call the local cops right away, okay?"

"Absolutely. Whatever else happens, this has been fun."

"I'd like to keep it that way," John told him.

He ended the call and started to move ahead at close to 20 miles per hour.

Los Angeles, California

"Get lost before I run you in," LAPD Captain Terry Adair told Rebecca.

She'd stepped between Adair and Emily right after he'd made his creepy, implicitly threatening plea for reconciliation with his lost love.

"You know who I am?" Rebecca asked.

"Yeah, a recent immigrant," he said. "I checked. You used to be a Mountie up in Canada." He twirled an index finger in a dismissive gesture. "Whoop-ti-doo. Doesn't mean shit to me. You don't leave right now, I'll arrest you for refusing to obey a police order."

Rebecca stayed put; her only movement was to hold out both arms.

Inviting the asshole to put handcuffs on her.

Before he could respond, Emily stepped up and stood shoulder to shoulder with Rebecca.

"You dumbass," she told Adair. "You didn't look to see who she's married to — a fed, the Director of the BIA's Office of Justice Services. The guy who the President is going to nominate to her Cabinet. He's tight with the Commander-in-Chief. Is that whoop-ti-doo enough for you?"

In case it wasn't, Rebecca added, "Besides all that, if anything unfortunate were to happen to me, you'd lose all that pretty hair of yours when he scalps you."

All that did give Adair pause. Still, he was trying to sort out how much, if any, of it was true. He hadn't drawn a conclusion when Emily shook her head and told him, "Listen, Terry, you should have taken me at my word months ago. The problem is, you're a spoiled brat who's approaching middle age. You can probably count on one hand the number of times you've been denied something you really want."

The LAPD captain pulled his head back as if he'd been slapped. Whether that was due to Emily's character assessment or a fear of aging was impossible to say.

"All I want is one last chance to explain myself," he said. "If you're still not interested in any future with me ... well, all right, so be it."

Emily stared at him for a moment and then managed a small nod.

"All right. Meet me at my house tonight. Six o'clock. Don't bring flowers, candy or anything else. Just think about what you want to say. Rehearse it, if you want. See how it sounds to you. If it comes across as bullshit even you can recognize, don't bother coming."

Adair took a moment to process all that and said, "Okay, I'll do that."

Rebecca let her arms fall to her sides and told him, "You leave first. I don't want you to write me a ticket."

The look the police captain gave Rebecca would have scared most people. The fire in his eyes said the two of them would have a day of reckoning, no matter who she had to back her up. But he left without saying anything Emily could hold against him.

Once he was gone, the two women got in Rebecca's Audi and headed back to their office.

Emily asked Rebecca, "Would your husband really scalp someone?"

Rebecca laughed. "No, I don't think so. Arcelia might, though."

Emily grinned. "Now, that wouldn't surprise me at all."

"John would do something … unexpected. I could see him staking that guy out on a mountaintop. Let him grow weak and desperate from exposure, starvation and dehydration, and then get one last burst of adrenaline as vultures circled, landed and began to pick him apart just before he died."

Emily shivered. "Jeez, that's some sick imagination you've got. I'm going to like working with you."

"Yeah, I'm a million laughs, but what about you? What were you thinking, saying you'd talk to that creep one last time? That'll only encourage him. He'll never go away."

Emily told her. "I didn't say I was going to talk to him alone."

Rebecca smiled. "Tell me the whole plan."

She did, and Rebecca approved wholeheartedly.

Emily said, "He shouldn't have insulted the RCMP. You think there might be a couple of Mounties attached to the Canadian Consulate-General in L.A.?"

Rebecca gave her colleague a light punch of approval on a shoulder and said, "I'll be more than happy to find out."

Farnam Street — Omaha, Nebraska

Wilbur Rosewell, the ethics-free private investigator and former killer cop, rode in the box truck driven by Petrovich, the no-first-name Russian emigré. Rosewell got nervous whenever Petrovich was behind the wheel. He'd never said anything about it, but now he worried maybe a cop might pull them over, the way Petrovich drove. If Brice Benard were tied up in the back, along with who knew how much of his gold, things might go as wrong as they could get.

They might have to shoot any cop who stopped them, and that was never a good career move. Rosewell's heinie started to pucker just thinking about it. He finally came out and said, "You know what, Petrovich, you drive like a foreigner."

The Russian spared Rosewell a sidelong glance. "I drive with an accent?"

Rosewell coughed up a nervous laugh. "Yeah, goddamnit, that's right. You not only watch for oncoming traffic and whoever might be coming up from behind, you look like you're checking out every manhole cover in the street in case someone might pop up with a bazooka. And you keep looking *up,* for Christ's sake. What's that about? Attack helicopters or flying saucers? You make jerky lane changes for no good reason. You can't do any of that shit once we grab Benard and the gold."

Petrovich stopped for a red light and looked at Rosewell. "No?"

"No. In America, patrol cops watch for erratic driving."

"I have been driving here for two years, and I have never been stopped."

Rosewell shook his head. "Is that the way you operated back home, counting on dumb luck?"

The light turned green, and Petrovich checked out every angle he could see before he put the truck back in motion with an abrupt burst of speed, until he cleared the intersection, and then he slowed down until he was under the speed limit.

"At home, no one would dare to stop me," he said.

"Yeah, well, those days are o-ver. If you've been here for two years," Rosewell said, "you've seen how Americans drive, and I don't mean the crazy asshole kids or the geezers."

"Geezers?"

"Old people. The ones who don't have the muscle tone to push the gas pedal down more than an inch."

Petrovich nodded. "Yes, I know both these types."

"Okay, so what you should do is shoot for somewhere in the middle and, for Christ's sake, be relaxed about it, like you don't have a care in the world."

"Perhaps that is the problem," Petrovich said.

"What is?"

"You ask me to do something for God, and I am an atheist."

Rosewell just barely stopped himself from saying, "Jesus!"

He was working to keep a pulsing vein in his forehead from

bursting when Petrovich asked, "Would you like to drive the truck after we take Benard and his gold?"

"Yeah, I would."

"Then I will accommodate you."

"Thank you."

"If the police stop us on the way to Benard's office, I will be humble and cooperative."

"Exactly right. That's absolutely the best way to play it."

They caught another red light at the next intersection. Rosewell had long felt certain that every traffic engineer in town was being paid off by OPEC. Maybe the mayor and the city council, too.

As they waited, Petrovich said, "You know, of course, that I do not use my own name."

Rosewell hadn't given that a moment's thought, but it made sense. "Yeah, fine."

"Do you recognize my name from your school reading?"

"What?"

"I've chosen the name of a character from a famous novel."

"No kidding," Rosewell said, clearly not interested.

"You are not familiar with it?"

"No."

"The novel is called *Crime and Punishment*."

That got a grin out of Rosewell.

The Russian continued, "Petrovich was an investigator who got a fellow to confess to two murders he committed — after someone else had already confessed."

Damn traffic light stayed red long enough to let a 100-car freight train pass by, Rosewell thought, and now the damn Russian was talking literature. Shit, next it might be chess.

Petrovich said, "I mention this to let you know I will get Benard to tell us where *all* of his gold is kept, and how to get at it. So I hope you will forgive my Russian driving."

Rosewell sighed and nodded. "Yeah, okay. Sorry about busting your chops."

The light turned green, and Petrovich moved through the intersection in a normal American fashion, accelerating but not racing.

He told Rosewell, "I thought as a former policeman you would know *Crime and Punishment,* but if you do not read ..." He shrugged.

Rosewell gave the Russian a dirty look. "Hey, I read books. When it comes to stories about guys like you and me, I just like Elmore Leonard better."

After a moment of reflection, Petrovich said, "You know, so do I."

A few minutes later, he backed the truck up to the loading dock at Brice Benard's office building.

Eppley Airfield — Omaha, Nebraska

Marlene Flower Moon landed in Omaha after a smooth, quick trip from Albuquerque. Despite having to pick up the tab for her transportation, she was in surprisingly good spirits. By putting her expenses in proportion with her net worth, she realized that what she'd had to pay for the flight was less than a trifle.

In her own right, she'd earned a small fortune from assisting the late movie icon Clay Steadman in the production of his last movie, *Texas Mean.* She'd later come into a far greater sum, and a continuing revenue stream, when she'd learned Clay had left his 33.33 gross points in the film to her, as well as any subsidiary rights that might later be exploited.

Clay's executor had explained to Marlene that the actor had felt a true kinship with her and wanted to express his gratitude appropriately. Marlene thought he already had by involving her, a complete novice, in his farewell performance. She'd seen immediately that he hadn't had long to live, despite being more physically vigorous than anyone might have suspected.

"It isn't often that I'm surprised," she'd told the executor.

Only Tall Wolf had surprised her again just recently. She wondered if the shape of the universe was changing — and what that might mean for Coyote.

The executor had warned her: "The studio might try some trick to weasel out of compensating you appropriately, but Clay said you'd be more than a match for them."

Marlene smiled politely, shook the man's hand and said thank you.

Then she went to see the studio head. As predicted, he tried to screw her financially.

He told Marlene, "We won't contest the legitimacy of Clay's will, of course, but you should know that because he was getting older and his appeal to the youth market had been waning for years, and because the material itself was of a risky nature, we all agreed that Clay would take net points on this deal."

Net points, also known as monkey points, were those that got paid only after the studio deducted all of its overhead from the box office receipts. Nobody with any real prominence in the Hollywood ecosystem *ever* took net points as part of their deal. Gross points, those that came straight out of gross revenue figures — screw the damn inflated studio expenses — were the only way to go for stars.

As long as Clay Steadman had drawn breath, he was still a star.

The studio head, being unfamiliar with Marlene, thinking she was only some babe who'd sunk her claws into a fading old man, had expected her to do no more than plead, haggle or at worst threaten a lawsuit. The movie boss was betting the studio had more and better-connected lawyers than any gold-digger did.

Marlene didn't take the bastard's throat in her teeth as she had done with Bodaway. Nor did she piss on him. Instead, she seized his throat in her right hand, piercing his wattled flesh with what felt to the bastard like an iron claw. She didn't go deep enough to kill him, but the pain and the shock were sufficient to cause him to wet his own pants.

She walked out of his office not only with the gross points Clay had left to her but also with half the gross points the studio had held on the film. Put together, she had taken in more than 50 cents of every dollar *Texas Mean* brought in. That was a hundred million already, and a steady stream continued to provide more.

Clay's other heirs had congratulated Marlene on her negotiating skills.

As the chartered jet came to a stop, the cabin steward told her, "Your limousine is waiting for you, Ms. Flower Moon. It's been a pleasure to have you aboard today."

She tipped him $2,000 and told him to split it with the flight crew as he saw fit.

Getting settled in the limo, she took out her phone. She had thought of heading straight to the Omaha Marriott Downtown, the place where Tall Wolf said he was staying. She'd bet all her movie money that the place charged more than federal guidelines allowed.

That was when a small revelation occurred. Tall Wolf had his own sly ways, didn't always play according to the rules. There *was* a streak of kinship between them. Not in terms of blood but in spirit. A sense of mischief, at the very least, was something they held in common.

Not that Marlene was ever going to get sentimental about it.

Rather, it was always helpful to know a potential adversary's tendencies.

She made a call to Tall Wolf. "I'm in Omaha. Where are you, your hotel?"

Since Marlene hadn't bothered with a hello, John didn't either. "I'm about to confront a guy I think ripped off a Native American medical researcher, and tried to con the local tribe out of something valuable, too."

"The Omaha?"

"Yes." John remembered a point that Cale Tucker had raised with him. "Would you know any tribes that had a hostile relationship with the Omaha back in the old days? Or even recently?"

Cale had said maybe Brice Benard had native blood.

If it was also *bad* blood toward the Omaha …

"The Lakota Sioux," Marlene said.

"Yeah? Serious stuff?"

"In 1855, a mixed-blood Omaha chief named Logan Fontanelle was on a buffalo hunt with a number of his men. During a lull, he left the others to go pick gooseberries."

"Really? Pick berries?"

Marlene chided him, "It wasn't the Sunday picnic activity it is now, Tall Wolf. A Lakota war party came across him. They took Fontanelle prisoner, killed him and scalped him. Presumably made off with his berries, too. What does all this have to do with anything?"

"The guy I'm going to see is named Brice Benard, a big-shot real estate guy. Someone suggested to me he might have native blood and be a traditional enemy of the Omaha."

Marlene laughed. "I see you still know how to recruit good help."

"The best," John said. "That's why I called you."

"Benard sounds French to me," Marlene said, ignoring the compliment. "The Omaha and the French have long intermarried. There's also an overlap between the French and the Lakota."

"But is there still a serious rivalry?" John asked.

"There's always friction of some sort between various groups, and on a one-to-one basis anything is possible."

"Yeah, just look at us," John said, "the best of enemies who can still get along."

"Don't push your luck, Tall Wolf."

"Okay. You can meet me back at the hotel then … after I go see Benard. Maybe I'll have to call the cops, if I need to shoot it out with him and, you know, any thugs he might have around."

"You really think you can play me that easily, Tall Wolf?"

John said, "Unh-uh, I just thought you might enjoy being in on the action."

Marlene stewed for all of ten seconds, couldn't see a way out.

Didn't want to, really.

Having made peace of a sort with Tall Wolf or not, she was still in the mood to enjoy shredding *someone's* ass.

"Give me the address where you're going," she said in a flat voice. "I'll meet you there."

John did and told her, "I look forward to it."

Los Angeles, California

The recruiting effort took a couple of hours. Everyone Emily, Rebecca, Arcelia and Emily's neighbor, Colonel Donahue had called agreed to show up at Emily's house by late that afternoon. At the colonel's suggestion, they also consented to wear their dress uniforms. Medals for valor, of course, would be polished.

Rebecca had called the Consulate General of Canada in Los Angeles, identified herself as a former inspector with the RCMP and asked if there were two members of the Force available to help her as part of a gathering that would include female members of the LAPD, the United States Marine Corps and the front office of the Los Angeles Dodgers.

Once Rebecca's bona fides were established, Consul Edmund Wolcott came on the line and said, "Sounds like you're planning quite the event, Inspector. Have you secured a parade permit, by any chance?"

"Won't need one, sir," she said. "The show's being held on private property."

"Everything will be well within bounds, both legally and in terms of general decorum? Can't do anything to cause a fuss in Canada's fourth largest city."

Rebecca laughed. Los Angeles was jokingly given that title for the estimated million citizens of Canada who lived at least part time in the metro L.A. area. She said, "Everything will be proper and peaceful. Might even be a nice bit of publicity to display back home."

"Any chance I might be able to observe?" Wolcott asked.

"I think we could arrange a living room window view for you. That is, assuming you have the free time."

"I do. You asked for two female members of the Force to attend. Would it be agreeable if I brought a third? We have a Deputy

Commissioner Eileen Murphy visiting us, and she claims to know you. She'd also like to be on hand."

A warm glow filled Rebecca. "I'd be honored to have the deputy commissioner join us."

"Another seat in the living room is available?"

"If she has her dress uniform with her, I'd love to have her stand with us, sir."

"By happy coincidence, she does. Will there be press in attendance?"

"A reporter and a photographer from the *Times*."

"Good. They should be happy to share with our newspapers."

The troops were massed in Emily's living room at 4:55. Colonel Donahue and nine other Marines, as was their custom, would be the tip of the spear. They'd be followed by ten officers of the LAPD. Arcelia, in a San Francisco Giants jersey, and the two women wearing the Dodgers jerseys would each have a baseball bat at her shoulder. Rebecca, Deputy Commissioner Murphy and two Mounties from the Consulate General would form the honor guard for Emily, who would be the last to step through her front door.

The women exiting the house would form two parallel lines along the walkway leading from the house to the public sidewalk. Inside the house, watching from the wings would be Leland Proctor, Emily's dad, along with the President of the L.A. Police Commission, Bob Sifuentes, who'd cleared the LAPD officers' participation, Consul Edmund Wolcott and Detectives Eloy Zapata and Wallace MacDuff, who'd stopped by to see how Emily was doing and, being miffed that they hadn't been included in the plan, refused to be budged.

Emily mollified each of them with a kiss on the cheek and told them if circumstances dictated that they could come out shooting, making sure they didn't hit any of the wrong people.

The photographer from the *Times* was also inside the house, and he'd shoot Terry Adair over Emily's shoulder. The newspaper's reporter would appear on the sidewalk outside the house and try to get a comment from Terry as he beat his expected retreat. The reporter might also use his iPhone to take some video, if he was willing to risk getting the phone smacked out of his hand.

Emily thought she was going to look like a great big doofus if Terry didn't show.

But he rang the doorbell right on time.

Omaha, Nebraska

A big guy in green coveralls who must've handled shipping and receiving for the building came charging out of a door leading out onto the shipping dock. He was a solid 240 pounds, if he was an ounce, Rosewell thought. Looked like he might've played college football at some small school 30 years ago. A linebacker who could deliver a big hit when he didn't have to run too far to get to the running back.

He waved a thick index finger at Rosewell and Petrovich as they climbed the steps to the dock. "You guys can't park that truck here. You're not on my list."

He held a clipboard in his left hand. A sheaf of neatly stacked papers clamped to the board apparently told him whom to allow into his grimy domain. No surprise, their truck wasn't on the list; they hadn't told Brice Benard they'd be bringing it.

Rosewell stepped forward with a smile. "Last minute call, Stan." He'd read the man's name on his coveralls. "Mr. Benard called for us. If you get him on the phone, I'm sure he'll tell you it's all right. I've got his number, if you want it."

The loading dock boss gave them both a look. It was clear he'd recognized Benard's name, and he didn't really have a problem with Rosewell, but he didn't like Petrovich's looks. Rosewell understood why when he saw the Russian look Stan up and down like he was deciding where to shoot him first.

Before Rosewell could give Petrovich an elbow to straighten him out, Stan turned his back, and walking away said, "I've got the number, too. I'll be right back."

"Lighten the hell up," Rosewell whispered to Petrovich. "We haven't even gotten into the building yet."

"You get cooperation your way," the Russian responded, "and as you shall see, I will get it my way. Remember to tell Benard what I told you."

There'd always been some tension between Rosewell and Petrovich, neither willing to concede to the other who was boss. Still, after a half-dozen jobs, they'd always managed to make their scores and not kill each other. This time, Rosewell thought, would be the last time he worked with Petrovich, or maybe any other damn foreigner.

He stepped aside to make his call to Benard. Stan should have had time by now to get an okay from the man. That was confirmed when Benard answered his call.

"Mr. Benard, it's me, Rosewell. I'm downstairs with the man I told you about ... The truck? He's just come from another job. If you want, I'll tell him we can do it another time ... Okay, we'll do it now, only he doesn't want anybody in your office to see him ... Yeah, he's real careful. So if you want to let your people go home a few minutes early, then we'll be right up ... That works for you? Good. See you soon."

Rosewell ended the call and looked up to see Petrovich talking to Stan. Petrovich was speaking Russian. Rosewell didn't understand a word, but he could see Stan was breaking a sweat on a day the weather definitely didn't call for it.

Petrovich wasn't holding a gun on Stan, and Rosewell thought that was the only thing that would equalize a fight between them, and then only if the Russian got off a first shot. So what the hell was going on? Rosewell decided it was better not to intrude.

Petrovich didn't need to belabor whatever point he was making, and Stan soon began to nod repeatedly. Satisfied, Petrovich clapped him on the shoulder, turned and rejoined Rosewell.

"That guy's Russian, too?" Rosewell asked.

"Polish. His parents brought him to this country as a child. His English is good, but there is still a trace of his homeland in his voice. That was what I heard when we arrived."

Roswell hadn't heard it but didn't argue. "Poles can understand Russian?"

"Many of them learned the language when we managed their country for them. This one heard enough at home to understand me."

"So what did you say?" Rosewell said.

"I asked him to be a good fellow and shoo away any other trucks that might want to pick up or unload while we are here."

"No witnesses." Rosewell nodded. "That's good."

"You made our arrangements with Mr. Benard?"

Rosewell nodded. "He should be sending everyone on his floor home right now."

"Good. Then all should go well."

"What about Stan? He's seen us."

Petrovich shrugged. "He hasn't seen us do anything illegal, and I have the feeling he will soon forget we were ever here."

Rosewell was inclined to think the same, but he wasn't entirely persuaded.

Knowing just what he was thinking, Petrovich added, "Of course, if you are not satisfied, well, you've told me you killed two men. What would one more matter?"

Rosewell knew it would matter if they got caught. The guy who didn't do the killing could rat out the one who did. Get himself a lighter sentence.

Thinking about things in terms of eliminating witnesses, though, it'd be better for both of them to kill each other. Eliminate the need to split the haul. Leave *no* witness to what they were about to do.

"Perhaps you wish to abandon this job?" Petrovich asked. "You seem uneasy."

Rosewell couldn't bring himself to do that. Maybe that was the power of gold.

"No," he said, "let's do it."

Los Angeles, California

LAPD Captain Terry Adair, wearing a bespoke gunmetal gray merino wool suit — instead of his uniform — drove around the block where Emily Proctor lived three times looking for signs of trouble. He felt alternately smart and foolish for doing so. If Emily had set out a pile of poop for him to step in, while wearing his killer Ferragamo loafers, he'd certainly want to avoid that. On the other hand, what woman in her right mind wouldn't recognize the mistake she'd made by trying to give him the brush-off?

Maybe that tall, pain-in-the-ass Canadian broad for one, but she hadn't known the pleasure of spending a night with him. Let her do that and see how she'd feel. That notion sparked an idea in Terry's mind: him, Emily *and* the Canadian babe.

That'd make for some long-lasting memories.

After they were done, he'd give that foreign frost-queen the old heave-ho.

And if her old man did try to scalp him, he'd show that Indian how the West was won.

He was chuckling to himself as he pulled to the curb. His watch, a Breitling Navitimer, told him he had a few minutes yet before he was supposed to rap on Emily's door. He'd run through any number of scenarios of how he should announce himself. Wear his dress uniform and bang on the door with a billy-club. Some women he'd known would like that … but not this one. He'd considered dressing the way he was now and bringing some crazily expensive gift … only Emily had told him specifically not to do that. So he'd only got dressed up in his best suit and shoes, and added just a dash of Tom Ford Oud Wood cologne. If that didn't buckle her knees … hey, maybe the Canadian broad was more than just a friend.

Hell, if Emily was like that, all she had to do was tell him.

He'd say *adios,* no hard feelings.

Not that he still wouldn't like to corral both of them on the same Tempur-Pedic.

Terry got out of his car. He no longer had any time to spare looking for signs of a trap, but his eyes still went to the house on his left, the one with the old broad who had an assault rifle and claimed to be a Marine officer. Shit, wasn't that half of the world's problems, women pretending they could do a man's work?

The other half being people of both sexes not being content to stay right where they'd been born. Not just Mexicans. Put Canadians on the list, too.

People from out of state, too. Especially New York.

By the time he'd analyzed all of the world's problems, and it looked like the hard-assed old biddy next door wasn't at home, Terry rang Emily's doorbell. He was pleased when he heard her call out, "Be right there."

The quick response was gratifying enough, but the tone of Emily's voice said she was happy. Glad to see him. Made him overjoyed once again Mom and Dad had sent him to the best orthodontist in Beverly Hills.

He was smiling molar to molar when the door opened.

And who the hell should he see but the crone from next door?

Wearing a goddamn Marine dress uniform. Looking fierce enough to scare an addict away from his needle. Jesus Christ, she hadn't been kidding. Terry took an involuntary step backward.

Colonel Maeve Donahue clamped a vise-like hand on his shoulder and said, "Don't go rushing off, sonny. Emily will be right out. She's just saying goodbye to a few friends who dropped in for tea."

Terry blinked as a bright light went off in his eyes.

His mind was too awhirl to realize he'd been photographed.

The colonel stepped past him, and here came another woman Marine in a dress uniform. She looked like she might cut his heart out, too. And then there was another and another and ...Then came a line of female LAPD officers in Class A uniforms. For just a second, Terry's spine stiffened, until he saw the same look of contempt in each pair of eyes that met his own.

There was no fear, no respect, not even a bit of deference.

No chance they'd follow any order he might try to give them.

He thought things couldn't get any worse but, what the hell, here came three women with baseball bats on their shoulders, two wearing Dodgers jerseys, one in a Giants jersey. He feared he was about to catch a serious beating, was about to turn and run when the broad in the Giants jersey caught his sleeve and told him, "Emily will be right out. Hang on another minute."

He wasn't sure he wanted to, but then he saw what was coming next.

The goddamn Mounties, four of them, again in dress uniforms. One of them was Emily's sassy pal; three others were strangers. One of them was another old biddy and she looked just as tough as the first one. The fantasy of bedding *any* Canadian woman died a sudden death.

Then, at last, Emily stood in front of him. In contrast to all the others, she wore an old T-shirt from a Neil Diamond concert at the Hollywood Bowl, a pair of cut-off jeans and raggedy flip-flops. She held two open cans of Coors beer in her hands. She handed one to Terry.

It was still cold.

Emily told him, "My friends and I are having a little party tonight, Terry, but you're not invited. Still, it would be rude not to offer you a drink. One for the road, since our paths will never cross again if I can help it. What do you say? Can we end things, once and for all, on a civil note?"

Terry didn't have to turn around to know that every woman who had passed him by was staring at him now. They'd descend on him like Patton's Third Army if he tried anything physical, maybe even if he just got foul-mouthed. For all that, though, he was relieved. If Emily had done anything less dramatic, he would have kept coming back at her.

Now, he knew he had to put her behind him, no two ways about it. Just the two old broads would probably kill him in his sleep, if he caused Emily any more trouble. He raised his can in a gesture of salute.

"You're too tough for me, Emily."

She clinked her can against his and they both sipped.

"Be good, Terry," Emily said.

"As good as I can," he told her.

"Terry?"

"Yeah?"

"Each of the women here? All of us will come to her aid, too, if she needs us. We got to talking today about women standing up for each other. That idea is going to spread across town, across the country and around the world. So learn to take no for an answer."

For just a moment, Terry looked as if he might object.

Until Arcelia and Rebecca stepped forward.

Arcelia gripped her bat like she'd swing for the fences and added, "Learn fast."

Omaha, Nebraska

The outer cubicles and offices of Brice Benard's real estate empire were empty when Rosewell and Petrovich got off the elevator. The door to Benard's corner office stood open, so the two men walked right in. Before either of them said a word to Benard, they caught sight of the large bar of gold sitting in the middle of his desk, gleaming like it was lit from within by its own personal sun.

Sonofabitch, Rosewell thought, how could a chunk of metal hold such power?

He'd never before seen gold in any form bigger than a gaudy ring. But this thing, it made him think of kings, conquests and the power to have any damn thing he wanted. Rule the whole frigging world if he could get enough of it.

Intruding on his flight of grandiosity, Rosewell could sense Petrovich reacting in much the same way. Only the Russian hadn't lost the ability to speak. He said to Benard, "You make quite a first impression, sir."

Benard smirked. "That damn thing is quite an ass-tickler, isn't it?"

Remembering his earlier conversation with Petrovich, Rosewell said, "That's a standard bar, right? How much does it weigh?"

Dazzled more than a little himself by his treasure, Benard lost sight of the fact that Rosewell's question evinced a knowledge of the subject at hand that most Omaha cops and PI's wouldn't possess.

"Yeah, it's a standard bar," Benard said, "and —"

Petrovich held up a hand. "Let me guess," he said. He studied the bar of gold, seemed to be communicating with it in some silent way. Then he nodded as if he'd heard an answer. "Four hundred ounces."

Benard sat back in his chair. "Sonofabitch, that's exactly right."

Rosewell turned to the Russian. "What's the price per ounce today?"

"Thirteen hundred and fifty-one dollars."

"So that one bar is worth?"

Petrovich had no trouble doing the math in his head. "Five hundred and forty thousand four hundred dollars."

That feat of multiplication did make Benard uneasy.

"Who the hell is this guy?" he asked Rosewell.

The Russian held up his hand again. "One moment, please."

He closed the door to Benard's office. Petrovich's training and experience told him that a man such as the one he was about to rob would not shy away from placing his employees under video surveillance, and might even record their conversations. It was always best to learn early who might be plotting against you.

On the other hand, any wise ruler always strictly guarded his own privacy.

"What the hell do you think you're doing?" Benard said to Petrovich. "I already sent everyone home, and the cleaning staff won't be here for hours."

"How many hours?" Rosewell asked.

"Three hours. They don't come in until eight. Two hours after the rest of the staff usually leaves. They were happy about getting off early, I can tell you."

"May we sit?" Petrovich asked.

He was pleased Rosewell had spoken up and asked the same question he'd had in mind. That diverted Benard's attention, made the question seem less out of place, less threatening even if the fellow had bothered to take his head out of his rectum.

"Yeah, go ahead, both of you. Let's get down to business already."

Rosewell and Petrovich sat.

The Russian said, "If we might delay for just a moment, may I ask, by any chance, have you read Dostoevsky?"

"Who?" Benard asked.

"The famous Russian novelist, the author of *Crime and Punishment*."

"Are you kidding me?" Benard turned to Rosewell. "Is he kidding me?"

Rosewell didn't answer directly. He only asked, "How about Elmore Leonard? Have you ever read any of his books?"

"*Da*," Petrovich said, "Leonard was one of *your* countrymen."

"*Da? Countrymen?* Are you two serious?" Benard looked from one of his visitors to the other. He clearly thought they'd both gone nuts. "I don't think I should trust either of you bastards. Get the hell out of here."

Neither man moved.

Until Rosewell disappointed him worse than the last time. He pulled a gun and pointed it at Benard. Then Petrovich did the same. Benard looked at the two of them bug-eyed ... until his gaze shifted to the bar of gold on his desk. The one valued, for the moment, at better than a half-million dollars.

"That's what this is all about?" Benard asked. "You came here to rob me, you sonsabitches?"

"We did," Rosewell said calmly.

Petrovich elaborated. "Only not just that one bar. Everything you have here, and all that you have at your home also. With people like you, there is always some treasure at home. In fact, that's usually where most of it is."

The expression of hatred on Benard's face told the two thieves Petrovich had it exactly right.

"Fuck the both of you," the real estate tycoon said. "I'd sooner die than hand over all my gold."

Petrovich nodded. "I believe you would, if only we would be so kind as to kill you quickly. However, that is not our plan. Wilbur knows something of my past. He has even seen me ply my tradecraft a time or two. No one on the four continents where I've worked has ever resisted talking to me or has even held out very long. I am very good at what I do." Petrovich smiled. "And I do enjoy it so."

Benard put his eyes on Rosewell. "You are a scumbag sonofabitch."

"Pretty much, yeah," Rosewell agreed, "but I'm getting on to retirement age. So I need to start putting money aside." Then he turned to Petrovich. "You do know what's even more important than the gold now, right?"

Without taking his eyes off Benard, the Russian said, "Of course, I do, Wilbur. Mr. Benard was willing to pay us a very large sum of money to kill someone. The only reason to do that is he stands to take in even more money than he would pay out."

"A *lot* more than a half-million," Rosewell said.

"Yes, well, you are more familiar with capitalism."

Benard jabbed a finger at Petrovich, and said, "You commie bastard."

Taking no offense, the Russian looked at his partner in crime and said, "I agree, Wilbur. We will have to learn *both* of this proud capitalist's secrets: who he wants to have killed and how richly he expects to be rewarded."

Rosewell nodded. "And we need to get him and all of his gold out of here before the cleaners show up. Then grab the gold he's got at home."

"As well as any loose cash he has lying about," Petrovich agreed.

Smiling at Benard now, the Russian added, "Even being raised as a Socialist, I never let an opportunity to make money pass me by."

McGill Investigations International — Los Angeles, California

After thanking Colonel Donahue, Deputy Commissioner Murphy, and all the other women who'd made the banishment of LAPD Captain Terry Adair possible and promising to be available to help any of them if they were ever confronted by similar circumstances, Emily, Rebecca and Arcelia said farewell to the male guests who'd taken in the show from Emily's living room: her dad, Lee Proctor; President of the Police Commission, Bob Sifuentes and Canadian Consul Edmund Wolcott.

Hugs, handshakes and congratulations on a job brilliantly done were the order of the day. Rebecca was told by the Consul to be sure to attend as many of the cultural and social events at the General Consulate as she was able. The year-round warm weather in Southern California was great but contact with her native culture would be a tonic for any case of the missing-home blues she might feel. Her American friends would always be welcome, too.

As the visitors were departing, Bob Sifuentes handed Emily his business card.

"Just in case Adair loses all his marbles," he said in a quiet voice.

Emily thanked him, but she honestly didn't think he'd be back.

Lee Proctor hugged Arcelia and Rebecca as well as Emily.

"I always thought having another daughter or two around the house would have been nice. Now, I know I was right." He took a manila envelope from his briefcase and handed it to Rebecca. "Here's the material you asked for, Rebecca. Hope you can make good use of it."

Both Emily and Arcelia immediately wanted to know what was in the envelope.

"I'll show you when we get back to the office," Rebecca said. Being the boss, she could make that kind of decision. "You want to go in this evening or wait until tomorrow?"

Emily and Arcelia voted for that evening.

Emily took the wheel of her Audi and they made the trip in

fifteen minutes.

The three women convened in Rebecca's office.

"Okay," she said, "we have photographic evidence that Jack Murtagh can forge a signature. That was an essential step in building a case that he could have done the same thing for Angelo Renzi: forge the signature of our client, Keith Perry. Now, Walt Wooten puts Murtagh together with Angelo Renzi for us, but I wanted to see if there's photographic evidence of a relationship between the two of them."

Emily nodded. "So you called my dad, having gotten the idea that he's well connected in this town."

"And has a staff that knows how to do research. I was counting on that."

"Did he give you a family-discount rate?" Arcelia asked.

"Or did he comp it?" Emily said, feeling uneasy about accepting a favor from her father's law firm.

"Neither," Rebecca said. "I told him we'd pay the going rate and charge the expense to our client. He said, and I quote, 'Hooray!' This office will be run strictly on a professional basis."

"Good to know," Emily said.

"Let's see the dirt," Arcelia told Rebecca.

Rebecca pulled the 8x10 color photographic prints from the envelope, an even dozen of them, nicely divisible by three. Each woman studied her own batch and then passed it along. They didn't do glance-and-shuffle inspections. Each print got a careful scan, top to bottom and side to side. One shot was a simple buddy picture: Renzi and Murtagh, arms around each other's shoulders. Eight exposures showed the two men standing in front of various Murtagh paintings. Three more were prints of Murtagh's paintings with neither man in the frame.

A note from Lee Proctor said all the shots were used in a magazine layout of Renzi's home. The publication's name, *Coastal California*, was stamped on the backs of all of the prints. On the nine prints that included the two men in the shot another line of stamped information indicated: *Photos taken May 14, 2016.*

On the three exposures showing only the paintings them-selves, the second line on the back of the prints said: *Photos taken June 7, 2016.*

None of the three women missed the discrepancy.

Rebecca, Emily and Arcelia all searched for some significance. Had the photos featuring only Murtagh's paintings also been shot in May with the others? Had they been out of focus or poorly lit, requiring a reshoot? That didn't seem likely. All of the images were crisply defined and well composed. A pro, someone whose work was consistently top-notch, had taken them.

So what was the need for a reshoot? A magazine editor had simply wanted some stand-alone shots of the paintings? Or had Murtagh asked for them to emphasize his work?

The women asked themselves those and other questions.

Then Rebecca came up with the question they'd yet to con-sider.

"What if Angelo Renzi asked for the re-shoot?"

"Why would he do that?" Emily said.

None of them had an answer, at first.

Then it hit Rebecca. She smiled tentatively and then reviewed all the photos again, pulling three of them with the two men in frame and put one down above each shot of the paintings-only images.

"Tell me the difference you see between each of these pairs of photographs, other than the two guys not being in the bottom row of shots."

She moved aside so Emily and Arcelia could lean in for close inspection.

Emily caught the discrepancies a heartbeat before Arcelia did.

She said, "The stand-alone paintings have been altered."

"Right," Arcelia agreed. "Something in each of them has been removed."

Rebecca nodded. "Those perverse visual jokes that Murtagh likes to put in all his work — having a child molester watch kids dancing — somebody painted them out."

Emily said, "You can bet it wasn't Murtagh himself."

"So you know he's going to be one pissed-off painter," Arcelia said, "somebody screwing with his work."

Rebecca smiled. "Yeah. Up until now, we've had evidence that Murtagh can do a terrific job forging a signature and he has a close professional relationship with Angelo Renzi. That should be good enough to get a favorable ruling for Keith Perry in civil court. So our client should be free to pursue his own new business and we chalk up a win in our first case, but…"

Emily knew where Rebecca was going, "If we get Murtagh pissed-off enough, which shouldn't be hard, he might be willing to testify that Renzi used him to perpetrate a fraud."

"I like that," Arcelia said, "but wouldn't Murtagh do some time, too?"

"Depends on the deal he cuts with the D.A.," Emily replied. "Renzi is the big fish; Murtagh's the marginal 'artist of the moment.'"

Rebecca came up with another important consideration. "You know what? With all of us being new to the private investigations business, I think we'd better check with our big boss and see how he wants us to play this situation."

She called the home office in Washington, DC, even though it was getting late back east.

McGill was in. He listened to their story and said, "Go for it."

Farnam Street — Omaha, Nebraska

John was standing in front of the building where Brice Benard had his offices when Marlene's stretch limo pulled up to the curb. A chauffeur got out and walked briskly around the rear of the colossus to open the door for Marlene. He extended a hand to help her out, but she waved it off and exited with a dancer's grace.

Without bothering to say hello to John, she asked him, "Do you have your own transportation, Tall Wolf?"

John nodded. "A Chevy."

She addressed her driver, "Find somewhere nearby to park. I'll call when I need you."

The man only nodded and handed her a card with his phone number on it.

As the limo pulled away, Marlene stared at John for several seconds.

He broke the silence by telling her, "The President wants me to take your place as Secretary of the Interior."

"And?" she asked.

"I don't want the job. I've been trying to think of a way to bow out gracefully, but I haven't come up with anything good. Any suggestions?"

Marlene said, "Pretend it's me asking you, or even *telling* you, to do something."

John laughed. Then he said, "Had a good time with Mom and Dad, did you?"

Marlene's eyes flashed. "We'll talk about that later."

"Okay, I've got a proposition for you, but we can discuss that later, too."

John opened the door to the building for her.

She looked at Tall Wolf as she passed by. "I was thinking on the flight here that you and I have a few things in common."

John joined her in the building's lobby. "We're both sly devils?"

That brought Marlene up short. Made her wonder if Tall Wolf understood her *too* well.

Before that idea could be discussed, a man's voice called out, "Help you, folks?"

They both saw a uniformed security guard addressing them from his perch behind a highboy desk adjacent to an elevator bank. His name tag said he was Eugene.

John walked over to him with Marlene at his side. He showed his BIA identification and said, "Federal officer."

Gene read the particulars of John's ID. Then he asked, "And the lady?"

"My boss. I'm just the muscle."

"Well, you're big enough. How can I help?"

"We're looking for Mr. Brice Benard. Would you know if he's still on the premises?"

Eugene said, "Just a minute." He checked the laptop on his desk. "His car's still in the building, so I imagine he is, too."

"He never leaves the building on foot?" John asked.

"Goes to lunch at some restaurants nearby. At the end of the day, he takes his car."

"How about other people in the office? They stay late when the boss is putting in long hours?"

"That's a pretty smart question for a guy who's just muscle," Eugene said.

John told him, "I work at self-improvement. I bet you do, too."

"I'm taking a couple of community college classes," Eugene admitted.

"So are there other people up there with Mr. Benard?" John asked.

Eugene shook his head. "The whole place cleared out early. Never saw that before. As far as I know, it's just Mr. Benard. You going to arrest him?"

"I think so," John said. "Can't say for sure yet, but it looks that way. You don't know if he carries a weapon, do you?"

"Never heard that he does. Never saw any bulges in his suit coat." A thought flashed across Eugene's mind as plainly as a neon sign. Only he didn't like the message. With great reluctance, he asked, "You want me to give you some back-up?"

John pointed a thumb at Marlene.

"The boss takes care of that."

"What if things get rough?" Eugene asked.

"That's how she likes it," John told him.

Eugene told them Benard had his office on the top floor.

John and Marlene got in an elevator and exited two floors short of their destination.

***

The building had 40 stories according to the numbers in the elevator; John and Marlene got out on the 38th floor.

John said, "Don't want Benard to hear the elevator ring and know someone's coming."

Marlene responded, "Two questions: Do you think a two-floor cushion is enough to keep someone from hearing a bell?"

John looked at her. "Not for you. For most people, yes. What's your other question?"

He opened the door to a stairwell and they headed upward.

Marlene said, "You think a white man would have thought of this precaution?"

"You mean are they as naturally sneaky as us Injuns?"

"Exactly."

John grinned. "Yeah, some of them are. The ones who had their own reasons to learn misdirection young. Like when they picked gooseberries in a rough neighborhood."

They came to the door to the 40th floor. It was locked, as an adjacent sign advised. They'd have to go down ten flights to find a door that opened from inside the stairwell. John said, "I can pick the lock. Took a class at Glynco."

The Federal Law Enforcement Training Center at Glynco, Georgia.

"Don't bother," Marlene said.

She took hold of the doorknob and turned it easily, as if it was unlocked.

Only John heard metal shearing and pieces falling.

He didn't say anything as Marlene opened the door and held it for him. Smiling wide enough to show her killer incisors. He'd have had to admit he was impressed, if she'd asked him, but she didn't.

What he wondered, though, was if Benard heard the lock assembly deconstruct. Maybe, but unlike an arriving elevator, the sound would be hard to identify and characterize as a threat. Still, a paranoid personality, or someone who'd stolen a computer from a federally funded research facility, might investigate any unexpected sound he heard.

John turned to whisper a warning to Marlene. Only she was no longer standing next to him. Or anywhere else he could see. He understood she was showing off for him, defeating the door and then disappearing, but it was still impressive.

The darkened office space had an open floor-plan, except for a few small, dark offices to John's left and an enclosed area that had two perpendicular walls separating it from the rows of desks, sans cubicle partitions, which filled the large majority of the square footage. The large enclosed space had a thin line of light showing at the bottom of its door. That had to be Benard's corner office. John had to decide how to approach it.

He could move along the outer rows of desks to his right, but that border area was dimly lit by the ambient light from downtown Omaha filtering through the windows. Taking that path might reveal him as a silhouette, if Benard stepped out of his office. He could eliminate that problem by dropping down beneath desktop level and do a combat crawl, but that felt wrong to him. He was a senior federal officer with good reason to suspect Brice Benard had committed a crime. He had to take charge.

John decided the way to go was to take the most direct route, the central dividing line between the rows of desks that was wider than all the other spaces between workstations. Bestride Main Street to arrest the big shot. That was the way to go, and just what he did.

To be careful, though, he took his Beretta in hand and clicked off the safety. Keeping his mental focus on the center of his visual field, John let his peripheral vision and subconscious mind take in less immediate surroundings. None of the desks he passed had so much as a paperclip on it. The boss had to be a neat freak. It was always good to know the other guy's personality type.

The other thing that struck John was that he saw no sign whatsoever of Marlene. He knew Coyote was capable of many things but he hadn't ever heard invisibility was one of them. Then, as he reached a point just short of the closed door to Benard's office, she was standing beside him again.

Without having made a sound. Without a visual cue to her approach. She was just there.

Marlene pointed to her ear and then at the closed door.

Taking her cue, John heard voices, plural. Two of them spoke casually as if not worried about being overheard. One spoke English in flat Midwestern tones; the other spoke accented but understandable English. Eastern European, John thought. Slavic. Russian?

A third voice, again Midwestern, this one loud enough to hear every word clearly, said, "You bastards are *not* getting my gold! Break every damn finger I've got. Go ahead and shoot me. I don't care. I've got a bad heart. It's gonna pop any second now anyway."

Before he even turned to look at her, John could feel Marlene's sudden interest.

Coyote, it seemed, was numbered among the legions who lusted for gold.

He caught her eye and pointed to himself and then the door. He was going in, and he was going first. He made his move before she could either object or disappear again.

John threw the door open. He was lucky nobody had thought to lock it. His misfortune was Wilbur Rosewell had a gun in his hand and the one who'd been working on the man he took to be Brice Benard with a pair of pliers, and definitely looked Russian to John, put his tool down and stuck his now free hand inside his coat.

From the gruesome look of things, the Russian had already broken four of Benard's fingers.

Rosewell was definitely the jerk Great-grandfather had tripped in DC, and his eyes bugged out at the sight of John. He froze for the moment, possibly thinking other feds might start pouring into the room. Even so, he managed to yell, "Petrovich!"

The Russian started to pull his weapon out.

John intuitively said to him, "Порфирий Петрович, нет?"

Porfiry Petrovich, no?

John had taken another college course: Russian Literature — Two Semesters of Hard Labor.

The Russian went rigid, stood motionless. How could this tall stranger not only correctly infer the literary reference of his pseudonym but also voice it in his native language? Certainly, he had to be an agent of fate. His unexpected appearance had to be a development of fatal consequence. Petrovich felt he could do no more than stare at the man and await his inevitable demise.

Dostoevsky could not have written a more fitting end to his life.

By now, Rosewell had other feelings about the prick who'd already had him locked up once. He took Elmore Leonard's approach to how a bad guy should act and shot John while he had his eyes on the Russian.

All of which happened just as Marlene entered the room. She saw John fall and blood spurt from his chest. The two men with guns might have shot her, too, only they waited a heartbeat too long and Marlene was gone.

Replaced by Coyote.

Huge enough to make the two of them try to crowd behind Benard for cover. The real estate mogul could only close his eyes, hoping that his end would be swift, and come after those of the two bastards who'd been torturing him.

Benard heard the monster's jaws snap twice, followed by what sounded to him like bones being crushed. He knew he'd be next and he braced himself for the end, but it didn't come. Instead, a hand slapped his face, resounding with a loud crack.

Benard's eyes popped open, blurred for a second before they cleared. That fucker Rosewell and the bastard Russian were gone. There wasn't a trace of either of them anywhere. The monster had vanished, too. In its place was a gorgeous woman who looked like *she* might murder him.

Instead, she handed him a business card and said, "Call my driver. Tell him to have my car out front by the time we reach the street. And bring the computer you stole from Dr. Lisle with you."

She picked up the bloody big guy like he was a baby and stormed out of the room, leaving Benard alone. Nonetheless, he didn't hesitate to do exactly as he was told. Who the hell knew where the monster was? Maybe it'd take its time with him.

Linger over the third course of its hellish meal.

Benard, carrying the laptop, caught up to Marlene as the elevator came.

Leaving behind the bar of gold on his desk.

Tall Wolf was still breathing as Marlene got him and Benard into the back of her limo.

The nearest hospital, the limo driver told her, was only three blocks away.

He'd get them there in under a minute.

Even so, Marlene snarled into John's ear: "Don't you dare die on me, Tall Wolf. I don't want to live under your mother's curse forever."

Los Angeles, California

Jack Murtagh, perhaps thinking no one would either desire or dare to call on him at home, let his address be listed online. Apparently, he'd done well enough online to live in a neatly renovated home in the Silver Lake neighborhood, not far from Chavez Ravine where the Dodgers played baseball.

Arcelia, who'd insisted on tagging along, thought Murtagh might like her wearing her Giants jersey in that locale. It might stir up the locals. Considering that possibility and a few others, Arcelia had brought her baseball bat with her. Rebecca and Emily had to get by with their pepper spray and tactical flashlights.

Emily parked her car and the three women walked up to Murtagh's house. Rebecca rang the doorbell. They'd all felt the moment to strike was that evening. Rub Murtagh's nose in what Angelo Renzi had done to his paintings, and see if they could get him to rat on the bastard right away.

It took a minute but Murtagh came to the door. He recognized Rebecca and Emily and said, "I don't give refunds. Your check has been cashed."

Rebecca said, "That's fine. I don't want the money back."

Murtagh relaxed and then noticed Arcelia's jersey. He smiled and said, "You've got some nerve wearing that in this neighborhood. You ever think of posing nude?"

She said, "I *have* posed nude. Tastefully, of course."

The artist laughed. "Where's the fun in that?"

Rebecca held up a hand, cutting off that line of conversation.

"If it's all right with you, Jack, we stopped by to talk about your art. You mind if we come in for a few minutes? We discovered something you really should know about."

Suspicion clouded Murtagh's face. He looked at Emily.

"Don't know why I didn't see it before, but you're a cop." He turned to Rebecca. "You, too." Finishing with Arcelia, he said, "Not you, but you just might be the badass of the three."

Rebecca told him, "Ms. Proctor used to be LAPD; I was a Mountie in Calgary. Ms. Martin is one tough cookie. Now, we do private investigations for Jim McGill's local office."

Murtagh knew the truth when he heard it. He said, "I'll buy all that. So why shouldn't I slam my door in all of your faces?"

Arcelia said, "We've got some photos to show you. Not naked ladies, but you'll still find them interesting."

Emily added, "We also think you're the kind of guy who likes to get even when people screw with you."

Rebecca concluded, "Especially when someone screws with your art."

Murtagh frowned and then stepped aside to let them enter and said in a low growl, "Show me."

It took him less than a minute of inspecting the photos of his paintings to see and agree that they'd been altered in ways that Murtagh considered vandalism. He told them, "I'm gonna kill that bastard."

Emily said calmly, "That way gets you locked up for life."

"And you won't get any canvases, oil paints and brushes in the joint," Rebecca added.

"Be smart," Arcelia told him.

Then Rebecca gave him their pitch. Confess that he'd forged Keith Perry's signature for Angelo Renzi, testify against him in court, get a slap on the wrist for what he'd done and enjoy seeing *Renzi* rot in prison for years. While he continued to paint as he saw fit. Maybe, who knew, he could even sell his story to a movie studio.

With the idea of moving pictures and the fame that came with them in mind, Murtagh confessed while Rebecca shot the video with her phone.

She'd just put a wrap on the production when her phone rang.

A woman who introduced herself as Captain Anne Marie Meyerson of the Omaha Police Department told Rebecca that her husband John Tall Wolf had been shot in the line of duty and had just been taken into surgery.

She was advised to fly east as soon as she could.

Omaha Indian Reservation

After Marlene saw Tall Wolf into the hospital emergency room, she had the limo driver take her and Brice Benard to the Omaha Reservation. Along the way, she called Thomas Emmett, the tribal chief, and Dr. Yvette Lisle and Alan White River.

They were all waiting in Emmett's office when Marlene dragged Benard in by the scruff of his neck and flung him to the floor in front of the chief's desk. Then she handed the formerly missing iBook computer to Dr. Lisle.

"Please check your machine to make sure all your data is present and uncorrupted," Marlene told Dr. Lisle. "This worthless creature swears he didn't download any files to any other device or server."

"I didn't, I swear," Benard echoed in a whimper.

White River was the first to sense something was amiss. "Where is my grandson?"

She told all of them what had happened to Tall Wolf. Then she pointed to Benard and said, "This rodent is part Lakota Sioux. He disgraces all those who are his ancestors. He thought swindling the Omaha would be a great coup and enrich him obscenely. I've persuaded him to make appropriate compensation to your tribe: $500 million. I'd suggest you contact the Lakota to have them participate in deciding his ultimate fate. He needs to make compensation to them far beyond money."

Emmett asked, "What about the civil or criminal courts?"

Marlene smiled in her predatory way. "His accomplices will not be available to testify. The Lakota will have to reach justice on their own. Your people will have to make peace with theirs."

"And if we are unable to come to an agreement?" Emmett asked.

"Then I will return and help everyone to see the right path."

The threat implicit in Marlene's words was clearly understood.

Dr. Lisle looked up from her laptop and said, "All my data look to be present."

Marlene nodded, glad that something had gone right.

"I want to see my grandson," White River said.

So did Marlene, assuming he was still alive.

University Medical Center — Omaha, Nebraska

John was out of surgery and in an intensive care recovery room. Medical orders stated that he was not to receive any visitors until his medical team decided he was … well, going to live, for one thing. The bullet that had hit him entered his body on a downward, transverse trajectory, starting just below the right clavicle and exiting through the interspace between the fourth and fifth ribs, nicking each of those bones in its flight.

A far more serious concern was that the projectile also lacerated the brachial artery. By rights, even though the patient had been rushed into the hospital within minutes of being shot, he should have bled to death. Only by some unguessable means that major blood vessel had been neatly, if imperfectly, cauterized. There'd been a significant but not immediately fatal blood loss.

The woman who'd carried the victim into the emergency room in her arms had immediately left the hospital, so there was no chance to ask her for details. The man's wallet had contained his identification and his wife had been located and contacted. Not that she'd be able to explain what had happened.

Still, she was on her way, and she'd said the victim's parents and even her own parents soon would be en route, and they were to be given the same considerations regarding visiting the patient that she would have. The medical team felt somewhat better that their patient was well loved. If he didn't make it, they hoped he'd hang on long enough to be with his family when he passed.

What they didn't know, no one knew, was that John Tall Wolf was already in the presence of one of the most important figures in his life. In the form of a surgical nurse, Marlene stood at his bedside, holding his hand. Not a word passed between them, but they communicated nonetheless.

"Are you leaving us, Tall Wolf?"

John knew that voice immediately. It wasn't St. Peter talking to him.

"I don't know. Seems possible."

"I won't ask you to stay, if that's asking too much."

John might have laughed, except he thought that would kill him.

"You know, I had something to tell you. I'd better do it now while I still can."

"What is it?"

"I was going to put a provision into my will saying that when I die I want my body to be placed on a sepulture in the Sangre de Cristo Mountains. In the very same place where Coyote first met me, if there's isn't a planned community there by now."

Marlene didn't know what it was to weep, had never understood it.

Now, she did.

"Anyway, there should be someplace nearby where my remains could be left, and if Coyote was still interested and could choke me down, bon appétit."

"Don't leave just yet, Tall Wolf. I'm sure your wife and your parents are on their way. Your great-grandfather is already in the building. He wants to see you."

"Please bring him to me ... but don't take too long."

Changing her appearance to that of a large male doctor in surgical scrubs, Marlene brought Alan White River to John's bedside. The old man didn't say a word. He only took John's hand in his, and at that moment John saw Awinita, Alan White River's wife, and his own great-grandmother.

She was not alone. Bly Black Knife, John's biological mother, was with her. So was his biological father, the man whose name he'd never known, but did know now, Hok'ee Bates. More than that, John knew that *hok'ee*, in its native language, meant high-backed wolf. Tall wolf. The universe could be a very small place.

Many others, spanning countless generations, stood with Awinita and his blood parents.

John felt sure this could mean only one thing —

Until Awinita told him, *Your time is not yet. Take good care of my husband, your great-grandfather. His counsel to you will always be wise. I have told him it had better be.*

This time John couldn't help but laugh.

That sound wasn't often, if ever, heard from patients in that wing of the hospital.

It brought three nurses and a doctor on the run. By the time they arrived, though, John was alone — and all of his vital signs were steadily improving. When Rebecca, his parents and hers arrived, the medical team was cautiously optimistic.

BIG MEDICINE

CHAPTER 5

Tuesday, February 14, 2017
Montecito, California

There were too many *Carcharodon carcharias*, great white sharks, in the water off Butterfly Beach in Montecito for Byron DeWitt to give John Tall Wolf his first surfing lesson. Some of the brutes trolled for the unwary just a few yards off the sand. That didn't discourage every surfer, of course.

The hard-core wave riders had paid good money for their boards and wetsuits. Their taxes helped cover the costs of maintaining the beaches. What the hell had the sharks contributed? Okay, one good book and its movie spinoff. Other than that, they were just a real nuisance.

Sure, the bastards might *eat* your ass, and the rest of you, too.

Then again, people died every day on the freeways.

You decided where you'd take your chances was all.

John and DeWitt had resolved that their big gamble that day would be sunstroke. They jogged at a lumbering pace along the wet, hard-packed sand at the edge of the ocean. A week in the California sun had darkened both of their hides, and brought out gold fringes in DeWitt's hair.

Both of them wore sunglasses and baseball caps: Dodgers for

DeWitt; Giants for John, courtesy of Arcelia Martin. Given the demographics of the neighborhood, both movie and rock stars were beach *habitués*. The celebrities tended to recognize others of their kind and offer polite nods and waves. The general public had to make do with minimal pro forma smiles or averted glances from the famed.

Asking for an autograph on the beach was a request to be fed to the sharks.

Even so, just about everyone, including those who saw their own names in lights, peeked curiously at John and DeWitt. Here were two tall, athletic males, in the primes of their lives or just a bit beyond, gutting their way along the beach. Surely, they'd recently been able to move with far greater speed and grace.

So what kinds of misfortunes had laid them low?

A better question would be: What kind of treatments were bringing them back?

When the elder Wolfs and Bramleys, along with Rebecca, had arrived at University Hospital in Omaha, they were pleased to hear the medical appraisal that John had gotten past the crisis stage of his gunshot wound. There would, of course, be a prolonged period of recovery and rehabilitation.

The three Bramleys could only offer their encouragement and availability to be on hand and do anything they could in the way of physical assistance. Hayden Wolf, on the other hand, presented his medical credentials, and Serafina Wolf y Padilla related her published scholarship in the area of herbal medicines. They said they would evaluate the local physicians' planned course of treatment for John and offer their advice.

In reality, they quickly assumed responsibility for their son's recovery.

They had his power-of-attorney to do so.

Their efforts were aided when Marlene Flower Moon offered the use of her beach house in Montecito as a place to convalesce. Serafina made a point of checking it out first but then agreed to bring John there. Rebecca seconded the idea. Montecito was less than a two-hour drive from Westwood.

With James J. McGill's blessing and best wishes, Rebecca was given clearance to manage her husband's return to health and the L.A. office as she saw fit. That was because McGill was a *mensch* and Rebecca's new client, Keith Perry, would represent a substantial cash-flow for years to come.

Once word reached the White House about John Tall Wolf being shot and recuperating in Montecito, Byron DeWitt had told his wife, President Jean Morrissey, "I've got to go out there and help John."

She'd replied, "I'll buy that you want to help a friend, but you want to get back in the water, too."

"The reward for doing a good deed," DeWitt told her.

There was an additional benefit for the former FBI deputy director. Hayden and Serafina became aware of his medical situation, too. They examined him, read his medical history online and began to prescribe herbal medicines to supplement the prescription drugs he was already taking.

As a devoted student of Chinese culture, DeWitt had a great respect for the power of nature's pharmacopeia. He checked in with the President, as a good husband would, and got her blessing to give it a try.

Within a week, both John and DeWitt had made significant progress in their recoveries. In less than two weeks, they were plodding along the beach, a day after the senior Wolfs and Bramleys had returned to Santa Fe and Calgary respectively.

Great-grandfather, Alan White River, had returned to John's apartment in Washington, DC. Dr. Lisle's grandmother on the Omaha Reservation was described as a lovely woman, but she already had a boyfriend. White River had called John's upstairs neighbor, Barbara Lipman, and they'd agreed to keep an eye on each other.

Rebecca had felt it would be all right to drive down to L.A. and put in an appearance in the office for a day, but she planned to be back that night for a Valentine's Day date.

"Lucky dog," DeWitt had told John. "We'd better go for a run and whip you into shape for a hot night."

John replied, "A hot night will be if I don't fall asleep before things get good."

It turned out John wasn't the only one who got lucky.

The President of the United States and a contingent of Secret Service agents, straining to be discreet if not invisible, were waiting for John and DeWitt when they returned to the beach house. Jean Morrissey sat in a wicker chair on the front porch. She looked at her husband and John, sweat-drenched from their run, and said, "How am I supposed to keep this country up and running when all its best men are out lolly-gagging?"

"Madam President," DeWitt said, coming to a posture of attention, "I stand ready to serve in any way you wish, and by the way, why are you here?"

"It's Valentine's Day, and you are my valentine," she reminded him.

DeWitt grinned and said, "Oh, boy. I believe I'll go take a shower."

He left John alone with the President.

She told him, "Some people will do just about anything to avoid becoming Secretary of the Interior, but you didn't have to go and get yourself shot."

Following DeWitt's example, John straightened his posture. "Madam President, I, too, will serve in any office in which you'd care to place me. Regarding the Interior job ..." John tried to find the words to express his feelings in a way that would be meaningful to Jean Morrissey. "Having me do that job would be like putting a basketball player on a hockey team."

Jean Morrissey thought about that for all of two seconds before she started to laugh. She told John, "All you had to do was tell me that right off."

Chagrined, John said, "Sometimes the right words don't come easily. So, I can keep my present job?"

"As long as you like ... as long as I'm in office."

"You'll be able to find someone else for Interior?"

"I already have. Ms. Flower Moon has agreed to return to the post. So the two of you will be working together again." The President looked around. "That shouldn't be a problem, seeing how she's letting you use her house. Nice place, by the way."

"It is."

"You and Byron both seem to be doing remarkably well here."

"Mom and Dad know their stuff, Madam President."

"Glad to hear it. I think I'll go see if Byron needs any help washing his back."

"Yes, ma'am." John pointed the way, while looking at his feet.

Nobody ever wanted to think of either their parents or the President of the United States having sex. Especially in a shower. John hoped DeWitt's recovery wouldn't be set back.

He'd have to consider his own jeopardy when Rebecca returned.

That idea was interrupted by a house phone ringing. Might be Marlene. He'd have to thank her for taking the Interior job, and letting him use her house. He jogged into the kitchen and picked up the phone. "Hello."

"Director Tall Wolf, it's me, Cale Tucker."

"Hello, Cale. How are things at the NSA?"

"Busy is all I can say."

"Of course."

"I heard about what happened to you. I wanted to tell you I was glad to hear you made it."

"Thank you. I'm glad, too. May I ask how you got this phone number?"

"Sure, your wife, Ms. Bramley, gave it to me. Everyone knows she works for Mr. McGill's L.A. office."

"Of course."

"I did have to work a little bit to track you down. I tried your parents' house first but they weren't home, apparently."

"They were here with me," John said. "Went home yesterday evening."

"That's good ... but I found out something when I tried to

reach them."

John heard the uneasiness in the young man's voice. "What's that?"

"Somebody's tapped their home phone."

"What?"

"Yeah. I checked and was happy to find out it's not one of ours or anybody else in federal, state or local governments. It's an illegal wire."

John did his best to stay calm. "Do you know whose it is?"

"We're pretty good at backtracking these things. I can't tell you how we did it, but we obtained a store's security video of a man buying a disposable phone in New Mexico. He used it to test his tap. We ran his face through a federal database and got a hit. He's an army vet named Thomas Bilbray."

A chill ran through John.

"He used a fake credit card to buy the phone," Cale said. "The name on the card was—"

"Bodaway," John said.

Someone else, it seemed, who was hard to kill.

PREVIEW OF POWWOW IN PARIS

The sixth novel in the John Tall Wolf Series
Available from amazon.com

CHAPTER 1

Wednesday, May 23, 2018, Washington, DC

"One hundred and five?" Alan White River asked. "I don't feel a day over a hundred and four. Why, last year, I was thought to be only 99-plus."

"I'm just telling you what your epigenetic clock says, Mr. White River," Dr. Caroline Laney said.

The physician was young and more than a little amused by her venerable patient.

"C'mon, Doctor," White River said as he sat on the examination table. "You just got your microscope out and looked at the number of rings in a strand of my hair, didn't you? Maybe you miscounted."

The doctor laughed. So did John Tall Wolf who stood behind her in the examination room.

"What do you think, Grandson?" White River asked. "Could I really be that old?"

Alan White River declined the use of the word great as a noun of direct address for both himself and his great-grandson.

"We'll keep the awful truth from Ms. Lipman," John said.

Barbara Lipman was a cellist emeritus, late of the National Symphony Orchestra. A comparatively young octogenarian, she lived one flight up in the Washington townhouse where John and his great-grandfather also lodged. She was Alan White River's lady friend. He joked that he was her groupie.

The reason for the visit to the doctor was neither illness nor injury. John and White River were going on a trip. John thought it wise to get an informed opinion as to how well great-grandfather would hold up on a trans-Atlantic flight. That and see if he would still be eligible for a traveler's health insurance policy. The cutoff age, unfortunately, was 100.

John had thought that age limit to be remarkably benevolent, even if the premium was astronomical, but now it turned out to be insufficient. With the European public health care systems accepting neither Medicare nor Blue Cross Blue Shield, White River would have to pay his own tab if he fell ill or stumbled on uneven pavement.

The comforting fact here was the heroic old Indian who'd masterminded the theft of the Super Chief had earned more than a million dollars net on the lecture circuit in the past year, and John had persuaded him to keep a quarter of his earnings.

White River had given the rest to causes he considered worthy.

Ironically, his generosity had provided him with good publicity and raised the speaking fees he was offered.

Dr. Laney told White River, "We gave up the ring-counting method a long time ago. We use DNA methylation these days. That's why we took your saliva and blood samples, Mr. White River. But you need to remember, there's chronological age and then there's biological age: how well your cells are functioning and how much spring you have in your step. You're a good 10-to-15 years younger than a calendar reckoning would say."

White River beamed and stood up with surprising fluidity for someone his age.

He extended a hand to Dr. Laney. "May I have this dance, young lady?"

"There's no music playing," she said.

White River began to hum.

Recognizing the melody, Dr. Laney grinned. "*The Blue Danube Waltz.* That's my grandfather's favorite. He taught me the steps."

The two of them danced around the examination room for a minute, as White River continued to hum and John stood back and marveled.

White River told the doctor, "If I didn't already have a girl-friend, I'd take you on my trip with me."

Dr. Laney said, "You know, I never heard where you'll be going."

Producing another broad smile, he told her, "Paris."

Friday, May 25, 2018, Washington Dulles International Airport

The control tower gave the flight crew of Freddie Strait Arrow's new Gulfstream 650ER permission to take off, and the captain relayed the news to his passengers. "Ladies and gentlemen, we're on our way to Paris, Charles de Gaulle Airport. Expected flying time is just under six hours. Please make sure that your seatbelts are securely fastened."

For a centenarian, Alan White River looked as excited as a small boy. He looked to his left and told John, "I love this part, Grandson. It makes me think I am on my way to see Awinita."

He turned to look out the window for the spirit of his late wife.

The sudden thrust of the plane's two Rolls-Royce engines also made John Tall Wolf think they might be launched toward heaven and possibly the afterlife. The plane gobbled up its 6,300 feet takeoff distance in the seeming blink of an eye, and then they were climbing into the sky at a rate commercial airliners never approached. Their cruising speed would cut almost two hours off the standard flight time to the French capital.

Seated to John's left, also staring out a window and watching the earth fall away below, John's wife, Rebecca Bramley, was herself excited to the point of shivering.

"Are you okay?" John asked.

She turned to look at him with a smile. "Okay? I'm ecstatic. I'm with the man I love, going to the City of Light, flying in what has to be one of the most luxurious planes in the world, and … why haven't we gotten our glasses of champagne already?"

"I believe the flight crew is also buckled in at the moment," John said.

The people keeping them airborne, alive and pampered were the pilot, the co-pilot, the relief (i.e., emergency) pilot and the two cabin attendants, male and female. The other passengers aboard were Freddie Strait Arrow, the aircraft's owner, and his translator/ language instructor, a tall, stunning female member of the Osage tribe named Nijon, who looked like she might have stepped off the cover of *Vogue*'s latest issue.

John had whispered a joke to Rebecca earlier: "She's teaching him to talk dirty in French."

"And why not?" she'd replied. "You like it when we do it."

Rebecca had grown up bilingual in Canada. John had learned French in college, which was to say his fluency was functional but not subtle. He enjoyed refining his command of the language with his wife — when they had the time to spend together.

John worked in Washington; Rebecca toiled in L.A.

A situation they agreed that couldn't go on much longer.

At the moment, though, Rebecca was more than happy that she could lean to her right and give her husband a kiss. She asked, "Your great-grandfather will be busy with his counterparts from around the world, won't he?"

Alan White River was the guest of honor and the featured speaker at that year's convention of the Congress of Aboriginal Peoples, CAP for short. The gatherings happened on a biennial basis in the capitals of former colonial powers. Each meeting began with a historical review, always educational and often embarrassing to the host nation, of how it had treated the people of the territories over which it had assumed dominion.

The political elites of the host countries often suffered redfaced embarrassment when their sins were paraded before the world's mass media. The citizenries, however, were often educated and indignant about cruelties that had been perpetrated in their names and were now determined to see that such behavior would never again be committed by their politicians.

Alan White River was expected to inform his fellow native peoples from around the world of the many sufferings Native Americans had experienced. To her credit, President Jean Morrissey had promised to listen closely to White River's speech and voiced her full support to implement as many of the reforms he suggested as she might ram through Congress.

Rebecca had asked John if his great-grandfather's speech would be televised and streamed around the world.

He'd said, "I don't know the full media plan, but I'm sure it will get wide distribution."

As Freddie's luxury aircraft reached cruising altitude, John whispered a secret to his beloved. "We should have a fair amount of time to ourselves in Paris, but shortly after we arrive, we'll be going to the Élysée Palace."

"What?" Rebecca's response was loud enough to draw a few looks.

White River glanced at Tall Wolf and his wife. "Everything okay?"

"We're fine," John told him.

He gestured to the male cabin attendant that his help wasn't required.

After everyone calmed down, Rebecca whispered, "We're going to meet the French president? I'm not dressed for something like that."

"You look wonderful, as usual, and our attendance is not strictly required."

"But I'd like to meet him. I hear he's charming."

"Then you'll have to suck it up as a proud Canadienne and go as you are."

Rebecca nodded, and then she frowned. Dropping her voice to the softest of whispers, she told John, "You knew about this. You could have given me a heads-up."

"Grandfather wanted to surprise you. I probably shouldn't have said anything at all."

Rebecca tried to cling to her indignation, but couldn't. The pilot announced that the passengers could now move about the cabin if they so wished. The female cabin attendant appeared and asked if John and Rebecca would care for anything to drink.

Rebecca asked for the champagne she'd thought of earlier.

John requested a Perrier.

Opposite them, they saw that Alan White River was now dozing. He wore a smile on his weathered face. The male cabin attendant gently wrapped a fleece blanket around him.

Freddie Strait Arrow and Nijon were tucked away in a private compartment aft.

Looking at his great-grandfather, John told Rebecca in a quiet voice. "Dreaming of Awinita."

She nodded. "What a sweetheart he is."

"When he's not out stealing trains," John said.

"Yeah." Rebecca took John's arm in hers. "So you have any more surprises in store for me?"

"Me, personally? No."

"You mean someone else might?"

John said, "Who can tell? It's a crazy old world."

Having expressed that thought, John wondered what Marlene Flower Moon was doing.

She was supposed to find her way to Paris, too.

Maybe she was already there. Or she might arrive at the last minute.

***

ABOUT THE AUTHOR

Joseph Flynn has been published both traditionally — Signet Books, Bantam Books and Variance Publishing — and through his own imprint, Stray Dog Press, Inc. Both major media reviews and reader reviews have praised his work. Booklist said, "Flynn is an excellent storyteller." *The Chicago Tribune* said, "Flynn [is] a master of high-octane plotting." The most repeated reader comment is: Write faster, we want more.

Contact Joe at Talk to Me on his website: *www.josephflynn.com*

All of Joe's books are available for the Kindle or free Kindle app through *www.amazon.com*.

Printed in the USA
CPSIA information can be obtained
at www.ICGtesting.com
LVHW022338100424
777071LV00007B/241